TO SEARCH THE NIGHT

A JAZZ NOVEL

ANTHONY SWANN

Roadrunner Publishing Company
Bemidji, MN 56601

To Search the Night
COPYRIGHT © 2018 by Anthony Swann

ISBN: 978-0-692-03581-8

Printed in the United States of America 2018

This Book is dedicated to Morris Wilson, whose soulful sax kept us emotionally alive in the inner city.

Best Wishes!
Anthony Swann

Out! Out!

Out into the night,

to prowl the existential night,

following the spontaneous truth of the jazz mind—

searching the circuit for a band to deliver,

 The Holy Sound,

our sacrament,

elusive elixir,

blessing our ears until it vanishes phoenix-like,

leaving us to search the night.

1

SARAH 1963

Sarah watched her mother Ruth with pride. Two of Ruth's paintings had been accepted in a juried art show at the Jewish Community Center in St. Louis Park, Minnesota. Judges had just placed ribbons; giving Ruth second place. It was her first show and Sarah could sense Ruth's shyness, her barely concealed nervousness. Ruth was dressed like she thought an artist would look, in a blue denim shirt and designer jeans, a bright yellow scarf around her neck. The effect, Sarah thought, was more Jewish matron than artist. The younger female artists were bohemian casual in tight faded paint-stained jeans, vests, braless tops and roguish hats. They ignored Ruth as if she were invisible.

A lot of viewers had congregated in front of two large powerful paintings: One a dramatic abstract which carried the first place ribbon, the other a nude study of a black woman. A young man dressed in denim came forward and Sarah overheard one female artist say he had done the paintings. Ruth and Sarah watched him. He was pacing around the edge of the crowd, avoiding people who might want to talk. He glanced around seeking an opening to bolt through and escape. A couple of young women managed to approach the blonde disheveled artist but he ignored their attempts to start a conversation by heading to the refreshment table for a cup of coffee. Ruth walked up to him and began talking. "Excuse me; are you the artist who did that powerful painting that won first place?"

"Yeah, I guess that would be me. And you won second, didn't you?"

Sarah knew she could walk over and join the conversation. It would be just that easy. The young artist was charismatic, but not her type. She was surprised at her mother's forwardness starting up a conversation with a male stranger, something she would not do if her husband were near.

Sarah left the building to have a cigarette. Soon the blonde artist came out to join her for a smoke. His lips were curled in a snarl.

"What's the matter? Did my mom upset you?"

"Who's that?"

"My mom, that older woman you were talking to. Did she upset you or something?"

"Oh no, not at all. She's nice. Good painter too, damn good. She should've got first. You know it's ironic she just stayed back while all those younger artists acted so cocky." He blew some smoke, "Oh, some button-down Brooks Brothers asshole insulted me."

"Really? Face to face?"

"Indirectly. I heard him commenting on my abstract, the one that won first. He said it looked like a piece of shit in color. Then he drooled over my nude and made lewd remarks. I felt like decking the bastard so I came out for a smoke. I'm about ready to book. They didn't have wine here at an opening. Pin that. Where can I catch a bus that will go back to the city? I'm not used to the suburbs."

"St. Louis Park isn't the suburbs, not anymore."

"It's still the burbs to me," he scored, pointing toward the well-kept neighborhood with a gesture of dismissal. He was like a wild animal that had strayed too far from the inner-city jungle. Sarah noticed he wasn't used to dressing up. His jeans bore traces of oil paint. On sudden impulse she asked, "Wanna ride?"

"Sure, if you're done looking at the show," he said, pulling a drag from his cigarette. "Your mom's still here though, I can catch a bus."

"Oh no, I'm done looking. I just wanted to see Mom in her moment of glory. She's so proud to be in a show with an artist like you and other young people."

"She should be proud. Her work is strong. By the way, my name is Jim K. Jensen. May I ask yours?"

"Sarah. Sarah Rosen. Nice to meet you." Sarah quit nervously fooling with her long black hair and extended her hand to Jim.

"My pleasure, Sarah. And yes, I'll take you up on that ride then, as long as your mom's got one."

"Oh yeah, she's got her own car here. I was glad to see her go somewhere. All she does is paint, paint, paint, and dig flicks."

They quickly left the gallery and Sarah led Jim to her bright red, year-old XKE Jaguar in the rear parking lot.

"Wow! What a short! You actually own this ride?"

"My dad gave it to me if I promised to stay in college and graduate."

Jim had no personal interest in cars, but, as an artist, he was aesthetically impressed by the XKE's aerodynamic design. Sarah was pleased whenever anyone enjoyed the sight of it. And while she hadn't taken it for any long rides out of the city, it symbolized adventure and freedom from the restrictions of living at home.

With the Jaguar purring along on Minnesota State Highway 7 headed toward Lake Street, Sarah asked Jim where he wanted to go.

"I just need to catch some air. Openings make me claustrophobic. I could use some good music to cut loose with. Wanna dig some jazz?"

"Sure. I love jazz!"

"Okay. When you get into the city, take University toward St. Paul. It's a club where my buddy Gil goes...he might be there." Jim noticed how deftly the rich Jewish girl shifted and handled her car. She was cool. Naïve probably, but she fit the scene. The sleeveless red summer blouse, short red skirt, and red purse all matched her red XKE Jaguar. The wind was playing with her long black hair and it billowed out whenever she accelerated. The tight fitting blouse reminded Jim of the first thing he'd noticed about her at the art show: She was "built for speed," as Lady Day or Billie Holiday would've put it, just like her car. Unlike most foxy women, she seemed modest. She wasn't wearing makeup or jewelry. Modest or not, Jim thought, she could be Ray Charles's "lady with the red dress on" to the blacks and railroad employees at the jazz club. He knew he'd have to look out for her.

# # #

It was after ten when they walked into the club called Road Buddy's to music by a black jazz group that was covering Wilson Pickett's "In the Midnight Hour," and Jim knew from the astonished look on Sarah's face that she'd never heard, nor seen, anything like what they were witnessing. The place was electrified with raw voltage; railroad employees and their women, dancing like demons, loose and hot, drinking down, and letting go with all their booty-shaking sensual smoothness, doing the jerk and mashed potato. Single black men made eye contact with Sarah and moved closer to her, so Jim made ready to ask her to dance, if they pressed.

As they walked toward a table, Jim noticed the black bass player smiling at Sarah, watching her like a lost desert wanderer eyeing an oasis. He was a big man with a moustache, which, along with his size, made him resemble a walrus. As he played, one of his hands left his upright bass to reach into a pocket of his sports coat to procure a pint of Bacardi rum, which he opened with his teeth while his other hand deftly pulled notes as he drank. Eventually he pitched the empty bottle out a huge window behind him which had been opened for ventilation. The song ended with strong applause, whistling and yelling, "RIGHT ON! RIGHT ON!"

The big bass man then began a lead-in to a Latin version of "Green Dolphin Street." DOOM DOOM baa…doom doom doom… DOOM DOOM baa, the bass resounded. Then a Puerto Rican conga player laid in his basic beat, steadily rolling it forward, while the pianist began groovy Latin chords, and the sax player picked up a flute to dance the melody above. People began to mambo.

Sarah had never seen live Latin dancing. She was fascinated. The dancing was sexy and hot. So hot! Yet sophisticated too, totally seductive. The dancers were mostly black and they knew the dance as well as a Latino man in a white suit and white shoes. His Latin girl wore a black silk dress and a red hibiscus flower in her hair. Sarah could see the enjoyment in their flushed faces, feel it in their movements. How free they must feel, she thought, being able to dance that way!

Looking upstage again, Jim waved to the drummer, a friend of his named Dean, who in return, struck his drum sticks together above his head in salute. The bassist began a solo. His face, which had been all come-on smiles for Sarah, now became completely serious as he concentrated on his deeply resonating bass. An intense energy began flowing through his solo. It crackled about the whole stage like a demonic possession. With his body bent to the bass, some supernatural creative force moved his fingers with unimaginable skill.

When the other musicians came back in, the mysterious energy remained, to move through them all, electrifying them and, in turn, everyone in the place. The crowd stood up from their tables and the rest stopped dancing, all yelling "ENCORE! ENCORE!"

The bassist gave an exaggerated formal bow from which he came back up too quick and forcefully. Losing his balance, he toppled backwards right out the big window behind him, down a few feet into an alley below. A few drunks laughed, several women screamed, and the place fell silent. The drummer jumped up and ran outside to help his friend.

"That poor man could've hurt himself," Sarah said.

"Yeah, I know. His name is Carl and my friend Dean went outside to check on him. Let's go see what happened."

# # #

The bass player was clutching his leg. "It's fucked up, man. My leg is FUCKED UP! I can't get up on it." The grimace of pain in his face intensified with anger when he saw Jim and Sarah approach.

"Who are these fucking people? What do they want?"

Dean turned. "That's my friend Jim… I know him. Carl, you need to get some help, man. That leg needs to be set if it's broken."

"Jesus man, I don't need any surplus ofays right now. I'M IN PAIN! I ain't goin' to no hospital either, man. My green ain't long enough for that shit."

Sarah, who overheard him, surprised herself by speaking up. "I can help you. I've got some money."

Seeing Sarah, the anger and pain in the big bass player's face quickly changed to charm mode, and a soft smile. "Well, well, who do we have here?" he asked.

Sarah approached, timidly at first, after speaking up so quickly. Her respect for the musician's talent had given her the boldness. Seeing him smile overrode her hesitation. "I'm Sarah," she said, "and this is my new friend, Jim." She grabbed Jim by the arm, surprising herself again at feeling bold enough to tuck Jim in close to her.

"Well hello! I'm Carl. And where did you come from, my little angel of mercy?"

"Carl, I can help you if you want to have that leg looked at. I'll pay for a doctor."

"Well, I guess, if it's broken…I jus' don't have the bread, no long green like that. Say, I could use some painkillers, right away, I mean-- first things first. This pain is horrible!"

Sarah was processing the realization that she had been over-whelmed by Carl's cologne the second she got close to him. English Leather! She recognized the sexually powerful musk as one a college boy wore, a boy who had been after her, until she managed to put him off. The charisma Carl created for her was from the solo he'd just played, the presence of a deeply gifted person.

Dean went back to the club to get the painkiller Carl requested; it was his favorite liquor, Bacardi 151. After drinking half the bottle, Carl got into Dean's car with Jim's help and then he and Sarah followed to the Hennepin County Medical Center. By this time they got there Carl was roaring drunk. The admitting nurse tried to be as patient as possible with Carl yelling in her face. She managed to coax out his full name then had Dean fill out the form for Carl.

"Your religion, sir?"

"Rastafarian."

"How do you spell that?"

"He knows, Dean knows. Just put R-A-S-T-A!" Carl said, almost falling out of the chair.

"Are you allergic to anything, sir?"

"Yeah. Country western music. Fuck this! Fuck this paperwork crap! I need a doctor to give me some painkillers. I'm in PAIN!"

It took two strong male nurses to restrain Carl while his leg was set in a cast and a brace. Sarah signed for payment of the bill including the cost of a set of crutches. Carl eventually passed out. They got his dead weight out to the car by wheelchair. Sarah and Jim followed Dean to his south-side house where they hauled Carl out of the car and lugged him into his bedroom.

# # #

Afterwards, Dean rolled some joints and they all relaxed. Sarah had never smoked grass as powerful as these musicians were smoking. She paid attention to everything they said as if she was on the set of a powerful drama they were all involved in, a drama slowed down to a profound state of revelation.

"Carl and Bacardi 151 do NOT mix," Jim said.

"Tell me about it!" Dean replied. "He shouldn't drink at all; he's on tranks and shrink meds."

"What for?"

"Depression. He just lost his wife… a wonderful white woman. They were living in New York City and he was just beginning to make it in the jazz scene while she supported them with a good secretary job. He was gigging with some heavies. He even played with Coltrane. Then his wife was struck by a car and died instantly. He's never gotten over it. He couldn't do anything…came back here just in shambles."

"Yeah," Jim said, "I remember he was a holy terror when he started to stay drunk all the time."

"I got him a shrink through the county," Dean continued, "hoping he could quit booze if he got some tranks for his depression. But now he does both-- and he can't handle it. I have no control over him. He does what he wants and I can't stop him."

"Kick him out," Jim offered. "Give him an ultimatum: Quit booze or get out."

"He has no place to go. His family's distanced themselves from him. He can't go to them."

"So you're stuck?"

"Well, if I kick him out he'll be on the street and end up in an institution. They'll just up his meds and he'll end up not being able to play at all."

# # #

After saying their goodbye's to Dean, Sarah drove Jim home. She tried to bring herself to ask him where she could score some grass. Finally she just came out with it and asked, looking straight ahead, too nervous to ask face to face.

"I could probably get you some. I don't deal but I've got the same dealer Dean does."

"Oh wow! That's dynamite stuff. It's a lot better than what I've had."

"Okay. You wanna front me twenty dollars? It's twenty a lid. I'll pick you up one next time I cop, in a week or so. If you give me your phone number, I can call you when it's ready. Maybe after I get to know you better you can cop for yourself." Sarah gave Jim her phone number and thirty dollars.

"What's the extra ten for?"

"For your service."

"Oh no, I don't do that. Here, take the ten back."

"Okay, but how about giving me your phone number?"

"I don't have a phone."

"Really? Why?"

"I don't like the goddamn things. They interrupt me when I paint."

Pulling up at a warehouse address, Sarah raised her eyebrows, "You live here?"

"Yeah. For the time being. I get free rent for caretaking the place. The tenants are expatriate Czech artists and filmmakers. Nice meeting you, ah, good night, I guess."

He slid out of the car and disappeared into the night.

Sarah watched the young artist enter the big building. She was struck with the realization that she'd just met a set of people living in a world entirely different from her own.

That night she made a journal entry: *Met an artist today named Jim who took me to a jazz club. He opened a door to another world, a world of people really getting down! Who, I could tell, must live harder and deeper than anyone I know. The music was so hot and sophisticated it makes what I'm used to sound like child's play. I helped one of the musicians out who had an accident. He's a stormy, foul-mouthed character who plays bass like an angel (or demon!). It made me feel good to be able to pay his hospital bill.*

# # #

Her old life and routines now seemed dull. She missed the excitement the jazz people had brought, and that she'd actually been in the middle of it for a very short time. Was she in wonderland, falling down the rabbit hole to discover a land ruled by music with a new set of pleasures and exotic people?

She wanted more of this kind of sensation but didn't know where to find it. Jim hadn't called. Maybe he decided she was a risk. She wondered if she'd ever have the courage to go back to Road Buddy's by herself. She wanted to hear more of that sparkling, seductive music; and maybe meet someone to talk to.

Meantime, she began looking for notices of jazz playing at other places, but there didn't seem to be any– unless she just didn't know where to look. Jazz, it seemed, was not in demand.

She felt isolated. High school friends were either married or off at other colleges. Her university classes were so large she never sat next to the same person twice or got the chance to talk to anyone. Living in a dorm would have allowed a social life but she'd promised her dad she'd live at home until graduation.

However, there were jazz concerts from time to time at Coffman Union and Northrop Auditorium. Also foreign films, shown by the University Film Society; in Italian and French, "new wave" films that were so much hipper than the cumbersome monstrosities Hollywood made. Once, after seeing a French film, "Web of Passion," she took down the film poster from a kiosk on the university mall to put up in her room. The film starred Jean Paul Belmondo, a young French actor who oozed animal magnetism. On-screen he moved with the natural charisma of a big male cat combined with a casual arrogance that suggested reckless criminal potential. He stirred sexual excitement in her so intense it felt uncomfortable, frightening at times, a kind of frenzy that made her palms sweat. She couldn't wait to find him in another film.

Life at home was glum. For a long time she had known that her parents' marriage had gone sour. Her father, always serious about something; never talked about his feelings. Her mother, knowing he wished to be alone, retreated to her basement studio to paint. There was an evening meal which Ruth instructed the maid to prepare, but it was usually eaten in silence by the family. Sarah missed the clever banter her parents used to have. The few remarks they managed now were strained. Rachel, her sixteen year old sister, was often sent to her room if she disturbed her father in the least.

"What am I going to do, Sarah?" Ruth asked. "I can't talk to your dad about Rachel anymore. He hates her and she hates him. He comes down too hard on her. She doesn't respect him at all. I know she's going to try to run away again. She's constantly in trouble at school. I have to go see one of her teachers again tomorrow."

It was difficult to see her mother so upset, so Sarah decided to talk to Rachel. The door to her room which Rachel left open when they were closer as sisters was now always closed. Sarah never knew if Rachel was there unless she knocked and when she did, Rachel resented it. Sarah knocked.

"Rachel, can I come in?"

"NO."

"Please, just for a minute?"

"Why?"

"I'd like to talk to you for a minute, that's all."

"Oh, alright, but make it quick, I'm expecting a phone call."

Rachel snuffed out a cigarette and sat back on the pillow propped up at the head of her bed. She was wearing cutoff jeans, an oversized grey sweatshirt, and dirty sockless sneakers. She'd made the bedspread dirty by keeping her shoes on, but she didn't care. The room was shorn of all the girlish things Rachel had once kept around. All that remained was a poster of James Dean.

"Rachel, I just want to ask what's been upsetting you?"

"Fuck off, Sarah, mind your own business."

"Why are you so hostile? We used to be really close. What happened?"

"I said it's none of your business!"

"Maybe not. Maybe it isn't, but you've got Mom upset and THAT really bothers me. Do you want her upset?"

"Leave me alone!" Rachel snapped. She brushed her unkempt black hair out of her angry eyes. Her mouth was tight with fury.

"Why are you in so much trouble at school? That's REALLY got Mom upset...I know you and Dad aren't getting along. Is that it?"

"FUCK OFF! DADDY'S LITTLE GIRL! You're daddy's little darling, aren't you? Can't do any wrong. That's why he gave you the car—your own XKE; it's a reward for being such a good little Daddy's girl. All he gives me is shit! Leave me the fuck alone. Go on; get the hell out of here!"

Sarah turned and left the room.

2

STANLEY

Sarah resigned herself to continue driving over to the lonely campus and then coming back to the empty streets of St. Louis Park. Her only release was listening to the jazz she bought in record stores or heard on the radio. Sarah was thankful for a private phone line in her bedroom when Jim finally called to tell her he had scored her "smoke."

Jim wanted her to meet him at 26th and Nicollet, an inner-city location she was unfamiliar with. He said it was near the art school he had attended. She was to go to Butler's Drug Store and either wait outside in her car or go in for coffee. He would find her. With her city map, Sarah found the place, but felt uncomfortable just sitting in her XKE. People were gawking at it and it made her feel like she and the car were on display. Car and foot traffic were heavy and exhaust fumes and dust were irritating. As she got out entering the drugstore, a black man yelled from across the street, "That car gets it, Lady! Most cool thang eva made. You gotta RIDE, Lady, you gotta ride!"

Sarah smiled and mumbled "thank you," and ducked into the drug store. It was Friday, busy with people cashing paychecks and meeting for lunch. Sarah found an empty spot in the café and relaxed. She was excited, anticipating the "smoke," the code word Jim had used on the phone for the grass she was about to "cop." But when he was a half hour late, she began to worry she'd been stood up. She was on her third cup of coffee when he finally showed, forty-five minutes late. He nodded her way, but stopped to talk to a couple in a booth. She was miffed at how nonchalant and unhurried he was but she didn't let it show. She smiled and greeted him when he finally joined her. He politely suggested they go out to her car to take care of business. When she had the grass secure in her glove compartment, she asked, "Want a lift anywhere?"

"Oh, I'm just going up the street, but yeah, I'll take a lift. That way you can meet Stan if you like. He's an artist. I've got a lid for him too."

They drove north on Nicollet Avenue, a few blocks past Franklin, parked, then walked along a block between Nicollet and First with little nondescript storefronts no longer in use. Jim approached one. It had no sign or markings anywhere. The door and windows were covered from inside by cardboard.

Suddenly the door opened and a woman stood there for a moment and blew a kiss to someone inside. She quickly stepped outside, and slammed the door shut. Sarah stared after her. She was all legs in a miniskirt and Nancy Sinatra boots. No blouse, just a skimpy halter, loose brown hair, and plenty of makeup. Seeing such a woman in that area wasn't surprising, but when Sarah saw her face as she turned to look back at them, she was shocked. The woman looked exactly like Miss Martindale, her English Lit teacher at the university. But it couldn't be… could it?

Miss Martindale was a prim, cultured thing; intellectual to the bone, who wore long tweed skirts with tan knit stockings. She kept her hair up in a bun, buttoned her blouses to the top, and never wore any makeup. She read the New Yorker, studied Virginia Wolfe, and wouldn't be caught dead looking like a hooker.

The woman who had just appeared was bold! She looked exuberant. Her face was flushed and she was ecstatic. No doubt she was high.

"Hey Jim!" she called to him with enthusiasm, while walking away, her hips moving in complete sensual freedom, while her purse swung at her side, trying to match her stride.

"Bye Cynthia!" Jim shouted after her. "Wow! Is she turned on!" he said to Sarah.

"Did you call her Cynthia?"

"Yeah, Cynthia. An' she surely has the hots for my friend Stan. She's like a bitch in heat."

Sarah looked perplexed. "What does she do for a living?" she asked.

"She's a college teacher, believe it or not. But she likes to dress sexy when she comes to see Stan."

"College teacher? What college?"

"The University of Minnesota."

Sarah was stunned. No doubt, that was her English Lit professor!

Stan, pale faced and sweaty, pulled aside a piece of brown cardboard behind the door, enough to peek out, then opened the door.

"You got time to see us?" Jim asked, knowing Stan had just had sex, "Or are you all wore out?" he said with a wink as he introduced Sarah.

"I'll put some coffee on," Stan ran his hand through his dark reddish hair and beard. "I didn't know Cynthia was coming by today. She usually calls but she also likes to surprise me. It's like an adventure for her, you know?" He pulled on a black tee-shirt with several holes. It went well with his paint-stained work pants and old sneakers. "You guys want anything to drink? I've got some whiskey."

Sarah took coffee and looked around the dimly lit room while Stan and Jim sipped whiskey. There was a small bed near the back. A dirty blanket lay on the floor. The sheets were messed, presumably from Cynthia's visit. Stan had made a working studio out of the front area and an improvised living space in the back. There was a tiny sink and simple toilet, a crusty hotplate and tiny icebox, but no kitchen. Sarah wondered how he washed his dishes. No bathtub or shower, so how did he bathe?

Stan put on a Thelonious Monk album. "I can't afford many records. I just play Satch or Monk while I work," he said. Various styles of painting hung on the walls; Stan had experimented during his years at the Minneapolis College of Art and Design. A black female nude caught Sarah's eye. It reminded her of the nude Jim had in the show where they met. She wondered if the same black woman had modeled for them both.

The men got up and moved to the opposite side of the work area. It looked as though garbage had been spilled there.

"What the hell?" Jim said. "This is far out!"

"Oh, my junk art. I'm just having fun. I take the shit people in our consumer society throw away and work it into a collage: cig butts, candy wrappers, beer cans, bottle caps, used condoms, ticket stubs, sardine cans, dried turds, you name it. I don't take it seriously, but Manuel, my teacher at MCAD, says it's a statement about our disposable culture, dig?"

"Yeah! Yeah, man, real funky! Can I buy one of these?" Jim was amazed at the creativity inherent in the work.

"Hell, no. You can't buy one. You can have one. You're my friend. Take as many as you want." Jim selected several paintings and they concluded their visit.

Later, back out on the street, Sarah asked Jim if the black woman in Stanley's painting had modeled for them both.

"She did. She modeled for us at the same time, right there in his studio." They climbed into Sarah's car and shut the doors. "Monique is a pro. Not a pro model, but a prostitute. We paid her for the modeling, but he also pays her for sex from time to time. She was the only woman he ever had sex with before he met Cynthia. Stan's a different breed of cat, very shy and very vulnerable. He's on some very powerful shrink drugs that make him reclusive. Tranks."

"Tranquilizers?"

"Yeah, his parents put him on them."

"His parents?" She turned on the heater and rubbed her hands together.

"Yeah, yeah. They're both shrinks in New York. His dad's quite famous. Wrote some book that's a standard in the field. They diagnosed their own son as paranoid-schizophrenic. They wanted him to stay with them in New York, gave him a studio in their basement." He looked out the window.

"Just turn left when I tell you. Anyway, Stan talked them into letting him come here for art school so he could get out on his own. He lived in the art school dorm 'til he graduated. The kids at school really dug him. They looked out for him. He moved to that storefront after graduation. That way he's only paying rent once for a crib and studio both. His parents send him a monthly allowance, but it isn't much. Not much left after rent. I think that's one reason he looks so sickly. He buys cheap food. He can't afford any luxuries beside cigs and whiskey now and then, unless he sells his work. But his stuff is too far out for most people."

Sarah pulled up to the warehouse Jim directed her to.

"Oh, this isn't the same warehouse I dropped you at before, is it?"

"No. This is a different one. I'm renting my own studio in this one," Jim said with pride.

"Do you have a phone in your studio?"

"NO, I told you I'll never have one of the goddamn things ever. But you can come up there during business hours. You take the elevator to the fifth floor. By the way, I hope you don't mind, I gave your number to Dean. He and Carl are giving a barbeque in Dean's backyard. They want you to come. They appreciate how you helped Carl. Watch out for him, though, he's a wolf to put it mildly."

3

RACHEL

One day when Sarah's only afternoon class was canceled, she drove home before noon to have lunch with her mother. Ruth was sitting at the kitchen table and didn't respond when Sarah greeted her. Her usually kind, composed face was raw, eyes red from crying. She just stared at Sarah, lost for words.

"What is it, Mother, what's wrong?"

"Your father. Heart attack. He left us. He's gone, Sarah, he's gone." Sarah gasped and fell into a chair across from Ruth. Her father was dead.

The next few days were unreal. Ruth practiced Jewish law forbidding elaborate funerals on the principle that all are equal in death. The synagogue in St. Louis Park took over most of the arrangements and the body was sent to Solomon Brothers who would ready it for burial, which took place as soon as possible after death. The body was not embalmed or cremated. While alive, Morrie had purchased a family plot for himself, Ruth, and the girls. Sarah thought the plain pine box was more fitting than any of the more expensive coffins which they could have easily afforded.

The short funeral service conducted by the rabbi was for family and friends and after the blessing, the coffin was wheeled out to a waiting hearse and burial took place in the family plot. Ruth was surprised to see Morrie's brother Saul Rosen there. The brothers had been estranged and Saul had not notified Ruth of his attendance. He looked upset and was extremely courteous and kind in his sympathetic greeting to her and Sarah. He left soon after. Ruth struggled through the burial but collapsed going home.

Ruth practiced sitting Shiva or mourning for three days after the burial which was held at her home. Friends and family brought food to the house and were urged to take the money they might have spent on flowers and send it to Morrie's favorite charity, the St Jude Children's Hospital founded by Danny Thomas. Giving had been important to Morrie as it is to all Jews. He never spoke of it, but after the funeral Ruth disclosed that he had given thousands of dollars yearly to help the Jewish community.

Ruth was becoming very distraught over her worry about Rachel's disappearance. She had covered up for her not being present at the service, but somehow she felt her wayward daughter might not ever come back. She thought back to a discussion she and Morrie had about a month ago. "Ruth, Rachel is jealous of Sarah. It's so obvious. We have to get her some support. I want a psychiatrist to see her weekly, talk this out. I don't think Sarah has a clue as to how much Rachel hates her–and me."

Now he was gone. Their financial support was gone, too. The man who ran the show, who'd built and maintained their security, their home and fortune. Sarah soon began to realize how much strength her father had provided. The first earnest prayers of her life were made asking God to be able to help her mother and for Rachel to return.

Soon Ruth began talking to Sarah about "the business." Two big clothing stores: Morrie's, the clothing store downtown that sold men's suits and ladies' fashions at reduced prices; and Sammy's, the working man's clothing store on Lake Street. Sarah had worked at Sammy's the year before starting college. It was named after Samuel Rosen, Sarah's grandfather, who'd invested his New York savings in Minneapolis. There was also the third entity to contend with; the complicated web of investments worth more than the stores combined.

# # #

Rachel showed up after sitting Shiva was over. Ruth found her in the kitchen gorging on the food brought by the neighbors to comfort the family. Her worn backpack with its emblems of rock bands unknown to Ruth lay on the floor beside her chair. Her clothes were dirty, hair unkempt. Rachel glanced up for a second as if to tell her mother she didn't belong in her own kitchen. Her look suggested that Ruth was completely trivial to her, a mere nuisance. Ruth wanted to chastise her but didn't have the heart, knowing it would only prompt her to leave again.

Rachel spent her first night at home stealing what looked like was the most valuable of her mother's jewelry and dying her hair blonde; while her older sister was out at a concert and her mother in the basement painting. After years of rebellion against her Jewish identity, Rachel had begun to consider herself a Gentile. Now she would look and live as one. Her blonde hair would've set her dad's anger blazing, but he'd never see her now. He had refused to let her work a part-time job after school because he knew she'd use the money for running away. Now she had to steal from her mother, in order to join Steve, her boyfriend whom her father had forbade her to see. She was banking on Steve's help because she didn't even have enough money of her own for one night in a motel. He said he could set them up until they got jobs. No one could stop her now. She would not wait one day longer for her new life.

When Rachel was sure her mother had gone down to the basement to paint for the evening in her studio, she took her backpack and slipped out into the night. She took a bus to a downtown bar that Steve could get into with a false ID

# # #

She walked in expecting to see Steve right away. Knowing she would be carded if she waited for him, she went back to wait outside. An hour later she began to watch for someone she could stay the night with, but no one she knew showed. Finally she took her chances, went in and tried to order a drink. She handed the new bartender Sarah's university ID and he noticed that the photo of 21 year old dark-haired Sarah did not look at all like her with the new blonde locks. She knew she could be charged for carrying a fake identity as well as being a minor and quickly grabbed the ID back, and split. Standing outside again near closing time, she felt a strong urge to just give up and go back home. She had expected such an urge to occur, but was not prepared for one this strong. She steeled herself back to resolve that going home was not an option.

The Greyhound station! It was close by. At least she could think there without being hassled too much. She made herself comfortable in a bus station chair, thinking maybe she could catnap the night away, when a policeman came in the door and asked if she had a ticket. Did she have somewhere to go? She quickly left the bus station.

She tugged at her too-short skirt as she walked down to the late night Burger King. It was filled mostly with drunks devouring food and drinking coffee. She knew time was running out. When this place closed she'd be out on the street again. She tried not to panic. Maybe she could sit in bus shelters on the mall until the morning. Then she could hit the pawn shops with her mother's jewelry. Something must've happened to Steve and she'd better have some money until she could find him again. With a few nights in a motel, she could look for work. She wanted to score some grass but that would have to wait. She'd have to get by with liquor.

She sat waiting for the Burger King to close, staring out at Hennepin Avenue, spread out like a big Midwestern main street, now a virtual no-man's land. Fear had ruined her appetite. Halfway through her fish sandwich she left it, along with the fries and the malt.

A tall, lean black man walked over to her table. Rachel did not recognize him at first. She took in his black pinstripe suit, expensive white shirt and the big shiny diamond in the tie clasp on his paisley-patterned tie. Where had she'd seen him before?"Hey, you're the guy…we were talking downtown and my sister butted in and ruined it."

"Yeah, I remember," he said as he handed her a cup of steaming coffee, "my name is Reggie Washington." He sat down next to her. "What's a pretty girl like you doing out here so late?"

Rachel was taken in by his deep voice and his concern. It had been a long time since anyone had listened to her, and she found herself telling him her whole story. Reggie seemed so understanding. He offered to put her up for the night. He said he even had some pot. They could do some up; maybe have a taste of wine, too. He could give her a lid on credit.

They left the fast food restaurant and headed for Reggie's small apartment just two blocks away. Rachel felt this was the answer to everything she'd been longing for. They entered an older building and walked up three flights of stairs to an apartment without a number. They entered and she was immediately offered a joint and a glass of wine. Reggie arranged the lights, turning on one lamp and lighting some candles. The pot was strong and the wine incredibly fine tasting. She felt lush. Her appetite returned. A hunger not only for food, which he'd prepared for them, but for him, his virility, which she keenly sensed. She ate the omelet and French bread—it was delicious. Everything was good, good, good. She felt secure. He'd been fully tuned into her body that night and gave her an orgasm. She awoke the next morning without her clothes on, in a large bed with pillows all around. Then she heard Reggie's voice in the next room. He was on the telephone and his voice was hard. "I have a blonde bitch here for you–for the Big Apple –yeah– same price IN CASH. Pick her up in the van."

4

BACKYARD BAR-B-Q

When a week had passed and the police failed to find Rachel, Ruth became despondent. She had taken her husband's passing with normal grief, but now was severely depressed over her runaway daughter. She couldn't concentrate long enough to paint, the one thing that had brought her solace.

The house felt like a funeral parlor to Sarah. It was deadly silent until her mother burst out sobbing. "Oh, poor Rachel," Ruth cried, "she could be dead out there somewhere."

"Damn Rachel!" Sarah said, surprised by her own candor. "Damn her, she's so childish, so selfish! Her so-called problems are nothing compared to what you're going though; what we're going through. Dad's gone. She said he was the cause of all her trouble, but now he's gone. She ought to shape up and join the family again. I'm sorry, but her problems are so adolescent."

"Shame on you!" Ruth looked up at Sarah, "I know you're concerned about me—God bless you—but your sister could be in real danger right now. What on earth can we do? The police have come up with nothing, nothing at all. I have no ideas who else to ask for help, do you? Can you think of anyone, anyone at all that might know where or how to look for Rachel?"

"No. I would've told you if I did...wait! I do know someone, maybe, the only person I know who knows people in the inner-city. He's a new friend, ah... you know him, too, the artist who won first place in that show you were in. I can ask him."

"Do it, dear! Go and ask him, right now!" She started crying again.

Sarah did Ruth's bidding immediately. She drove to the warehouse district where Jim's studio was located. But all the warehouses looked the same. Why hadn't she written down the exact address when she had the chance? She had to return home completely frustrated at not being able to help her mother.

Coincidentally, later that night Dean called her. "Yes, I remember you. How is Carl? Oh yes, I would love to come. What's the address? By the way, I'd like to get in touch with Jim. Ah, yes? Yeah, I know that. Oh, he'll be there. Great! See you there." She was excited by the invite to the barbeque at Dean's house and yes, Jim would be there.

# # #

No one answered the door at Dean's address, but there was music coming from the backyard, so she walked around the side of the house. Through cracks in the fence she saw a mixed group of people; some artistic-looking and others straight looking. She opened the rear gate cautiously and stepped in.

"AH, MY LITTLE JEWISH ANGEL! COME IN! COME IN AND JOIN US!" Carl joyfully welcomed her. He stood over a grill basting chicken pieces with bar-b-q sauce. All eyes were upon her after his greeting and she looked around to see who she knew. Dean waved at her, but she spotted Jim. He was talking to dark-haired young man with brown eyes with trembling hands sitting almost on top of a beer keg.

After a friendly greeting and a hug, Sarah wasted no time making a pitch to Jim to see if he could help find Rachel. Jim listened sympathetically, asking questions about what Rachel was into, and where she hung out.

Then Jim put his hand on the shoulder of the man sitting on a beer keg. "Sarah, this is my friend Gil Montgomery. He might be better suited to help you than me. He knows more people in the kind of scene your little sister was into." He lowered his voice, "He's a drinker, an alcoholic actually, and knows all the bars. I smoke dope, as you know, and stay out of bars unless I want to dig music. Why don't you talk to him?"

She hesitated, "I don't know him…Oh, I don't think so."

Jim looked at Sarah. "Say, are you hungry?" She nodded in appreciation.

"I thought so. Let me get you a plate of food. You just have to try some of Carl's famous bar-b-q chicken and that delicious potato salad and sweet corn cooked in foil."

As an afterthought he said, "I'm going to get Gil a plate of food, too – get him away from that keg for awhile."

Sarah was hurt. Jim had just casually shifted her onto a drunk. She had sized up Gil's demeanor and actions. He had that manner of a lot of drunks who try to appear as if they were normal and everyone should just accept them.

But weeks of worry and frayed nerves had left Sarah weary, slipping into depression. Now Jim, the man she was going to pin her hopes on for finding Rachel, had left her staring with a mixture of anger and sadness at this hopeless drunk. The whole effort was jinxed and hopeless. She wanted to turn around and walk quickly away. But, something made her step back and take another look at Gil: He had on faded denim Levi's, work boots, a denim shirt and held a comical corncob pipe in one hand; a beer in the other, leaning on the keg, as if it were his best friend. He looked back at her, his brown eyes direct, "Sarah, I'll help you any way I can," he said sincerely. But then he fell back and caught his arm on a chair, "But I won't be able to do anything for you until I get back off my job with the railroad."

"Oh please! That would be so helpful. You've just given me the only bit of hope we've had so far. Thank you so much, ah, is it Gil? "

"Yeah, it's Gil, Sarah." Just then, Jim arrived back with the plates of food and everyone just loved the bar-b-q chicken and thought it was delicious. Jim looked over at them and said, "Carl uses Ken Davis Bar-B-Q Sauce."

Sarah looked over at him, "What's that?"

"I know Ken," Gil said. "He used to be a waiter on the Northern Pacific Railway's passenger train where I work. He made his sauce at home and would just give some to friends and sell a few jars now and then out of his station wagon. Nice guy. Good waiter. But the demand for his sauce got so big he quit the road and now he just sells his sauce commercially. It went national."

"Best chicken I've ever had," said Sarah, licking the tasty sweet sauce off her fingers.

"Go tell Carl how good it is. He loves it when people compliment his cooking." Although wary, Sarah went right over to Carl and congratulated him. Gil was right; a guest must acknowledge the hosts. She longed to be part of this crowd; to bond with these jazz people!

"Man, Carl, you cook on the grill like you cook with your bass! Thanks for the great food and inviting me to the party. How's your leg?"

"Oh its fine, my little angel, fine. I'm still limping a little, but thanks to you it's gonna be fine."

Just then some dynamite lyrics broke from the speaker.

"Turn that up!" Carl yelled back to Dean.

"Who is that?" Sarah asked, swaying to the beat.

"That's "Testify" by the Isley Brothers with Jimi Hendrix. It's a 45. We just got it."

"I wanna see your record collection." She looked at Carl.

"Most of them are Dean's. He finds good stuff. Go on into the house–his sides are in there, go right in an' have a look."

"Thank you." She turned. "I'm on my way!"

She passed a group of musicians trading stories at the biggest picnic table she'd ever seen. A trumpet and sax player each playing passages now and then. Little children, black and white, were playing tag with each other and two dogs joined them. Women socialized at another table, one cutting watermelon to give to the kids. Colorful men and women, wearing bright shades, some tribal, and all with some bit of adornment, necklaces, beads, pipes, hand drums, handbags, packs. A man dressed all in black --black shirt, pants and a fedora was handing another man a lid of grass in exchange for cash. Was he Jim's dealer? She wouldn't ask. She already got what she came for. A chance to meet Gil and that was enough; she'd leave it at that.

Dean was in the house spinning records. "Dean, thank you for inviting me! The food and music are great. And so are the people."

"You'll have to meet more of them."

"I'd love to, but I'll take a raincheck, please. I'm on a mission for my mom and I gotta get back and report to her. Dean, that last 45 you played was so HOT! Where did you get it?"

"A DJ gave it to me. Promo copy. You can have it. I can buy one. It's probably out by now." Dean picked it up and slipped it into Sarah's purse.

"Oh my God, thank you! Mind if I take a quick look at your record collection?"

"Sure, go ahead. It's in the living room."

The living room was filled with records all over, on shelves, tables, in boxes, jazz, blues, R&B, and gospel. Sarah could've spent hours going through them. She turned to bid good night to Gil.

"Oh, Gil, I just want to tell you that we'll want to pay you. Mom and I want to pay you for helping us."

"Oh no, it's okay. I can do this okay."

"No, we insist. Here's my card. When you get back from your train trip, call me and I'll bring you some money. Come out and meet Mom. God knows how much we appreciate you just saying you'd try!"

5

JOE: NORTHERN MINNESOTA 1958

"You may as well go home, Joe, I know you ain't old enough to get in here," The surly blonde bouncer at the Log Jam, an old dance pavilion near Lake Bemidji, stood by the door glaring at 16 year old Joe Citro. Moonlight danced a sparkling froth from the middle of the lake near the dock. Now and then the door opened, letting out people dressed in sporty, bright clothes; loud-talking, tipsy people, who released a tantalizing whiff of music with them, a much more sophisticated music than Joe had ever heard. It had a seductive melody and a swinging beat like some of his mother's big band records, so fascinating compared to the frumpy old polkas they played everywhere else. He didn't want liquor, hadn't come for girls. Music called him.

"Come on, Swede, can't you let me in if I don't drink?"

"Drink or not, kid, the law says you ain't old enough to even be in here and I ain't lettin' you. Come back when you're 21."

Joe now felt his whole night was ruined, and on top of it he needed to take a piss.

"I need to take a leak, Swede; can I come in just for that?"

"Go piss out back. Go on, kid, move." His spit landed within inches of Joe's new tennis shoes.

Disgusted and in urgent need, Joe hurried around back of the old log structure. Behind the parking lot stood a field filled with moonlight, blinking fireflies and the sound of crickets. He came to the back wall to relieve himself and there it was – THE MUSIC! The old wall vibrated with it. He realized he was standing right behind the bandstand, only a board's width away. While the front and sides of the dancehall were made of ancient logs, the back was just old grey planks. There were knotholes here and there, and golden light poured out from them.

He rushed up to one and peered inside just as the band leader raised his golden trumpet to begin playing. Hearing this haunting melody for the first time, Joe was mesmerized, left in a highly agitated state. He could see the bass and piano players too, but the drummer was out of his range of sight. He heard the people laughing and enjoying themselves. The beautiful women caught his eye, their bodies moving seductively in dance. But the song! He had to find out its name so he could buy the sheet music. It would, name or not, now forever remain stamped in his memory of this summer night. He scrutinized the way the trumpet man fingered the keys, trying to understand what notes he played. Later he would try to play the melody himself.

Joe was willing to hitchhike a hundred miles or more one way to hear such music from musicians like these. His music teacher said they were from Grand Forks and most of them taught school for a living.

He moved to another knothole so he could watch the drummer. Losing track of time, he listened as the band moved through numbers, alternating between fast and slow. His neck was getting stiff. As the band launched into "Stardust," an old man came out of the dancehall half drunk and swaggered across the parking lot toward his truck to get a bottle of liquor. "Hell's bells!" he blurted, stumbling on a rock. Looking up, he noticed Joe and yelled, "Hey, Youngblood, what the hell you doin' back there?" It startled Joe out of his reverie. The intrusion angered him. "Nothing," he yelled back. The old man's grin looked stupid, almost grotesque. He wore a new denim western shirt with pearl white buttons. Nicely pressed Levi's fell over cowboy boots, and his big silver belt buckle caught the glint of the lamppost.

"I'm just listening to the music," Joe added, hoping the old man would go away.

"Oh, a music lover! Well, come on in, son, I'll buy you a drink."

"You know I can't get in there, mister, I'm underage."

"Oh, the hell with that, kid, I'll get you in. Swede can't say nothin' if you're with me. I'll tell Adam you're one of my grandsons."

"Adam knows better. He knows me."

"He won't care as long as you're with me. Come on, let's try it. What you got to lose? You wanna hear some music? What's your name, kid?"

"Joe. Joe Citro."

"Nice to meet you. I'm Harvey. I know your mother. Let's go get us a drink."

"I don't drink liquor---just Coke," said Joe firmly, as he walked over to join Harvey.

The bottle of booze swung freely in Harvey's hand. Joe eyed it, knowing his father had died from booze and his mother drank too much, too.

"He's with me," Harvey said, waving the bouncer aside to lead Joe up to the bar and introduce him to his wife, Myrtle. She wore a frilly white blouse, gold vest and black skirt.

Adam, the owner, brought setups for Harvey's booze. He looked at Joe knowing he was underage, "Where'd you find this kid?'

"Oh, I know him. He's the Citro boy. He doesn't drink so just a Coke for him." Harvey poured whiskey into the two glasses.

"Whoa! Harvey." Myrtle said, "Leave room for some mix with mine."

Joe was caught between gratitude to this old man who had gotten him into the Log Jam, and for accepting his code, never to drink because of what it had done to his parents.

"Bottoms up," said Harvey. "This'll get us in the mood for your music. An' watch out for those redheads – they're dynamite!" He pointed out one on the dance floor and winked as though he knew a private truth about her. Joe could see all the musicians well now and how the dancers were responding. Each song they played was a rare and precious gem offered on this summer night.

As much as Harvey liked to talk, he shut up while the music

played. When the musicians took a break, Harvey grabbed Joe and they headed over to the jukebox where he selected a rockabilly song by Carl Perkins titled "Matchbox." Joe studied the juke. Mostly polks and corny hits of the day, like, "How Much is That Doggie in the Window" or "North to Alaska." But he found some older stuff and played Sinatra singing "Blue Skies" with Tommy Dorsey, and Billie Holiday's version of "Back in Your Own Backyard," with Lester Young backing her. By then Joe had finished sipping his Coke and when the band began again he felt he had entered innermost musical heaven. It ended too quickly. The musicians had played an encore with the leader doing his version of Bunny Berigan's, "I Can't Get Started," vocal and all, and now they were packing up, heading to the bar.

The musicians crowded in right next to Harvey and Myrtle at the bar so Adam could pay off the band leader and then poured them all drinks on the house. Harvey was pretty drunk and Myrtle was trying to get him home. But he roused himself. "Hey Cliff, I want you to meet Joe here. He's a big fan and a real music lover,"

"My pleasure," Cliff said, extending his hand. "Are you a musician, Joe?"

"Well, ah…," Joe stammered. "I play trumpet. A little."

"Hey, that's good, Joe. Keep playing, man. Nice to see you again Harvey, Joe, Myrt, we gotta book. See you all next Saturday."

They were gone and the music with them. Joe wanted to rush after them, attach himself, know them, hear everything they were saying to each other, know what they thought and felt about everything. He wanted to continue to search the night for a place where music never ended.

# # #

Five years later Joe turned 21. All the while Adam had let Joe into his bar, supposedly under the wing of Harvey, or Cliff, the band leader who, since Joe always sat in, said of him, "He's with the band." And because Joe never drank anything but Coke or coffee, Adam never worried about Joe at all. The sheriff had come in once because Adam had let the band play way past closing time on New Year's Eve. The sheriff even overlooked Joe being there, and after making a brief show of shutting down to close, when the sheriff left Adam yelled to the band, "Okay, boys, he's gone, strike up the band!"

Joe was in the bar legally now for the first time in his life and could order a drink, but he didn't. He ordered his usual instead, black coffee, which Adam never charged him and Joe always left him a tip. Adam had ordered a birthday cake from the bakery, and Cliff and the boys had pooled their money to buy Joe two jazz albums which Cliff ordered from the music store in Grand Forks, Louis Armstrong's "At the Crescendo," Volumes I and II, live recordings from a night club in L.A. by the master. They gave these to Joe with a card signed by all the regulars.

He was overwhelmed. These were the people he chose to be with, who had shared the best times he had ever had in his young life, playing music. They were the light that balanced the emptiness of life at home with an alcoholic mother.

After the first couple of years just listening, Joe began to bring his trumpet and sit in. Before long he was even able to fill in when Cliff was sick. When they played together, they would trade riffs and improvise taking turns soloing. But it became almost embarrassing for Cliff as Joe's playing had become better than his and everyone knew it. "Look at you, Joe," he said. "You were just a kid hangin' out back, and now you can blow circles 'round me, blow me right off the set. Go on ahead with your bad self, blow, man, BLOW!"

Joe had learned from his high school music teacher and from the piano man in Cliff's band, who was a college music teacher. But now he wanted to play jazz, and he instinctively knew he wouldn't be able to learn that from school teachers. As much as he loved these older musicians who had adopted him, he knew he had to move on. An ingredient was missing, something elusive that existed in a larger world.

"I think you should move to Minneapolis, man," Cliff told him. "A guy with talent like yours, you'd waste it stayin' 'round here. You go down there, you can stretch and learn. You gotta dig the black music down there, man, it's the best – much hotter than what we play. It swings twice as hard, it's twice as mellow, twice as heavy. You hear it an' you'll know."

Coming home from the Log Jam the night of his birthday, Joe found an empty house. His mother and her boyfriend Frank, whom she now let live with them, would be out somewhere at an afterhours party after closing the bar in town. Joe realized that his mother had completely forgotten his birthday. She left for the bar with Frank without even making supper. Joe came in from his weekend job to make his own cold sandwich, down it with milk, then clean up to go to the Log Jam. His mother hadn't even left him a birthday card.

He took his new treasures, the Louie Armstrong albums from the people who had remembered his birthday, into his bedroom to enjoy as much as possible before the drunks came home. The recordings were a revelation! All the big band records he had ordered in town were pale compared to Satchmo's genius, his incendiary passion, his authority. The records were pure joy. Joe would buy more – collect every Louis Armstrong album he could locate!

He heard them fumble at the door, laughing insanely, cursing, and careening around. He shut off the music immediately, hoping they wouldn't know he was up. His hatred of Frank was overwhelming. He wanted to physically throw him out. His mother had lost her job soon after Frank had begun drinking with her. They soon went through what was left of the insurance money from when Joe's father was killed in the car crash. Now Frank was trying to get his mother to put the house up for sale. He would not take a job and three of them lived on the grocery money Joe brought in from his part-time job.

Joe finally left his bedroom to use the bathroom. He saw Frank had passed out on the living room couch. His mother staggered up to Joe as he returned to his room. "What are those?" she asked, pointing to the records on the bed.

"Satchmo records. They gave them to me at the Log Jam."

"Who did? Why?"

"Cliff and Adam and the others. For my birthday."

"Oh my God! It's your birthday. I suppose you think what a mother, huh? I didn't even remember my own son's birthday. Well, by God I guess I didn't. I'm sorry, Joe. I wanted to buy something for you, but I didn't have enough money. Honest. I couldn't even buy you a card."

"Yeah, but you had enough money to drink all night, you and Frank both," he thought. She looked pathetic. Tears were forming in her eyes and he felt a mixture of pity for her embarrassment and revulsion at her condition, underlined as always by the deep sorrow that came from realizing how far gone she was and the improbability of any recovery.

In the morning Joe remembered that Myrtle, Harvey's wife, had called the Log Jam with a message for him to come by their place in the morning, saying also she was sorry Harvey hadn't shown up. That had puzzled Joe because he never missed a Saturday at the bar and he knew it was Joe's birthday.

"Come on in, Joe. Come in and sit down," Myrtle said as she led him to the kitchen. "I'm sorry Harvey didn't make it to help celebrate with you. He started in too early, drinkin' like he does, an' then I upset him by tellin' him what my doctor told me-- that I have cancer. He took it real hard when I told him the doc said its terminal. Thank God he passed out before he could drive to the bar like he was gonna do. He's still in there," she pointed to their bedroom, "hung-over, and sick as a dog."

"Gosh, Myrtle, I'm really sorry to hear about the cancer."

"Well, let's not dwell on that. That's in the Lord's hands. But it was your birthday and here's the cake I made for you."

She brought over a cake with 21 candles, and then reached for a pot of coffee and some cups. "Sit down. I'll light the candles. He always does that, you know."

"What's that?"

"Starts too early. Drinkin." She said, "He really wanted to spend some time with you yesterday. You're just like a son to him, Joe, the son we never had. Nellie moved away right after school and we never had any boys. Here's a card he left for you. And those keys there, they're for you too."

"Keys?"

"He's giving you that truck, Joe. The new one. He never used it 'cept to go to town. He always felt more comfortable in the old work truck, and since he stopped working much he hardly ever uses it. The workers do all the masonry work now. He just goes out to set things up and supervise now and then. When he's sober, that is."

"But, my God, Myrtle, are you sure he wants to do this?"

"Sure as the day is long, Joe, and you deserve it. He needs to feel like he's helping you, Joe; there's hardly anything else he enjoys anymore. But he thinks the world of you. Go on, take the truck. He won't use it."

Joe was on the verge of tears; trance-like he finished his cake and coffee, and then got up to hug Myrtle. "Thank you for everything. I'm so sorry to hear about the cancer. Please thank Harvey for me, tell him I'll come by tomorrow."

He drove his new truck straight to the parking lot at the Log Jam, his home away from home. He sat there trying to get used to the idea the truck was his. He opened the card from Joe and Myrtle. Inside were two crisp hundred-dollar bills and a transfer of ownership of the truck's title to him. Harvey had scrawled "Lots of luck, son!"

Joe let it out then, crying there alone. The truck was like a sign to immediately do what he really wanted before he could talk himself out if it – to leave for Minneapolis. There was nothing to stay here for but a subsistence level job while he watched his home life continue to disintegrate. He locked up the truck, left it there and began to walk home. He'd come back for it in the morning. Frank would covet it if Joe took it home now. Next morning he packed a small suitcase, left a brief note for his mother, and walked away from the house without looking back. He started the engine of his new truck, and then just sat there awhile telling himself it was really his.

He stopped at his real emotional homestead, Harvey and Myrtle's place, to thank them again before heading out. Harvey apologized for sleeping through his birthday. "I know you wanna blow your horn, kid, but you ain't gonna be a star overnight. You got any ideas what you're gonna do for work?"

"I don't know. Music is all I really care about. Work is just work. Anything I can get, I guess."

"You wanna do more construction work?" Joe was looking out the kitchen window at the piles of rock, the neatly stacked rows of bricks and cement blocks, at the mixers and the big storage shed that held the bags of cement and other tools and equipment he and the other laborers, more skilled, had used working for Harvey through the years. He had been working for him since he started high school. It was hard work but it was something he knew and trusted.

"Yeah, I'd do that."

"Well, it couldn't be any harder down there than what you've been used to here. I tell you what; I got a friend down there that's the head of the Hod Carrier's Union. He can get you a job doing labor on a construction site. I know he will if I ask him."

"Really?"

"Sure. Larry and I started out together right out of high school down there as laborers for a masonry company. We got in the union and he moved up in it while I started a cement business of my own and eventually brought it up here. Larry comes by the house here at least once a year when he comes up north to go fishing. Hold on, I'll call him right now."

He came back with a piece of paper. "Here it is– the address of the Labor Temple where Larry's got his office, and his phone number. He said he can line you up within a day or two after you give him a call."

As he pulled out onto the country dirt road to hit the highway for the Cities, Joe became one more soul in the perennial migration of youths, looking for opportunities and a freer way of life. The truck was running smoothly with all its potential power, and Joe felt fully alive with anticipation, if not a little nervous.

The closer he got to Minneapolis the better the music got on the radio. He found a station just as Billie Holiday began to sing "Fine And Mellow." As happy and excited as he already was, this piece of music was the icing on the cake, like it had come out of a realm of musical magic. It reminded him of the night when he was sixteen years old. He had a date with a high school beauty and a new-year Oldsmobile convertible loaned by a friend, to pick her up with. The girl stood him up. Her father came to the door and made an excuse for her.

Too depressed then to take the car into town, Joe drove it down to a lake to just sit there while the moonlight played on the lake and loons called. He had the convertible top down and a nice breeze was coming off the lake. It would've been a perfect place to park with the girl although he had planned on taking her to a drive-in for a snack after a movie then right back to her home, doing it right the first night. He switched on the radio to capture a station from far away. Billie Holiday was singing "What A Little Moonlight Can Do". He was mesmerized and there was no room then for any disappoint-ment about the girl, nor any self pity. Billie's voice was so naked, so poignant to cut him to the quick. Her naked voice crying out of nocturnal airwaves gave him the first knowledge that all human beings are fundamentally alone in the world but also present was the solace of song.

6

JOE: MINNEAPOLIS 1963

Moving from the outskirts of Minneapolis in toward the inner city, Joe began to notice black people walking on the sidewalks and driving cars and trucks. It was good to see them again. He was fascinated by how they moved. Some walked freely, effortlessly, as though their bodies were chariots of fluid motion. Others walked slowly, bent over by the weight of extra awareness, a depth of suffering he would never comprehend. He saw blacks for the first time as a boy when his dad drove him down to attend The Minnesota State Fair. He saw them again when his high school band made a trip to Minneapolis to partic-ipate in a competition. A black marching band with its powerful drum section won hands down. The rhythmic power astonished everyone. "That's exactly the way it was," his dad said, "when your mom and I heard Fats Waller live. He played at a joint in Nisswa, Minnesota. We were on our honeymoon down that way. He sat a full bottle of whiskey up on the piano and drank it straight and it was all gone by the end of the night. He sang and played that piano so well, he had everybody in the joint mesmerized." Joe had seriously listened to all those old 78's of his parents' collection and their new LP albums: Harry James, Bunny Berrigan, Benny Goodman, Glen Grey and His Casa Loma Orchestra, even records by Raphael Mendes, classical trumpet virtuoso. He finally settled on Basie and Ellington as favorites, but stopped listening to anything else after hearing Satchmo. He dug Charlie Parker and was amazed at how he and Diz could play together, but still loved Satch more than Dizzy's antics or Miles Davis's cool musings.

At Central and University Joe stopped at a place called Jim's Coffee Shop & Bakery, and took his road map in with him to get his bearings. He bought two doughnuts with his coffee and asked directions to the Labor Temple.

After thanking Jim, he walked over to the Labor Temple. He opened the big door and stepped in next to the desk of the head of the Hod Carriers Union. A big man with a ready smile, he was sitting at his desk lighting a cigar. "What can I do for you, son?"

"Well…ah…my friend Harvey, up north, said you might be able to help me find a job down here in Minneapolis."

"Oh, so you're Harvey's buddy, huh? I told him I could help you and I will. You wanna start out in this union as a laborer, is that right?"

"Yes, sir."

"Hold on a minute." He picked up his phone and dialed a number. "Let me talk to Curt , this is Larry over at Hod Carriers. You got any opening for a grunt, a laborer? I gotta lad here looking for a job. Friend of mine up north sez he's a good worker. Can you put him on somewhere? Okay, okay! I'll tell him. Thanks, Curt. Say, when are we going fishing?" After a few minutes the man hung up the phone. "Okay, Joe that was a foreman with Knutson Construction Company. They're on a job right now at the Minneapolis Auditorium, building an extension on it for a convention center. He'll have an opening in a week. Can you wait that long?"

"Yes, sir. I sure can."

"Good. He's gotta replace a kid who's going back to college. You can take that kid's place."

Joe was elated. He got a job that quick and a whole week in which to hunt for a place to live. He felt like celebrating. He wanted to find one of the black jazz clubs Cliff had told him about. He walked back to Jim's to buy a Minneapolis paper and a coffee to go. He sat in his truck and marked off the apartments to check out. He realized he was going to find it difficult to match their locations on his map. He called the most interesting looking place from a pay phone, and when he finally located the address after getting turned around once or twice, the landlady said she had just rented it to someone.

By then it was six o'clock and he was hungry. He had eaten only a sandwich and apple on his way to the city and craved a full meal. He found a restaurant called Embers on University Avenue that served breakfast all day. He ordered a full breakfast with orange juice and coffee and asked the waitress if she knew of the nightclub called Road Buddy's.

"Sure. Just up University here toward St. Paul a few blocks the other side of Snelling Avenue. You'll see it on your left." Joe remembered Cliff's words: "You're gonna have a peak experience, man, listening to black musicians."

He paid a five-dollar cover and went in. The bartender was sharper than any Joe had ever seen up north. "Music will be mighty fine, man. Too fine. I know you'll dig it. Stick around.

# # #

It was Friday night and the place was filling up quickly. Blacks and a few whites here and there, everybody enjoying themselves with food, liquor and raucous verbal jamming. It was a joyous place already, even without music, the energy tremendous, as if to promise some unimaginably exciting event. The music Joe was to witness on his first night in the Twin Cities, would put a stamp on his memory to last a lifetime.

The band was finished setting up. It swung, lifting its listeners in a wave of enthusiastic approval. It kicked like a mule, punched like Cassius Clay. It was a profound, almost terrible realization for Joe, that in the future music less than this would always be found wanting.

"Wait 'til you hear the band later on." Joe turned to the man at his side who'd been drinking steadily. He was dressed in denim, looked rough, and yet seemed friendly. Joe simply smiled.

"Hey, my name's Gil. You want a drink, man? I see you're just drinking coffee. I'll buy you a drink."

"Oh, no thanks, Gil. My name is Joe and I don't drink alcohol– just coffee."

"Okay, okay. Well, I'm gonna tip the bartender for you anyway. Reggie's a damn good barkeep."

A waiter came with a plate of smoldering barbeque ribs and set them down in front of Gil. A second plate held big cottage-fried potatoes, coleslaw and Texas toast. Even though he had recently eaten, Joe's mouth began to water.

"You hungry, man?"

"No, I just ate."

"Well, you ought to come here sometime and try these ribs. Best in the Twin Cities. Ol' Chet, the owner, is real particular 'bout his ribs. He smokes them the old fashioned way, all night long, and uses a special recipe for the sauce that his sister makes. This place is famous for ribs, man. Here, try one of these, even if you're not hungry. You'll see what I mean." The meat was tender and the sauce had a heady flavor as smoky and rich as the music in the place.

The band leader was at the microphone: "Thank you, thank you very much. Now I'd like to introduce our guest artist, the best sax player this side of Kansas City, Mr. Earl Saunders!" Several women in the crowd shouted their approval. The handsome, old, white-haired Saunders began a ballad, "Someone to Watch over Me," and Joe immediately sensed the man's total authenticity. He'd never heard this kind of artistry in a horn player before. He looked around the hushed club. People were rapt, completely attentive. Women were especially in awe and smiling. "I know that's right!" one woman exclaimed when Saunders finished his first solo. "Oh yeah! You KNOW that's right," another woman said. And applause came up all over the club for the old man's tasty playing. Joe knew he was witnessing a kind of artistic miracle, this unique art form happening live in this humble black nightclub of a Midwestern city. It confirmed his decision to move here and he knew in his heart the proximity of this music would be worth all the trials he would face trying to survive.

But then the last set was over and he felt good; the sustenance of it was in him to stay. It would last until he could return to listen and maybe play here himself one day. Now there was the reality of a decision – to find a motel or try to sleep in his truck to save money. Harvey had warned Joe that he would have to have an extra month's rent as a deposit, and he wasn't sure if he could cover that, let alone have enough left for food until his first check came in.

"Where you staying?" Gil asked. Joe explained his situation. "Don't sleep in your truck man, the nabs might spot you and hassle you. Don't rent no motel, either. You save that bread for your apartment. You can stay at my crib tonight. Maybe you can rent a place tomorrow."

Reggie, who had given his last call pitch, overheard them talking. "Yeah, we're going out on the railroad," he said, "Gil and I. Day after tomorrow. He's a cook an' I'm a waiter."

"Yeah, we go stock the car tomorrow – just for a couple hours, then we go out early the next day to Chicago, then across to Seattle and back."

# # #

Joe slept on a couch in Gil's "crib" and woke to the smell of coffee brewing. "I'm sorry I didn't get up earlier, man, I could've made us some breakfast. But I've got to head for the commissary in St. Paul after I have a little hair o' the dog here in my brew. Got to stock the dining car."

"You want a shot of grog in your brew?" he asked, fetching his rum. "Oh, that's right, you don't drink. Good for you. I hope you can stay off it, man, an' don't end up a souse like me." He handed Joe a cup of coffee, then spiked his own generously with rum, drank it down quickly, then poured another three-fourths rum, one-fourth coffee. " I see you brought in a trumpet case. You a musician?"

"Yeah, I play trumpet. Played dance music up north. I'd like to play jazz if I can learn how."

"Cool. Tell you what – check out The Blue Note, man."

"The Blue Note?"

"Yeah, little spade joint in North Minneapolis. They have jam sessions on Sunday afternoons, let guys sit in. You'd dig it. You could go there and just listen if you want to."

Like a hunter finding the next sighting of his prey, Joe felt a jolt of excitement. He walked over and picked up the cover of the album that was playing and read the back of it thoroughly. Gene "Jug" Ammons. Powerfully bold, almost brash sax. Urban yet funky. He liked the extra sound of the conga player, Ray Barretto, added to the group. He wished he had time to examine each one of Gil's records, really read and study them. He glanced around the place, trying to take it all in quickly, knowing they would soon leave. From the ceiling near the kitchen hung a bulbous skein of empty chianti bottles bearing Italian names. Here and there lay piles of books. A bookcase on one wall was handmade from recycled boards, bricks and cement blocks. He glanced at the titles of the books on the table where they sat: Another Country by James Baldwin and Steppenwolf by Hermann Hesse.

"You have a lot of books. Are you a writer?" Joe asked.

"I'm a poet. I'm trying to start a novel but I'm basically a poet. Look, I gotta book, but I'm gonna write down my address here and phone number. Keep in touch. And good luck, man. Wanna hear you play that horn someday."

# # #

Monday morning, Joe headed out to start his new job after renting a cheap apartment. He had scouted out the job site location in advance, enabling him to arrive a half hour before starting time, find a parking place for his truck, and prepare himself psychologically. He pulled into a parking lot across from the job just to look the area over and think a minute. He began pouring himself a cup of coffee from his thermos. A loud car horn startled his nerves and he spilled hot coffee on his work pants. A big, expensive looking black car sped towards his truck as if to collide, its horn continuing to blare long after the car had screeched to a halt. A man in a suit jumped out and ran up to Joe's window and pounded on it. Joe rolled down his window in disbelief. "CAN'T YOU READ?" the man yelled. His face was red, his neck muscles strained. "CAN'T YOU SEE?

THIS IS A PRIVATE PARKING SPACE! GET THE HELL OUTTA HERE RIGHT NOW BEFORE I GO AND GET SECURITY!"

Already nervous about starting a new job, Joe was now in fight-or-flight response mode. He looked up at the wall he had parked before and saw a name labeled there. Lot spaces were marked with the names of executives of a company. "Excuse me; I didn't know this was private parking."

"You must be blind then. Go on, get the hell outta here. This isn't for construction workers. Get your sorry ass outta here!" Joe rolled up his window and quickly pulled out of the parking spot and the whole lot. By the time he re-parked, workers were parking and walking in to work. Joe approached a couple of heavyset pipe fitters and asked them where he could find the carpenters' foreman. "That's Curt you want," one said with a friendly smile. "He's right over there." Joe noticed a very tall, slender man pointing out directions to some workers.

"So you're the kid Larry's sending me. Let's get you a hardhat from the trailer and get you punched in. I'm gonna put you with Sandy for a while, helping him shovel."

Underneath the steel girded outline of the first floor of a convention center being built as an addition to the Minneapolis Auditorium, a muscular black worker was shoveling sand from a pit. "That's where the boiler's gonna go," Curt said. "We gotta shovel a pit big enough for it to go in. Sandy just started on it this morning. He'll show you how to help him. I'll stop back later."

The solidly built black man extended his hand. "Name's Sandy. Nice to meet you, Joe. There's an extra shovel over there. Just shovel the sand out over one side or the other as far as you can toss it. And take your time – slow and easy." He smiled and went back shoveling in a natural, steady way, lifting full shovelfuls of sand effortlessly, tossing them well over the side with graceful ease. In half an hour Joe's muscles were aching. He didn't have a watch but he felt like he had been working for at least an hour. Sandy sensed Joe's growing discomfort. He stopped shoveling and came over. "How's it going, man?"

"Shit, I'm tired already."

"Just go easier. It's gonna take a few days for us to dig this all out. I forgot to tell you there's a water jug over there for us."

"What time do we get a break?"

"At ten o' clock."

"What time is it now?"

"'Bout a quarter to nine. Hang in there, man."

Joe felt a boost of energy from the coffee he drank when their break finally came, but half an hour later he felt weaker than ever. By noon he could hardly lift his shovel. They brought their lunches out into the sun and sat on a pile of plywood. Sandy told Joe that he was going back to college in a few days, back to the University of Minnesota Law School, and would continue playing football for the University team. He was a star player who wanted to go on to a career in pro football. When Joe told him he wanted to become a jazz musician, Sandy said, "All right! Cool. We'll have to go dig some jazz together sometime. Can you dig it?"

Back on the job, Joe watched Sandy shovel with the same ease he had early that morning. The man was a marvel – not a bead of sweat on his brow – like there was nothing to it. Joe's sweatshirt was soaked. His handkerchief was wet from wiping sweat from his face. His eyes stung. His whole body ached.

# # #

When the alarm clock went off in his studio apartment that next morning, Joe felt like every muscle in his body was sore and stiff. He didn't want to move at all. The whole second day was painful and torturous. He tried to shovel the sand high over the bank, but it often fell short to fall back in. Sandy understood but Joe was still ashamed. Pain shot through his arms and shoulders. He began to feel sick, lost his appetite. He forced lunch down anyway. "It'll be better tomorrow," Sandy said. "You'll see. Just try to rest as much as possible. No one can see us down here. Just try to make it one more day and we'll probably be outta here. I'll be in school and you'll probably be helping the carpenters. He's testing you out is what he's doing. If you make it for two or three days, he'll give you softer work. He does this with the new guys."

Because of Sandy's kindness, Joe held on another day. When Sandy would talk about football or college, Joe didn't know what to say. Several guys on the job said he was a fantastic football player, a star quarterback. To Joe it was more important he was a sympathetic soul.

Finally, on the fourth day, Joe was reassigned. Curt took him up top to daylight to work with the carpenters.

7

JEWISH BUDDHIST

Saturday morning was a good time to sleep in, but Sarah got dressed and went down to the kitchen to make coffee for Ruth. She poured a cup of her own while waiting for her mother. Looking out the window, she saw the empty streets that always seemed deserted. No one in sight. Everyone locked inside. Where are the kids? In the inner city kids roamed everywhere and people were out full throttle, bouncing around nonstop. Out here in this suburb, not one kid, not one soul anywhere in sight.

After a quiet breakfast of lox and bagels, and fruit, during which Sarah could only coax a few words out of her depressed mother, she decided to do the dishes, knowing that if she didn't they would still be there at lunch. Then she went back up to her room, wondering how she could get through the day with nothing to look forward to nothing but college homework. At 11:00 a.m. the phone rang.

"Hello Sarah? This is Mira. I'm calling from New York City. Sarah, how are you?"

"Oh Mira! It's so good to hear your voice! Well, actually I'm bored. Bored, lonely and quite sad, but I don't want to bother you with any of that, Mira. How are you, my best high school friend? How's New York?"

"It's great! I'm in college."

"Cool, so am I. What are you majoring in?"

"Oriental studies. I was going to major in anthropology, but I changed to Oriental studies. What is your major in?"

"English with a minor in French. I really like it—enjoy it really. But now that Dad's gone I might try to switch to Art History."

"I'm a Buddhist now."

"A Buddhist? I thought you were Jewish like me!"

"Of course I'm still Jewish. I'm a Buddhist now too. Seriously."

"Wow. Okay, Mira, I understand. That is really interesting. Now, how is your love life?"

"I'm engaged."

"You are?! Already? Oh my God, who to?"

"A gorgeous gentile named Spencer. He's my prince. Dad doesn't like that he's gentile but he's slowly accepting it. He knows it's my life. I don't know how he'll act when he finds out I now consider myself a Buddhist, too! Nothing says I can't do both! How about you, Sarah, do you still go to synagogue?"

"We go to synagogue only for Rosh Hashanah and Yom Kippur, but at home we light Sabbath candles and observe Hanukkah and Passover Seder. I like all those but now that Dad's gone I don't know if Mom will keep them up. I'll try to remind her...."

"You said you were sad, dear Sarah, why? Did you say your dad died?

"Yes, that makes me sad, and on top of that my sister Rachel is missing. She's been gone for two weeks now and the cops have no clue. It's killing my mom. After Dad passed, I need to watch over Mom, she's really down. If I had someone to talk to, I could handle it, but all my friends have gone away, like you, and I don't like any boys right now."

"Why not? You're good lookin' and sweet. A real catch."

"Oh, I get hit on now and then, but it's because I've got big breasts. I'm just average looking otherwise. Guys are always staring at my chest, not my face. It's like I'm just a pair of walking boobs; no head, no brain. Someday my prince will come perhaps. I'm glad yours did. Know what I do like now, though? JAZZ! I listen to jazz. It makes me feel better...."

They promised to keep up their friendship and signed off.

The call left Sarah feeling better emotionally.

# # #

Buddhism? Sarah went to her bookcase. There was *Think on These Things* by J. Krishnamurti. Next to it was *Siddhartha* by Hermann Hesse. Campus kids were reading a lot of his work. Hesse had made her think about Eastern spirituality. She would go to the university library and find a book on Buddhism. She was twenty two years old and soon would be graduating. Time for exploring life would be over. She'd have to find a job. She also wanted an apartment of her own someday after she graduated.

8

SAUL

Sarah and Ruth made it a point to share meals more often. Everything they did together had more meaning now that they were the only two left in the house. "Your uncle Saul's coming tomorrow," Ruth said as she poured breakfast coffee. "I asked him if he would look over our finances. Morrie said he had things all set up in a will, but I don't understand it or how the two stores are going to be run, much less all the investments."

Ruth sadly reflected, " Morrie took care of all that There's managers in each store, yes, and they're okay, I guess, but the whole thing scares me to death…that if left up to me it could all collapse."

She filled their coffee cups again, "I want your uncle's advice on what to do. He's going to go over it all with the bookkeepers and our lawyer."

With a wry smile she added, "Maybe I put the whole megillah, the whole schmear up for sale, see how that works, huh? Morrie would roll over in his grave! All that he built up with such hard work. But let's be honest, honey, all I ever wanted was a good home for you kids and to be left alone to paint. I should have paid more attention. So much for it. Life doesn't wait for shoulds."

"What's he like, Uncle Saul? I don't remember him."

"Oh he's a character! You'll see, just the opposite of your father. He talks to everybody, knows people all over, travels a lot. Trouble was your father thought he got in with the rackets. That's why he cut Saul off from us, wouldn't let us see him anymore."

"Got in with the rackets? What do you mean?"

"Oh, I don't mean he's a racketeer, a mobster, no, not Saul. He just took a job in the jukebox business, that's all. But Morrie was convinced that the business was run by organized crime, a Jewish mob like Kid Cann or Davie Berman. I don't know. I like Saul but God knows Morrie disowned him as a brother. He wouldn't even talk about him. End of story. But I need help now and I'm not proud."

# # #

After conferring with everyone, Saul returned to Ruth to report. "It's all set up," he said. "Morrie had it set in his will that when he passed, the whole estate, everything, goes to Sarah. The accountant explained that rather than putting everything in your name, it will already be in Sarah's when you pass, inheritance tax is controlled, everything in place. You're being provided for, Ruth, of course, no worries for you. The house will be taken care of, taxes paid, and your bank account, your personal account, will remain with practically unlimited funds, a huge balance that will be replenished as needed. Did you know that, did you realize you and…."

"Oh, come on, Saul."

"Really, Ruth, really. Morrie was not only a shrewd businessman; he was also a wise investor. With his own keen talents and help from a broker, he'd built up millions in wealth. The interest on it all is amazing! Here's the accountant's card. He wants to explain things to you in person. It will basically take care of itself after that. And here's the card of the manager of the downtown store. Sarah had worked at Sammy's for awhile and done a great job. Technically Sarah is now president of the organization, but she can take time to decide whether or not she wants to start taking an active role in it or have managers do it and perhaps give them raises. It's going to be run well in the meantime. I can tell you've had very loyal employees."

Ruth reached in her purse. "This is for you," she said as she tried to hand Saul a check for two thousand dollars. "We can't thank you enough."

"I can't take that, Ruth. Being able to see this part of my family again is good enough for me. I wish you and Sarah the best. How is she?"

"Oh, she's fine. She's almost done with college. She's been a good student, majoring in English, but her heart isn't in it, Saul. She's more concerned with this jazz music. That's all she talks about."

"That's good, Ruth, that's good!"

"Good? I want her to finish college, not chase around bars and nightclubs."

"But JAZZ, Ruth, JAZZ! Jazz is a great art form. It's America's gift to the world. There's nothing better to listen to. She'll be okay. Jazz is good for the soul. It's good to have an interest in something besides those dry college books. Ruth, you tell her I'm gonna come back next week with some records for her. I've been collecting records all over God's green acres."

# # #

Saul returned on a Sunday. Watching from the kitchen window, Sarah saw him get out of his new 1963 Cadillac. He was wearing a Brooks Brothers suit, a pair of two-toned brogues, and a panama hat at a jaunty angle. "My God, just look at you, young lady! Last time I saw you, you were just a little girl. Now I hear you're in college. How do you like it?"

"Oh, it's okay. It's going pretty good."

"Your mother tells me you like jazz. Is that so?"

"Oh yeah! It's really cool!"

"Well, I made this trip just for you. I happen to dig jazz myself. In fact, I'm an aficionado. I've got some records for you, boxes of them. Wanna help me unload them?"

"Oh, sure. I can't wait! I like your hat, Saul."

"My panama hat? It's not made in Panama, I got it in Cuba. I set up some jukes in the casinos, and man, what a swingin' place-- Havana!"

They brought the records into the living room and Saul sat down at the table. He was out of breath. He lit a Pall Mall and Sarah fetched an ashtray. "I used to collect these sides all over. Every town I'd go to, on or off the job, I'd find the local record stores, talk to people, go to estate sales, their houses, and find collectors. But you know, I've had these for so long I hardly listen to them anymore. I've got a whole garage full of boxes of them at home. I want these to go to someone who will listen to them. My wife hated jazz. I almost gave them to my black friend, Junior, who played jazz piano, but he passed away."

Sarah wanted to dig into the boxes right away, but she stepped quickly into the kitchen and put some coffee on, continuing to listen politely. Saul pointed at a particular box. "Look kid, before you make up your mind what you'd like out of all this, I want to point out a few of the greats, see, the heavy-hitters, so you won't miss 'em. You got great jazz singers in here, the greatest, like Satchmo–Louie Armstrong, who taught 'em all how to sing. You got Lady Day, Billie Holiday. Holiday had more soul in her little finger than most singers have in their whole body. She used to be on all the jukeboxes all over and on the radio all the time. You got Sarah Vaughan, sings right out of heaven, great chops, sings like a horn player, improvising with her voice as well as any jazz soloists.

"You got the guys in here, too; Billy Eckstine, Johnny Hartman, Frank Sinatra, Tony Bennett, Little Jimmy Scott, and my favorite, Herb Jeffries. I put a record or two by each of these artists in this box, but there's many more by them in the other boxes."

While he rested his hands on the box, Sarah got a good look at the rings he wore; on one hand a Star of David ring with a tiger eye stone under the silver star; and on the other hand a spinning ring of sterling silver with advice from the Kabbalah to read by rotating the ring. He lifted out a record. "Now here, Sarah, you wanna hear a singer's singer, listen to Ethel Waters. She was the mother of all the best lady jazz singers. She had a refined voice with great diction, could pronounce all the subtle things in the lyrics and she could belt 'em out and growl the blues too, 'cause she was tough. Like Lady Day, like Billie. Those women were scrappers, made of steel, but they had hearts like songbirds and men misused them bad. But I'm going on too much. You just listen to Ethel. Listen to her sing Gershwin's "I Got Rhythm." She'll wig you out. And Bessie Smith. Listen to Bessie sing blues. There's bedrock for you, Ole Bessie. They don't make 'em like those gals anymore. Yet who knows, some girl will probably come along, could be black or white? Mexican, Puerto Rican, or Chinese, who knows, who'll knock our socks off with new, raw talent. A new voice, see, it's bound to happen."

Saul continued to talk nonstop. " Okay, let's see…there's big bands, Count Basie, Duke Ellington, good white bands too, small combos, lots of sax players, Lester Young, Coleman Hawkins, Sonny Rollins, John Coltrane, I could go on and on about them. But you'll find your own favorites, sweetheart. I'm just glad I can leave these with someone who'll listen to them."

"The best music I've heard around here is black. Are blacks the best jazz musicians?"

"Personally, just personally I'd say they are USUALLY the best. But there's no such thing as the best because they're all telling their own stories best they can. There are great white players too. And don't forget your own people. We Jews got Gershwin; we got Irving Berlin, Russian Jews, both of those guys, great composers. Their parents came over here from Europe because the Czarist Russians were killing Jews before Hitler did. We got Benny Goodman, another Russian Jew, and we got Artie Shaw. Those guys were BIG, like rock stars. In classical music we got Jascha Heifetz, greatest violinist the world's ever heard. And we got Lenny, Leonard Bernstein."

"Black people created the blues, didn't they?"

"Oh yes, yes, they did. But we had a kind of blues in Europe, too. We had LAMENT. You can hear it in the Jewish music from the old countries, and then they brought it to New York. We were persecuted over there like the blacks are here. Gershwin would go into Harlem and black churches to listen to black music, then mix what he heard with lament and out came jazz. Jazz people put it all together. And when there's blues in it, everybody feels it because everybody in this world suffers. I'd say jazz is colorblind, sweetheart, it comes from deep inside, not from the color of the skin."

"I helped a musician out, Uncle Saul. He broke his leg and couldn't afford a hospital, so I paid for it all."

"That's good, Sarah, that's good! Doing mitzvah, helping people. God knows jazz people need support. Most Americans buy schlock pop music. They don't even know jazz. Jazz people have a hard time surviving while they make art. God bless you for helping them."

"Uncle Saul, I don't know how to put this. I hope I don't offend you, you've been so helpful to us, but Mom says the jukebox business might be connected to the mob. Is that true?"

"Well, Sarah, it's a business. Like all businessman it can get troublesome at times. Some guys might use a little muscle now and then when others aren't reasonable, when they get out of line. There might be some connection to the mob, maybe higher up, but I don't see any of that. What I do is clean. My job is to make jukeboxes available, get them installed and oversee them. Does that answer your question?"

"Yes, of course." She brought out two cups of good, strong coffee.

"Once in a while I do specialty jukes. I did one for the kids at the beatnik coffeehouse here in Minneapolis. They wanted an all jazz juke, so I fixed one up for them. Put on Bird, Charlie Parker, and Monk, none of that soft jazz crap but solid senders, and some blues too."

"What coffeehouse? What's it called?"

"Pan's Pipes. It's down at Seven Corners at Cedar-Riverside. I thought you'd know about it. They feature jazz there, and they got an old black man playing piano and singing blues on Mondays. Well, thanks for the coffee. I'm gonna have to hit the highway. I wish you and your mother God's mercy in finding your sister and all the best for you. And…maybe I shouldn't say this now, your mother will fill you in; your family's lawyer's got some real important news for you. Your mother will tell you all about it, okay?"

"What kind of news, Uncle, can't you tell me?"

"No, better your mother tell you. You two will need to talk it over. It's good news, real good."

"Okay, Uncle. Come back soon so we can listen to some jazz together."

"You know it! Here's my card. You need anything, you or your mother, just call. We jazz people have to stick together. You come visit me in Milwaukee. We can hit Chi-town too. Oy! I'll show you some real hot jazz clubs!

Sarah walked Saul to his Cadillac and watched him drive off. The wonder of it, she thought, that a guy like Saul is in our family. She felt he was a kindred soul, "I'm gonna listen to Ethel Waters tonight."

9

LUCY 1962

By the time the Perry Rutherford Revue reached its weekend engagement at the Ebony Room, a black supper club in North Minneapolis, Joleen's jealousy had reached a murderous pitch. Perry, her lover and boss, had seduced all the dancers in his show except the newest one--Lucy. She was holding out, and seducing her had not only become a challenge for him, it was an obsession. Joleen remained his "main punch," as the band boys liked to say, but now that he had made conquest of the others, Joleen was forgotten as all of his attention and free time was focused on breaking Lucy in.

"It makes me sick," Joleen said to Jackson, the band's road manager, "the way he hangs over Lucy constantly. Why doesn't she just put out and get it over with? I'd give anything to be rid of that bitch!"

"You mean that? I mean you really mean that?"

"I sure as hell do, why?"

"'Cause I think I could do just that, get rid of her…that is, if you could make it worth my time."

"Oh yeah? How's that?"

"I got some knockout drops, fix her good. I can put a Mickey Finn in her drink and we could leave her behind Sunday night, make it look like she's on the bus when she's not. You dig?"

"Oh man! I can really dig that!"

"How much is it worth to you?"

"I got 200 bucks I been saving. That enough?"

"Now Joleen, you know I'd need more than that. We're gonna be riskin' our asses. Perry find out, we'd both lose our gigs."

"How about 300? That's all I got."

"Okay, I'll do it, Sunday, after the last show, before they all hit the bus to sleep and it leaves."

That Sunday after the last show, Perry cornered Lucy. His red velvet show coat looked gaudy to her. His face was sweaty, his pompadour hair greasy looking. "Look here, baby," he said, "this is square biz. When we get to that hotel after the gig in Chi-Town, I got a separate room for you and me and you're gonna put out or you'll be looking for another job. Dig?"

Lucy turned and walked quickly away without replying.

"THINK ABOUT THAT! YOU GIVE IT UP OR YOU'RE FIRED!"

Jackson had been loading up the bands' instruments and equipment under the bus. He knew Lucy didn't hang after the show like the others and would be one of the first to board the bus. He was waiting for her and could see she was upset.

"What's the matter, honey? Didn't you get your drink? I'm fixin' me one now. Like one?"

"YEAH! Dig, make it strong too, will ya?"

If you only knew, he thought. He sat Lucy down on one of the two chairs he and Phil, the bus driver, used while waiting for the band. He picked up a bottle of whiskey and a cup with the Mickey already in it. He filled the cup half full of whiskey, and then added Coca-Cola.

"You been workin' hard, Lucy, real hard. Here, baby, this will calm you down." Lucy gulped it down and the drink hit her quickly, making her dizzy.

"Oh, I think I'm gonna throw up."

"Oh dear, let's get you over there." He guided her behind the bus to some trees at the edge of the lot. When she passed out he picked up her purse and took the bills from it. He took her coat and hat back to the bus and propped them up on a seat, then covered them with a travel blanket, setting her hat on top as though she were already there, sleeping.

# # #

The next morning Lucy woke in the wee small hours with no idea where she was or why she wasn't on a bus. She looked around and stared at the back of the supper club. Gradually it began to look familiar. The money was gone from her purse, but her ID was there. Not finding her coat or hat, shaking from cold, she got up and slowly approached the club. A black janitor came out the back with mop water he dumped to the side."

"Are you okay?" he asked.

"No! What is this place?"

"The Ebony, ma'am. You lost or somethin'?"

"Yeah. Missed my bus. Goddamn! What am I gonna do now?"

The reality of it hit her with a jolt of pure depression. The bus had to be hundreds of miles down the road and she was stuck in some jerkwater hick town called Minneapolis. Philly was a city; Minneapolis a little jive-ass town.

"I was with the band last night. I was supposed to be on the tour bus but I passed out and I can't remember why!"

"Pardon, ma'am, for me putting it this way, but you mean you drank too much?"

"NO! No. I didn't. I only had one drink. It was strong, but not THAT strong." A strong woman, she had never felt helpless before. Now she was destitute!

"Look, lady, why don't you jus' come on in here to the bar and sit down and think for a while. It's closed now, ain't nobody here to bother you. It's jus' Larry and I in there cleanin' up and you can take your time. Maybe we can help you some, you know, when you decide what you want to do. Okay? My name's Bill. Come on in a while."

Inside, Bill introduced Lucy to this coworker, who said, "You want a drink, Lucy, help yourself. Owner never knows. He don't get here 'til nine when they open. Go ahead, pour yourself a double an' take it easy. You want a ride somewhere when we get done we'll take you. We ain't got much money on us but you're welcome to it."

Lucy looked across the club to the stage sitting empty in the half-light. It seemed pitifully dull. It was hard to imagine they had sweat out their routines the night before on such a small stage. Sipping on a tall glass of scotch on the rocks, she remembered Perry's ultimatum, fuck or be fired. She considered all the nasty run-ins with Joleen, the daily doses of her jealousy and hatred. Maybe she should think twice about running to rejoin such people. Maybe she was much better off without them. But what a shock being stuck in a backwater. Maybe she could find some kind of work long enough to afford a bus to Philly. Hitchhike maybe. There was no one to call to wire her money, her parents long dead, her old friends scattered to the winds. She was working on a second drink when a new voice asked, "Who's your lady friend here, boys?"

"Hi, Mike, you're early."

When told of her situation, the owner sat down beside Lucy. He seemed friendly.

"So, you were with the show, were you?

"Yes, I'm a dancer."

"That's right! And a damn fine one too. Really enjoyed the dancing. Your boss was kind of a jerk to deal with, but you guys really worked hard and the people dug it."

"Jerk is right. A pompous ass. An' I ain't gonna chase after them people. Don't have money now to do anything."

"You ever a cocktail waitress?"

"Oh yeah. Done a lot of that before I started dancing."

"I just lost a cocktail waitress and if you want a job you got one. We can start you out tonight."

"I'll take it."

# # #

"A lot of bounce to the ounce," is how customers at the supper club began to describe their new waitress. In Philadelphia she was known as "Watusi Lucy" for her personal style of dance, how she liked to leap, hang in the air. Diners at the club liked her upbeat personality and tipped generously. In two weekend nights she made enough in tips for a one-way bus ticket to Philadelphia. She was tempted to split with her first paycheck but knew she'd also need a nest egg for Philly, so she tried to be patient. She felt grateful for the kindness of strangers, but the "town" bored her to death. How tiny the two black ghettos, one on the north side, the other south, two little islands in a sea of polka-lovin' ofays. In Philly you could enter the ghetto and forget whitey for a while, never see one nor deal with their abrupt distaste of you, never trespass the cold haunts they thought you were invading. In Minneapolis, you were lucky to find one, maybe two black owned jazz joints. Whites had some pseudo-jazz with no punch. The shit-kicking place was beginning to drive her crazy.

One day, just out of curiosity, she picked up a paper to see if there were any dancing jobs listed. She wasn't planning to stay around long enough to try one out, but she was curious. The first thing to catch her eye read:

UNLUCKY IN LOVE?
SEE MADAM CELESTE,
Fortune Teller
Tarot Reader

Lucy was used to having her cards read by her favorite aunt, whom she never asked for money, just advice. She jotted down the madam's phone number then read further. The only ad for dancers read:

EXOTIC DANCERS
Need young female dancers
for a career in entertainment.
Steady work, good pay.

Obviously a strip joint. No phone number. Apply in person. Lucy wrote the address down anyway.

On her next day off she went to see Madam Celeste. A young girl opened the door, and an Ethel Waters record was playing somewhere inside.

# # #

"Hello!" the girl said. "Have you come for a reading? Please come in. Have a seat and Madam will receive you soon."

The sitting room was plain. It was clean and simply furnished. Lucy was paging through an Ebony magazine when Celeste opened the door to her studio and called Lucy in. Celeste's white hair matched her simple white dress, her only jewelry a brown beaded necklace of African origin. Her eyes were amazing. A light and energy shone from them so intensely, Lucy sensed it might threaten the thin body that housed it.

"Please sit yourself down, child. Now, what would you like to know? I will tell you how I see your future, but do you have a question you really want answered first?"

The woman's eyes again. The spirit that filled the seer, glowing in her eyes, beamed like a searchlight straight into Lucy's soul. The questions she came with now seemed frivolous before this powerful woman's attention. Lucy voiced them anyway.

"I'm wondering how long I'll have to stay in this city and if I'll ever be able to dance for a living again…I mean dance the kind of dancing I really want to do."

Celeste nodded compassionately. "Yes, child. May I see your hands, please?" She did not examine Lucy's palms to read, but simply held her hands in her own. With eyes closed, she sensed Lucy's condition, past, present and future, while Lucy's eyes began to look around. No crystal ball or any of the other trappings. Behind the table where they sat was an altar bearing African ritual items and cowrie shells. A rosary-like mala of enormous brown African wood beads hung on the wall.

Celeste unwrapped her tarot cards from a black velvet cloth she kept them in, shuffled, cut and laid some out in a pattern. "I can sense your anguish, child, and I'm sorry I must tell you that you will not be able to dance as you wish for many years, not for a living, that is. However, do not despair nor succumb to depression, for your career will blossom later. And soon you will have good fortune in another department. I see a young man coming into your life who will bring sunshine into that darkness you now feel from the situation with the dancing, but also from some accident I sense you have just suffered. Be good to this man who comes. Love comes but once to most if it comes at all. Go now. The Holy Ones have blessed you with love and talent."

10

BORIS: 1963

When Papa Jack died, Boris lost his gig playing sax in the old blues singer's band and his money soon ran out. He could no longer afford to keep a room in town to go to when the band came off the road. His Air Force captain father disowned Boris when he dropped out of high school to join Papa Jack. "Go back to school or don't ever set foot in this house again and don't ask us for a damn cent," were his words. Through secret arrangements at homes of her friends, Boris's mother still managed to see her son without her husband knowing. She offered to help keep his room rented, but Boris refused the money, anticipating his father's wrath if he found out.

He found shelter in an old abandoned warehouse. He could hear rats scampering about as he entered the condemned building to crash. When he shined his flashlight toward them, he could see their red eyes regard him. The only safe place to sleep was in the office that had a door to keep them out. He got some revenge when he found he could shriek and screech at them with his sax and make them flee on those afternoons when he would practice long and loud.

Lately he had to work part time at a carwash while trying to find a gig, because one meal a day at the church mission wasn't enough. Then a break came. Some white kids wanted a sax player for their rock band. He gave the band a listen. He wasn't moved at all by what they were playing, but he needed to make some money, for his self-esteem, for regular meals and baths again. He decided to go on the road with them and drop them when they came back. As he fell asleep listening to the rats on the other side of the door, he remembered an admonition of Papa Jack's: "If somethin' don't feel right, don't do it! Just leave up offin' it an' do somethin' else."

After a couple of brief rehearsals with Boris, the band, which hadn't really found itself yet, went out on the road sounding rough. But the kids in the towns they played were all so starved for rock and roll, they were wild with excitement. Then came a one-nighter in an armory in Sioux Falls, to be followed by weekends in Fargo and Minneapolis. There were invitations to parties after the South Dakota gig, but the band opted to bring girls back to the motel. This raised an alarm for Boris, who at 21 realized he was going to have to act as babysitter for the other musicians who were 18 and 19. The girls they were taking to the motel were underage, but more disturbing; one of them was much older and didn't come off naturally. It seemed as if she was acting, playing a role. Boris tried to warn Nate, the band leader, that the girl could be a narc, but Nate shrugged off the suggestion, calling Boris paranoid. Boris threw up his hands. He had been looking forward to a good night's rest. Now he knew that in order to relax at all and avoid babysitting, he'd have to stay away from the motel while the kids partied. He accepted an invitation to join a black college student and his friends who said they had some wine and good jazz and blues records. These people were righteous, but Boris still couldn't relax completely for worrying about the band, how loose they could be with the grass they had brought along. A drinker himself, he didn't care what they did recreationally as long as they could play, but the Dakotas were notorious for draconian drug laws. Boris sipped his wine. The college kids were playing a new album, "Doin' the Thing, The Horace Silver Quintet at the Village Gate," getting a big kick out of one cut called, "Filthy McNasty."

"You know, Boris," said Clarence, the colored kid, "you should be in a band playing what you like. You should be with some brothers playin' what you FEEL."

"I can dig it, man." I'm jus' payin' dues. A man's gotta eat."

Boris rarely spoke for himself, but in high school his band teacher considered him a musical prodigy, gave him straight A's, even using him as an assistant. His math teacher, convinced Boris was a genius, gave him an IQ test. Boris scored 155. But in all other subjects Boris got D's and an occasional F.

"Something's fishy," Boris thought when he returned to the motel. The band's van was gone and the room seemed quiet. The door was unlocked. A detective who had been napping snapped to his feet.

"Boris Simpson?"

"Yeah, that's me."

"Listen, son, we had to bust your friends for using and selling. But they said you don't smoke pot. Is that right?"

"Yeah. Yeah, that's right. I just drink."

The detective searched Boris. He had already gone through his travel bag. "Okay, you're clean now," he said, "so I don't have to book you. But your buddies are gonna be in jail a long, long time. We confiscated their van, too. If I were you, I'd get out of town."

# # #

"Damn the luck. Middle of nowhere." After a short and restless night's sleep, Boris checked out of the hotel. He grabbed his travel bag and sax case and walked out into the quiet morning of a town just waking up. Cold wind came straight across prairie to cut through his thin jacket. He ducked into the town café to quell his hunger, get coffee and ask about a bus. He felt every one of the patrons' eyes on him as he walked in, a black in their town. They were all old men except for a woman and her two children at the counter where he was going to sit. The men's faces said we don't want you here. Boris turned and left. Back in the cold wind, he saw a farmer loading sacks of feed into his truck. The farmer had kind eyes. He gave Boris directions to a bus depot, sort of, a few chairs to one side of a little grocery store. Boris bought a cup of vending machine coffee and sat down to try to decide where he should go. Minneapolis, maybe. It was closer than Colorado Springs where he'd have to deal with his father again. In Minneapolis he'd have to start all over. Then

he remembered. His older sister Eileen had moved to Minneapolis. "*She always had a soft spot for me, he thought, and I just took that for granted.*" Boris felt a little guilty for not appreciating his sister as she deserved, but with her in mind Minneapolis didn't seem so formidable. He reached into his pocket, pulled out a quarter and flipped it – heads. Minneapolis.

Before leaving South Dakota on the bus for Minneapolis, Boris knew he should call his mother with his plan. During the three-minute conversation on a pay phone, she tried to talk him out of moving, and when that failed she managed to get him to agree to contact his sister Eileen when he got to Minneapolis. Boris said he'd consider doing so, but knew he really wouldn't call Eileen until after he was able to "get over," to be set up on his own. But as soon as their conversation was over his mother called Eileen, told her to look for Boris on the next Greyhound from South Dakota.

Eileen was there at the depot in Minneapolis, waiting to resume the role she forfeited by taking a teaching position in Minneapolis, that of looking out for her baby brother for all she was worth. Boris was glad to see her, glad to know someone in this city that was much bigger than the one he'd left. He found his newfound manhood threatened by how she was bound to smother him with protection. Hadn't he proved he could live on his own, hadn't he been out of his parents' nest for years now making it his own way, chasing his dream?

Her North-side apartment felt stuffy. Boris immediately felt out of place and confined. He had to quickly decide whether to stay or not. It would be much easier to leave then and there than later after she was used to having him. This meant living on the street awhile. The bus trip had taken most of his pay for the band's last fateful gig. What was left wasn't even enough for one night in a motel. He knew enough now, though, to live on the street when he had to. If only his mother hadn't tipped Eileen off to his coming, he wouldn't been free to live as he wished. Now both his mother and sister would worry if he hit the streets. "*Maybe I should do things their way this time,*" he thought.

# # #

Finally he decided to honor his sister and her desire to help. He'd stay until he had money coming in. For the time being he felt trapped in her middle-class lifestyle, forced to limit the hours he kept, when he could come and go and how much he drank. Life on the road with Papa Jack and the bluesman left him with a desire to drink whenever he felt like it. So he tried doing his drinking away from her as much as possible, but there were times when he got caught, passed out or was belligerent, frightening and upsetting her. Knowing she was actually concerned and worried about him, he began to feel guilty for disrupting her decent hard-working life. She didn't get angry like his father. Instead she internalized the pain Boris caused her. Once she got over the initial shock of his behavior, strong maternal instincts took over and she enjoyed cooking for him, caring for him in general, encouraging him to go clean and sober. She also tried taking him into getting his high school diploma, but Boris had no intention of plugging back into such a deadly boring system ever again. A beast in forced captivity, he looked for a way out. He was getting used to Eileen's home-cooked meals and laundry service, time to hit the street before he got too soft.

He got his break when he met an old man named Jake who owned a house near the grocery on Plymouth Avenue. He had just picked up a dish washing job on Broadway when he saw an apartment-for-rent sign on the old man's home. The old guy was on Social Security and needed extra income. They hit it off. Boris promised he wouldn't throw any wild parties, and Jake helped him soundproof the little basement apartment roof with egg case dividers, which Boris knew would work as well as expensive soundproofing tiles. He could then practice his sax day or night without bothering Jake, who was hard of hearing anyway. And, with a separate entrance, Boris could come and go as he pleased. Soon he was drinking as much as he did in Colorado. But this time he had a steady job to maintain.

His kitchen boss could smell the booze on Boris's breath now and then, but as long as he showed up and cut the mustard, the boss didn't say anything. Then he quit the suds-busting job for his first sax gig in Minneapolis, playing behind strippers in a pit band on Hennepin Avenue.

He got his drinking under control for this gig but he was smoking constantly, a two pack a day habit that came with a bad cough. One day when Eileen invited him over for lunch, she gave him some of her codeine cough syrup. He snuck another big swig of it before leaving. It made him feel so pleasant after calming his cough that he searched until he found a source to buy as much as he wanted from without a prescription. The high from it was better than booze. He began the "codeine cruise" he would continue for years.

# # #

Late one afternoon, Lucy came out of a movie theatre on Hennepin Avenue, walking along it for a while before turning off to find her bus stop for North, she walked right up on the club that had advertised for dancers of the exotic variety. Its name: The Torrid Zone. A strip club all right, with an afternoon session in progress. She knew it would be so, but it stung. How slack-assed sad! No serious dance gigs to be found. It would've been more depressing if she hadn't reminded herself, day by day, not to get too concerned with how things were in this town; she was going back to Philadelphia.

Disgusted as she was, she entered the club anyway for a couple of drinks before going home. Two uninspired, topless women were pole dancing to inane rock soundtrack crap music. She change her mind and was about to leave when she noticed a pit band was setting up. She changed her mind about leaving. One musician immediately fascinated her. She got a drink and moved to a little table near the band to watch the young good- looking player pick up a saxophone. She snagged a waitress/stripper to ask about him.

"That's Boris."

"What's he like?"

"I don't really know. He's real quiet, not shy really, but quiet." But when he picks up that sax, lady, he blows his little ass off! You'll see. They get to play a set of their own before they play behind us."

"*Boris*, Lucy thought, *you've already cast a spell on me before you've even played a note.*"

The little band played real jazz, the irrepressible voice of jazz cropping up again when and where it could, often in places frowned on by society, mongrel music, like mongrel dogs, tougher and more brilliantly resistant than sanctioned breeds. These men were stretching out, improvising, showing off some, pleasing themselves at least and a few random men who had come for this as well as the girls. Lucy stayed on through the first set of dance, hoping to speak to Boris on his break. The music was less interesting now, the dancing pedestrian, boring. But watching Boris she was lost to it all. Finally the band took its break and Boris came to the bar.

Lucy followed him. "I really dig your playing, man. That Latin piece you played in that first set was really special, beautiful."

"Oh, you mean 'The Shadow of Your Smile'?"

"Oh, is that what it's called?"

"Yeah, it's from Brazil, one of the new Bossa Nova things we're hearing now."

"Well, it was a stone groove and you really had it down."

"Why thank you. We don't get many compliments in here. Most of these people don't pay much attention to what we do – they're just here to dig the flesh."

"Well, they had an ad in the paper for dancers and I just came in to see what kind. I don't want to do this. I've done it before."

"Oh, so you're a dancer."

"Yeah, a show dancer, revues, what have you. But I'm looking for something more serious."

"I see. Well, good luck. I've got to play again now. I didn't catch your name."

"Lucy."

"Lucy, pleased to meet you. I'm Boris. You dancing somewhere now?"

"No, not at present, just waiting tables at the Ebony Room. Stop in sometime."

A few days later Lucy returned to remind him where she worked, which paid off as the very next day he walked into the Ebony and asked her for a date.

11

AT THE BLUE NOTE

The Blue Note sat on the edge of the ghetto in North Minneapolis where highways come into the inner city near warehouses and train tracks. It was a neighborhood bar that would leave its doors open for air and people walked in and out like it was their living room. It was a simple place with a bar along one side, a small stage at the back, and a few tables in the middle, but on weekends it was packed wall to wall with blacks who somehow made room in front of the band to dance. One co-owner of the club, a well-loved handsome black named Tommy also worked as a waiter on the Northern Pacific. On Sunday afternoons musicians were allowed to sit in with the house band and jam sessions developed. The band leader, Earl Saunders, was a tenor sax player who had arrived in Minneapolis from Kansas City. Earl's sound was so mellow and swinging that musicians and fans in the Twin Cities considered him a living oracle, and one musician claimed that, "every note Earl plays is like God's own, burnin' into your soul."

Boris Simpson learned of The Blue Note on his second day in town and showed up Sunday expecting a jam session. Some of the older musicians present that day tried to run Boris off at first. They knew he was trying for a modern sound he wasn't ready for. "Go back to the roots," one yelled at him, "back to the roots of the blues, learn your ABC's." "Why do you put up with him?" they asked Earl. "Give him some time," was all Earl said. Earl saw something in the kid, a kind of near-reckless energy that was generated out of sweat from testing in the wide open west, musicians experimenting freely in more open-minded environments. There was a kind of swagger to their playing, and freedom. You heard it best in Kansas City, where the blues started to really swing, to jump, a style that was ready to knock things out of its way.

James, the piano player, a big man with a ready smile, accepted Boris right away. His cap said, "SWEET MAN," which fit, but the two others, bassist and drummer, were cold. Sam, the drummer, had furtive eyes. "You must've come to the wrong place," he said, "'cause we don't babysit." With that remark, his constant sneer turned into a quasi-smile, revealing two gold teeth. Both he and the bassist, Lou, wore pinstriped suits which had lost their elegance with age. Sam wore alligator skin shoes, also old, which might've had a novel effect worn by someone else. When Sam's efforts to intimidate Boris failed, he remained overtly hostile and would deliberately throw off the rhythm during Boris's solos to trip him up. But Boris would skate through, making Sam look bad instead.

One Sunday, Earl, the band leader, was asked to play for a wedding party, and Tommy, owner, told Boris, "I need a horn player here and if you can tone yourself down a little and play some straight jazz, I'll pay you for the whole afternoon to fill in for Earl." So that afternoon when the band kicked off to find a groove starting with a laid back blues, Boris played down, as well as he could, to the bone of blues, knowing he'd never swing them like Earl.

When white boy, Joe Citro walked in the front door with his trumpet case, Boris knew he came to sit in, read him from jump street, the white shirt and tie, black slacks and unpolished shoes, knew he was showin' respect,but how naïve he looked!

Maybe, though, just maybe this ofay could play. Boris watched the kid find a table near the stage. He felt sorry for him, knowing what he was in for. Then he saw Tommy watching from behind the bar. Tommy would see he was treated right. And Charlene, a sister who dug white guys, was waiting his table.

"Welcome to The Blue Note," Charlene said. "What can I get you? Just coffee? You want some cream with your coffee or just black like me?" The kid blushed. "You gonna sit in? I see you have your axe with you."

As leader, Boris could call the numbers, so when the blues they warmed up on died out, he called for "Cherokee," and he jumped the tune, playing fast, running lots of changes swiftly with just enough references to the melody to inform the others. James smiled at their attempts to follow Boris. He knew "Cherokee," the Charlie Barnett tune, was what Bird, Charlie Parker, was playing when he had his breakthrough, thereafter revolutionizing the way jazz was played. This time Sam was right with Boris, using well placed rim shots and bass bombs here and there to break 4/4 monotony. He had that crazed look in his eyes he got on coke, but his timing was right on. Boris looked out into the crowd to catch the white kid's reaction. He looked somewhat puzzled yet fascinated. Boris decided to invite the kid to sit in, but waited to see if the kid would ask, and as soon as he announced, "Okay, we're gonna slow it down now," the kid came forward.

"Sure, kid, come on up. What would you like to play?"

"'My Foolish Heart.' Is that okay?"

Boris nodded and James began the intro. The kid started playing well from the start and kept it simple, the melody perfect with a pure tone, leaving the right breaks for Boris and James, their solos, his own solo very pleasing. But it struck Boris that the kid needed more bite to his style. The people clapped as his last pure note floated over them. They didn't bullshit in that place. They did NOT applaud just to be nice. But Joe Citro had no time to bask. Boris let James call the next tune and he counted right into "Lady Be Good," a standard he thought the boy should know. The kid tried but clearly flubbed, and James called a stop. Boris asked the kid if he knew "Salt Peanuts," and Joe smiled and nodded. He punched the Dizzy Gillespie tune like Diz himself, note for note, getting rises from the people including Charlene, who yelled, "That's right!"

James came up from the piano after to ask the kid his name.

"Ladies and gentlemen, that was Joe Citro on trumpet, Joe Citro, let's give him a hand!" The applause was generous. James and Boris smiled. The bass player looked vacant. Sam just frowned and spit into the corner.

Charlene brought a pot of coffee for Joe when the band went on break. "This is from Tommy," she said. Joe was elated. He relaxed. He was overwhelmingly glad he had been accepted by these people for whom jazz was central in their lives. This must be the Holy Place, he thought to himself. The strong black coffee Charlene poured put his senses on alert. He could hear the ice cubes tinkling in the drinks on nearby tables. His hearing was so heightened it reminded him of something Gil, the railroad cook he'd met at Road Buddy's told him –that Bird, Charlie Parker, said he could "hear rats pissing on cotton."

Joe felt more fully alive than he ever had up north. And the sax player, so close to his own age, had invited him to jam at his own gig!

Boris sat down and introduced himself. "You got a nice tone on your trumpet, Joe, where are you from?"

"I'm from Bemidji, Minnesota."

"Bemidji? Where's that?"

"Up north, way up by the Indian reservations."

"Wild, man, I've never been out of the city since I got to Minnesota. Anyway, I'm glad you're jamming with us. I like your sound."

"Thank you, but I know I'm really not good enough to play with you guys but I wanted to try."

"Hey, you did just fine. I know a place you can play all you want. Fact is, I got the house band. We don't get paid much but you might dig what we play. We do more modern stuff."

"Oh yeah? Where is this place? What is it called?"

"It's a coffeehouse, man, run by some beatniks down at Seven Corners. It's called Pan's Pipes. Hand me that bar napkin and I'll write down the address. Stop in sometime. It's real laid back."

When Earl Saunders returned to resume his place as bandleader, hearing Boris play he knew a time was coming when audiences, fickle as they could be, would tire of his own traditional style. In all of nature and humanity change was unstoppable, things died out, turning over for the new. And this kid had it, that fire, the white glow inside the core of a sax wailing, Boris had it.

"I'm coming for you, Old Man," Boris said good naturedly one Sunday after he knew Earl well enough. "We're gonna have a cutting contest, a shootout, you know, like in Colorado, and you can't hide!"

"Yeah, kid, but for the time being you just stay out of my hair, you little shit!"

12

PAN'S PIPES

Joe Citro found the coffeehouse Boris told him about in an area where two avenues, Cedar and Riverside, intersected. Historically it had been a Scandinavian neighborhood nicknamed "Snoose Boulevard" and was now becoming a gathering place for bohemians attracted by its low-key mystique and cheap rent. The exact address Boris had given him had no sign anywhere saying coffeehouse or "Pan's Pipes," but a single object sitting in its front window gave it up, a green statuette of Pan, the cloven-hooved nature god, playing on his pipes. Joe grinned. As he stood there, fascinated by the spirit of Pan, the door opened and a girl in a heavy knit black sweater with several prominent holes in it stepped out to pick up mail.

"Wanna come in?" she asked. Joe followed her. "Sit down and I'll be right with you." She hopped up on the stage to open the curtains for the front window. Sunlight revealed more of the dark interior. A beatnik couple were playing chess by candlelight. The walls were brick, which was soothing to Joe, reminiscent of masonry work with Harvey. The waitress took the mail over to the owner of the place, who was dealing with two Minneapolis police officers who'd come in off their beat to plant themselves at the coffee bar across from a huge copper espresso machine.

"You say there's steam in this thing?" one officer asked. "You sure this ain't a distillery unit makes some kinda drug? You don't make alcohol and sell it, do you?"

"No, no officer, I assure you, this is an espresso machine only! It makes nothing but espresso coffee. Here, I'll make you a cup. You try it, okay?

"I don't want anything with any drug in it."

"Okay, then you try it," Lorenzo said to the other policeman. The officers watched intently while the Italian manipulated the machine to produce a demitasse cup of dark aromatic brew. The officer accepted it warily.

"This is too bitter! It can't be coffee, it's too bitter."

"It's espresso. They serve it all over Europe. It's just pressurized coffee. The only drug in it is caffeine, same as in your regular coffee. It's very strong because the steam in this machine is forced through darkly roasted ground coffee. That's all it is, officer."

Officer Lewis looked up at the giant machine. It looked to him like a copper octopus, like something out of Jules Verne.

"Do the people who drink this bitter stuff get side effects?"

"No, no. No more than you'd get from a cup or two of your coffee at home. A little jittery, maybe, if you drink too much. But no, no side effects."

"I don't know. There's still something fishy about this machine I can't put my finger on. Listen, Lorenzo, you know we want to see your business be successful here, but the city will want us to close you down if they think you're dispensing any drugs in here or distilling liquor. We may have to monitor your place awhile longer yet."

"Okay, guys, meantime, anytime you come in, coffee's on me. We have regular coffee too, you know."

Joe overheard their conversation, "Sounds like the cops don't dig your espresso machine."

She handed him a menu, "Yeah, no wonder. It's the first one ever in Minnesota. Lorenzo had it sent from Italy."

"Wow! That must've been expensive."

"Oh yeah, Lorenzo's father paid for it. He's some kind of big restaurant owner in Rome, wants to see his son make it here. Cops don't know what to make of our espresso machine. They've been watching us. The jerk who owns the bar across the street's been putting pressure on locals to close us down. He thinks we're creating a bad image for the neighborhood. Meantime there's a drug dealer operating out of his bar. Nobody deals in here.

Joe ordered a regular coffee from the girl with the big ratty sweater and unkempt hair, noticing only her friendly smile.

"Is Boris here today?"

"Yes, he's downstairs rehearsing with the band. You can do go down if you like and I'll bring your coffee."

The stairway walls were covered by a collage of jazz images, hundreds of pictures of jazz artists ranging from Storyville to bop. The brick walls downstairs held paintings by a black artist. A stage sat in the middle of the cavern-like space to one side of which a life-sized replica of a human skeleton playing a real trombone was suspended. On the stage stood Boris, explaining something to his piano player by playing it out on his sax. Then the band picked up again with a new Boss Nova melody.

When Boris saw Joe, he came down from the stage to greet him. He introduced Joe to the band by saying, "This is the cat who blew a lot of good horn at The Blue Note last Sunday." Then he worked Joe into the rest of the rehearsal.

When it was over, Boris went to a record player at the side and, thumbing through a box of records, pulled out a Clifford Brown album and put it on. "Here's the horn player I want you to hear," he said. Joe heard a young, modern trumpet player with a beautiful tone and brilliant style who played runs incredibly fast yet coherent, smooth as clear, sparkling water tumbling over a waterfall. Joe was fascinated and immediately started to collect all "Brownie's" recordings. From reading Downbeat Magazine he learned that Brown did not use drugs or alcohol. Brown's artistry was proof that a musician could play as well or better without drugs at a time when many were hooked on heroin because their hero, Charlie Parker, used it.

Joe was hooked on one drug, and if no one else at the time noticed it, Boris did. That drug was music. It was the only thing the boy was using to ease the constant tension he carried around. Boris didn't as yet know many details of Joe's past, but sensed Joe had been paying some heavy dues to get so wound up. Whereas most people could enjoy music now and then as they pleased, Joe had to have it and lived for nothing else.

They began to hang out together, Boris breaking Joe into a city scene still new to him also, taking him under his wing and devoting side trips to various black places, including a black barbershop. There Joe sat and waited while Boris got a haircut. Joe listened intently as the blacks discussed news, music and sports freely but masked some bits in a private idiom of their own.

One day Boris took Joe downtown to the Cassius Bar, where he often came to sit and stare at the four large portraits the owner had commissioned. One was a painting of Jackie Robinson's slide into home plate in the 1955 World Series, and two others depicted Sugar Ray and Cassius Clay in moments of glory. The fourth painting especially fascinated Boris, a painting of Joe Lewis's victory over Max Schmeling. It became a personal symbol of his own desire to make it as a musician, to beat the odds. Joe Lewis had beat the odds by excelling in one of the few ways a black man could back then and he was hero, a symbol of victory over oppression. There he was, in a powerful painting, a huge, glistening portrait of the man in supreme action. Gazing at it gave Boris a recharge for rounds of dues paying up ahead.

That day Boris turned from gazing at Joe Lewis to regard the Joe at his side. He looked so tense. His fists were clenched tightly around his coffee cup and his body was rigid. Early on, Boris had sensed that Joe's tenseness could make others uneasy just being around him.

"You know, man, you need to learn how to relax. Carrying all that tension around all the time don't help you none. Look, man, I know you don't dig alcohol, but Doctor Simpson here would like to prescribe something for you."

"Oh yeah. What's that?"

"Just some boo."

"Boo?"

"Yeah, grass, marijuana. You just smoke a little now and

then – it'll calm you down, maybe teach you how to relax, let your muscles relax for a change, loosen up, dig?"

"I don't know…"

"You're such a serious dude, man, you need to lighten up. When you can't smile and joke around a little, life's a bitch. It's a bitch anyway, if you dig. Anyway, I can take that prescription to the Gypsy. He'll fill it for us. You don't need to stay on it, just try it out, and see if it can teach you how to chill.

13

SHORTY'S BRIDGE

Gil's job as dining car cook on the Northern Pacific Railway passenger train took him on a transcontinental trip from St. Paul to Seattle and back lasting five days. It was always easier to get through the long days if he knew there was at least one guy on the dining car crew whom he really liked. This trip it was the headwaiter, Tommy, a peaceful, gentle old black man and smooth dignified waiter whose personality was so positive it put everyone around him at ease. Tommy held double status for Gil, nice to be around, but also the co-owner of The Blue Note in North Minneapolis, one of the few real jazz clubs around, and one Gil frequented. It was difficult to watch him being disrespected by a belligerent waiter named Sherman as the waiters began serving lunch as the train headed west out of Chicago. Not only was Sherman treating Tommy badly, cussing him for no apparent reason, he was provoking Gil, too. Both Sherman and Gil had massive hangovers, which didn't help and the chef had to tell them both to shut up.

"What's wrong with Sherman?" Gil asked Tommy.

"Just try to humor him, Gil, if you can. Please," the headwaiter answered.

"I'll try, Tommy, but his attitude is BAD, man, bad. He's been getting his food from me faster than the other waiters, but he's still bitching and calling me nasty names. What's with him?"

"He's mad at me, son. I called him sloppy, out there, in front of the diners. He spilled coffee on two people at one table and dropped food at another and I called him out. He's furious now. And looped too. He's been drinking vodka on the job. I should have the steward write him up. His real problem is at home. He thinks Shorty is making it with his wife. ("Shorty" was road slang for the guy who took your place in bed with your wife while you were out on the road.) And he knows most of us know he's a cuckold. It's eating him up and he's staying drunk over it."

With lunch served and work caught up, Gil took a break in the dining car which was now empty. He sipped coffee and tried to relax as he gazed at the passing scenery. He caught a glimpse of a picturesque little railroad bridge over a mountain pass on the parallel tracks of the Great Northern trains. Older employees called it "Shorty's Bridge." By the time you saw Shorty's Bridge, Shorty would be in his stride – really sexing up your wife.

The men all joked about Shorty, but he was for real for some. Others were never completely sure their wives were one hundred percent faithful while they were gone. A seed of doubt could be a torment that bred suspicion. Cracking jokes relieved some of the tension. The proper thing, they'd say, was to leave out a new pair of slippers and a bathrobe for Shorty along with a bottle of good liquor. In turn, Shorty would have the bed warmed up for you when you returned.

Gil knew the thought of Shorty was twisting Sherman up inside. As he sat musing about Sherman and Shorty, Mr. Snead, the dining car conductor, was doing some musing of his own. He muttered to himself as he stared out the train window.

"Snead, what was that you were mumbling?" Gil asked.

"Oh, it's just a saying. It's something a Negro midwife I know says every time she delivers a baby. She always says …'this endless stream of life, from where does it come and to where do it go'?"

Snead went back to his post and put away some records he was keeping. Gil could tell he was upset. He was wringing his hands and fidgeting.

"Say Gil," Snead said, "I hear Sherman was causing you trouble back there in the kitchen. I had to watch him mistreat Tommy out here. I sure appreciate you trying to get along with that cuss. I guess I'll have to write him up. I just wish he wasn't on this crew. I might have to have the conductor put him off the train if he doesn't fly right."

That afternoon, Dining Car Conductor Snead gave waiter Sherman an ultimatum: Straighten up or be put off the train. Sherman stopped harassing Tommy, but back in the pantry, where Snead couldn't see or hear, Sherman was nastier to Gil than he had ever been, even taunting Gil to a fistfight. Out of respect for his conductor, Gil held back. He soon realized he was getting Sherman's goat by not responding at all.

Just before Sherman left on his Seattle layover he went to the bunk car to hunt down Gil for a fight, but Gil had already left the train car and was on his layover that included a trip to the waterfront and the liquor store.

When the crew went back to work after their layover, Sherman was reported missing. He hadn't come back. They thought he'd probably gotten into trouble in Seattle. No matter, things went better without him, even if they were short a waiter.

On the last night of the trip, when the last meal was served and the work all done, the crew played poker up in the bunk car. The waiters were loaded with tip money from the trip and they played poker with a passion, drinking, laughing, joking, cussing, yelling and singing, letting off steam from the whole trip, celebrating being free again. But Gil was still working. The kitchen had to be extra clean to turn over to the next crew. An inspector often waited in St. Paul to come onboard and check the pantry and kitchen with white gloves. When Gil finally got to the bunk car, he was exhausted. The poker game was wide open. He took a shower, had a few drinks with a waiter who wasn't playing cards, then fell into his bunk. He overheard the crew talking about Sherman: "Shorty's got Sherman running' scared," said Jelly Belly Robinson, "he must've got drunk and missed the train."

"Hey Jelly," the chef yelled, " what you figure YOUR ole' lady's doin' right about now, huh?"

"What about yours?" Jelly countered.

By now, Gil had begun to feel a little sorry for Sherman. He knew the worst thing about being a railroad worker was being gone for days at a time. He soon fell asleep midst the ever-constant rhythm, the eternal pound and clack of the train wheels beneath; a rolling rhythm ruling half a trainman's life.

# # #

Next morning, as the train sped toward the Twin Cities, Gil got up before everyone else to make coffee for the crew. There was no breakfast to serve, so the crew could just relax, as they headed home. Sitting there with his fellow railway workers on the iron horse, their home on wheels, Gil remembered a dream he'd had last night in his bunk.

He was standing by the tracks of the St. Paul depot with a group of black men who were waiting for the train. He was singing the blues, dream-blues coming through him strong and complete, the singer, the song, satisfying, as deep as his love for the black race.

It was payday and when Gil got off the train he stopped at the commissary for his check, and then went straight to Sugar's Bar near the depot, where they all cashed their checks. The chef and a few waiters were already there.

"Sit down, Gil," said Jelly, "and I'll buy us all a round."

Then John, the chef, bought one and Gil felt obligated to buy one, too, before he could get away. He was tired and the booze was going to his head too fast and too early in the day. He had to catch buses all the way back to his apartment in South Minneapolis.

Suddenly a black waiter from another crew rushed up to the bar.

"Say Jelly," he said, "didn't you work with Sherman?"

"Yeah, he was on this trip with us, but we think he jumped ship in Seattle."

"He's dead," the man said. "Sherman is dead. Shot yesterday."

He went on to explain that Sherman had flown back to Minneapolis from Seattle on a jet, determined to catch Shorty in bed with his wife. Full of jealous rage, he walked quietly up the steps to the front door of his house. His wife, who had gotten out of bed to mix her sexual partner a drink, spotted Sherman through a window and warned Shorty. Shorty jumped up, grabbed the loaded pistol Sherman kept in a drawer by the bed, and met Sherman at the door. When Sherman opened the door to his house, Shorty put two bullets in his chest.

After that, a saying was born on the road: "If you're coming home early, call first. Spend a dime to save a life."

14

SOFT EYES

After leaving Sugar's bar in St. Paul, Gil caught the University Avenue bus for Minneapolis, stopping off at Road Buddy's instead of going home. The place was early morning quiet. Two old blacks sat at a table talking. Only one person stood at the bar. At first glance, Gil thought it was a woman with a full head of long, shiny, well-combed black hair. Looking closer, he noticed it was Gypsy, the drug dealer standing perfectly straight and dressed all in black, with a black fedora.

Gil went to the jukebox and loaded it up with Nina Simone's version of "Solitude," Bird's "Parker's Mood," and several Billie Holiday tunes. The man in black turned around as Simone's version of Ellington's song began. Gil remembered that Gypsy's father had played clarinet in Ellington's orchestra.

"Where you been, man?" Gypsy asked.

"Just got off the road, Gypsy, what's going on?"

"Nada, man. I was just getting ready to book. I ran outta bread."

"Stick around. I'll buy you a few. Ain't every day I get to talk to someone who knows jazz."

"Likewise. I'll take you up on that. That way I'll also get to hear the rest of the tunes you just played. I blew it last night. I partied with a bunch of spades at their crib in Selby-Dale. They were too broke to cop, so I gave 'em my dope and we all smoked it. Bad biz, but good company. I stopped in here to get my head straight before heading home. How's the road?"

"Not cool. One of our waiters got killed by a guy who was sleeping with his wife. Guess that's why I haven't gone home yet myself. I still wanted to talk to someone about it."

"Yeah. That's bad. Extremely bad."

"Yeah, but I don't know why it upset me so much, because I really didn't dig the guy. He was on my case this trip, tried to start a fight. He's a sore head. No wonder his wife had Shorty, she probably couldn't wait for him to get out on the road. You drink rum, Gypsy?"

"Sure."

"Hey Jimmy! How much would you charge me for a new bottle of Bacardi and some ice?" Gil laid down a twenty and a five. "The five is a tip."

"Close enough." Gil also set a twenty down in front of Gypsy.

"What's that?"

"You said you ran out of money."

"Yeah, but I can't take that."

"Yes, you can."

"But you just bought this bottle we're drinking from."

"Sure, but someone who talks jazz like you is rare, even in Spadesville."

"Okay, Gil, I thank you, but you take this." Gypsy took off his fedora, slid a lid out of the hatband, and then quickly stuck it into Gil's shirt pocket.

"Oh no, you keep that."

"No, you keep it. I always got plenty of reefer, its just bread I run out of now an' then."

"But I don't use this stuff anymore, I'm just a lush," Gil smiled. "Give it to my friend Jim."

"Cool. He will dig it. He's one of my best customers and he's about due for some."

"Did you know he met a Jewish girl who lost her sister and wants us to help find her?"

"No. I'm not hip. What happened to her sister?"

"She's missing. Ran away from home. Police can't find her. I think she got nabbed by a pimp, forced into prostitution."

"Man! You are full of the world's woes this morning. First a guy you worked with gets shot, and now a Jewish girl forced into slavery. Peace, man, peace!"

They observed silence then, sipping rum, listening to Lady Day's voice.

"Yeah, a little soft conversation," Gypsy said when Billie's song died. "I can dig it. You can talk jazz too, Gil, but you know what I dig about you? You got soft eyes. You're gentle, unless you drink too much, then you get so goddamn angry!"

The remark caught Gil off guard. He never realized his anger when drunk. He changed the subject. "Where does the expression soft eyes come from?"

"From Prez. Lester Young. Haven't you heard that story? Towards the end of his days, Prez was holed up in a cheap room at the Alvin Hotel on Broadway and 52nd Street. He could watch the action on 52nd Street from his window-- the hookers or hatcheck girls as he called them, and the people going in an' out of the jazz clubs. He just hung up there, drinking his Gordon's gin and listening to Frank Sinatra or Basie records. He wasn't gigging much, alcoholic with cirrhosis, just plain wore him down. He had his wife and kids set up in a posh house out on Long Island, but he liked his little hotel room – only place he felt comfortable because of his life on the road. He went to eat at a little cafeteria around the corner from the hotel and went to see a lot of westerns in the afternoons at a fleabag 25-cent movie theatre on 42nd Street. And when cats would go up to try and get him off the sauce, all he'd talk about were the westerns. He was nearly gone, man, it was pathetic. Then Basie went up there, to try to talk to him, straighten him out. It made Basie real sad to see this man, this very pure poet of jazz, the guy they all called Prez, this guy Basie loved with all his heart, to see him dyin' like that." Gypsy sat back and took a sip of his drink and then continued.

"He sez to Prez, what do you want? Can I get you anything? I'll get you anything you want, man, except gin. Look at all these empty bottles, man, you're killing yourself! What do you want? I'll help you any way I can. And Prez said, 'Soft eyes. Soft eyes, man. I just want soft eyes…for and from everybody in the world."

"That's a true story," Gypsy concluded. "My father used to play with Ellington, and one of the guys in the band who was a friend of Basie's told it to my dad."

The quiet talk and stories continued until the rum was gone, and Gypsy finally said, "I gotta go cop some Z's. Thanks for the bread and soft conversation." He took his fist and struck his heart, then turned and moved gracefully toward the door. With his straight posture, stealth-like presence, and the sheen of his long black hair sashaying behind him, he reminded Gil of a Native American. When Gypsy opened the door to leave, a shaft of raw sunlight reached the bar, illuminating currents of cigarette smoke in the air as the jukebox they had so faithfully fed, fell silent.

15

FOR FIFTY BUCKS

The sun had risen but shed no warmth. It sat just above the horizon of what appeared to be an urban wasteland. Gil was sitting in a wrecked car in a junk car lot. Along with his usual hangover headache, there was a sharp pain in his mouth. Shivering, he rubbed his hands together for warmth and lit his pipe. One hand was covered with dried blood. His tongue told him he was missing a tooth. Two more teeth were loose. They would have to come out. He felt a bulk weight in his jacket pocket. A full pint of Bacardi still sealed! He couldn't remember how he had come by it, but was extremely grateful. He opened it and drank deeply to ease the pain in his head and mouth. He could not comprehend how or why he had ended up crawling into such a car on the edge of urban nowhere.

The rum began to lift blackness and pain from his brain and warm his body some. A fragment from the iceberg of his memory fell and floated to the surface: Two gorilla-like bouncers carrying him out of a bar to slam him down in the alley then pick him up to slam full force punches in his face. He drank more rum, seeking further relief and clarity. His billfold? It only held two dollars. Yesterday was payday. Where was his rent money? Rent was due and he needed to fix his teeth before infection set in. He drank more rum, stumbled out into the cold air to piss, then climbed back into the wreck of a car for what little warmth it had. More rum. He felt dizzy-headed but better, his mouth less painful.

A sequence began to emerge from his murky memory. All of yesterday's drinking had started at Sugar's when the crew cashed their paychecks. Then he had stopped at Road Buddy's where he drank with his friend Gypsy. After Gypsy left was when he should have put the plug in the jug and gone home, but he didn't recognize cutoff points anymore.

Then he remembered talking to Tommy at The Blue Note. That was it; he'd gone on to Tommy's place to tell him what happened to his coworker Sherman on his last train gig. Tommy had probably already been told, but Gil had been so maudlin and so obsessed over his death that he needed to to share his shock with a friend, which is where his memory ended.

But where had he been beaten up? Tommy didn't have bouncers like that. He tried to recall what happened. Tommy had not been surprised by the tragedy, "We knew Sherman was gonna run into Shorty sooner or later, but we thought it would be the other way around, that Sherman would blast Shorty. But it's done. It's over now, Gil, and you should go home and get some rest. Looks like you hit it too hard and too early."

"Yeah. And my rent was due a couple days ago when I was still out on the road."

"You better go pay it then or else leave that rent money here with me so I can hold it for you in case you go somewhere else tonight and get in trouble. I'm afraid that bread will slip away from you like some of those fine women you've had, when the fun is over."

Without a word Gil took the amount of his rent out of his billfold and handed it over. "Tell you what I'll do," Tommy said. He reached behind him and took a pint of Bacardi off the shelf. "You keep this sealed until you get home, okay? Don't fly off the handle and go to any more bars. Just go home and come back tomorrow and get your rent money. It's safe here with me."

"Thanks, Tommy, you're the greatest."

# # #

That explained where the pint had come from and the last piece of the puzzle came to light: On the way home from Tommy's, he'd jumped off the bus on Hennepin Avenue to buy a few drinks at The Midshipman, a cold place he had no real interest in, a place with a reputation for King Kong bouncers. He must've felt a challenge to try to drink there again after being eighty- sexed so many times.

Gil climbed out of the wrecked car and looked around, trying to get some bearings. He had to get to The Blue Note for his rent money. The landlord was probably knocking at the door for it right at this moment.

The doors of The Blue Note were open to air out the Pine-Sol smell from floors. Phil the janitor had just mopped and Tommy was setting up the till.

Seeing Tommy raised Gil's morale. Every time he encountered Tommy, he marveled at his elegance and genuine humility, an impeccable gentleman with a heart of gold. He was one of the best waiters the Northern Pacific ever employed, one of the old time waiters who gave full service with a smile. And off the road he ran his own club the same way, with warmth and style.

"Well, good morning, Gil. I see you made it through the night. Wait a minute; you got blood on your shirt. What happened?

While Gil explained, Tommy sat him down with a drink and brought over his rent money. Gil tried to buy a pint, "for medicinal purposes," but Tommy refused. "You need to get those teeth of yours fixed so they don't get infected and you need to pay rent. I don't want you drinking anymore 'til you take care of business. I'm going to the men's room. Be back in a minute."

Gil knew the janitor also worked as bartender. He was sure Phil hadn't heard Tommy refuse him. He quickly bought a pint from Phil. When Tommy returned, Gil thanked him and rose to leave. A morose looking black guy with a do-rag came in the door. Gil walked past the man on his way out and his attitude gave Gil a chill down his spine.

"Gimme a beer," the man snarled.

Outside, an Indian summer day was warming up. But Gil felt cold, weak, and more aware of how serious his condition had become.

His brain was throbbing again, his mouth more painful. At the bus stop he began sipping the pint he'd just bought, knowing it was a second pint on an empty stomach.

Then he heard gunshots! He turned in the direction they came from and saw the black man with the do-rag run out the door of The Blue Note, jump into an old car and speed away. OH GOD NO! Gil ignored the bus that had stopped for him. He ran back to the bar.

Phil was on the floor beneath the cash register, kneeing over Tommy's body. Tommy was bleeding profusely from the chest. Gil could not comprehend what he was seeing. It was inconceivable that anyone as gentle as Tommy could be shot so brutally. He was convulsing. Phil didn't know what to do to stop the blood spilling from Tommy's mouth. He was trying to speak.

"Junkie got me, Phil," he managed. "Please call Muriel." Then he fell limp. He had no pulse.

"Oh, Lord have mercy!" Phil moaned. He got up and went to the phone. His tears fell as he dialed Tommy's wife. No answer.

"For fifty bucks, Gil. That's all there was in the till. Fuckin' junkie killed Tommy for fifty bucks. I gotta call the cops now. I don't feel like dealin' with the man, but I better do it and get it over with. You can split if you want. I can handle this. Oh Lord. Lord have mercy."

"Okay, Phil. Listen, that junkie was driving an old beat up blue car. Looked like a '49 Ford." Gil was in shock. "If I can help in any way, call me."

In no mood to take a bus or deal with the people on it, Gil walked home, swigging rum, hoping it might kill the infection in his mouth; he walked slowly, crying. He remembered how Tommy, as headwaiter, had been so gentle with him when he was a new second cook. So many people loved Tommy, half the north side would be at the funeral. Tommy had brightened up the world wherever he might be, and someone put that light out for a measly fifty bucks. It was a long walk from north to south, and Gil walked it by instinct, avoiding people and traffic as much as possible. Hearing young men playing basketball on a south side corner, he looked up to catch a white guy nail a basket from half court. It was his friend Jim.

Gil stopped to rest and realized it was a bright sunny day, warm now, and the young players were enjoying it. Jim strode to the fence and yelled, "Where you going, Gil, you look really blasted. What happened to you?"

"Tommy's dead."

"Tommy who?"

"Blue Note Tommy. A fucking junkie shot him." Jim motioned to the blacks he'd been playing with to go on without him. He came and put his arm around Gil. "I'm sorry, man. Listen, Sarah's looking for you. Dean was gonna call you too. He and Carl are having a bar-b-que again today. Sarah will probably be there. They told me to invite her. I'm going over there after this game. You look really rough. What happened to your teeth?"

"Bouncer knocked them out. Midshipmen bouncers."

"I thought you were gonna stay out of there."

"I did too."

"You better take care of that mouth, in more ways than one."

"Yeah, I was in a blackout and shot my mouth off. I'm going to go see Sarah. I promised I'd try to help find her sister. I may be a drunk, but my word is my word."

Knowing Dean always left his front door open when home, Gil just walked in through the house to the backyard. Horace Silver's "Filthy McNasty" was playing from Dean's stereo speakers. The smell of chicken on the grill made him hungry, but Gil knew he couldn't chew until his two loose teeth were removed. He went for the keg in one far corner and sat down. Sarah stood nearby talking to an attractive black lady. The expression of animated pleasure on her face turned to shock when she noticed Gil.

"Tommy's dead," Gil said to no one in particular. Nothing else mattered.

"What the fuck you talking about, man?" Carl said. He'd left his post at the grill to be by the sexy black lady. "What Tommy?"

"Blue Note Tommy."

"JESUS CHRIST! DEAN! GET OVER HERE! TOMMY'S DEAD! What about you, man, you chase the killer or something? Your mouth's all fucked up."

"No, I got punched out by the goons at Midshipman's. But I saw the man who shot Tommy. He is a strung-out smack head, a do-rag spade. I had just talked to Tommy and was waiting for a bus when I heard the shots. I saw the dude run out of the club and jump in an old beater, but I couldn't get the license number."

"I hope the nabs catch that evil mother and hang him. May his soul rot in hell!" He turned to look for his friend. "Hey, Dean! Put some blues on, the heaviest goddamn blues you can find. This is a wake. This is a wake now for Tommy. God have mercy!"

Sarah took Gil by the arm and helped him up from the chair. "Gil, I can help you, get you to a doctor, dentist, but I still need to know if you are going to help us look for Rachel." Gil looked at Sarah. He seemed puzzled. Sarah wondered if he'd even remembered what she was talking about. When he wiped his face with the cuff of his dirty shirt, fresh blood appeared on his lip where he had been smashed in the face and apparently lost teeth. He looked sick, ready to pass out. His misery was repulsive, yet the pity she felt made her deeply sad.

"I told you I'd try to help. I will."

"All right. Let's get you some treatment and an antibiotic. I'll pay for it. You've probably already got an infection." On the way out with Gil behind her, Sarah noticed Jim had arrived and was helping the black lady keep Carl at bay. "Animal!" she said. "He was pawing me. He's the kind of dude chases anything in a skirt. I'm glad you showed up to talk to. He seems to respect you."

Later Sarah wrote in her journal: *Today Gil finally showed up. His life is a shambles. He was beaten up. I got him help and antibiotics then got him to his landlord so he could pay his rent before he could blow it all on drink. What a fool I am to expect that we can count on this pathetic drunk, this sad-assed jazz baby drunk, to help find Rachel. But he's all we've got so far.*

Another bar-b-que in Dean's backyard. Heavy jazz and blues. Blues later because some railroad worker was killed. Carl trying to paw a sexy black lady guest. He leaves me alone. His lust is disgusting but I also remember what Jim once told me. 'He's a damn brilliant musician. And it's not just women. He has a voracious appetite for everything: music, art, food, drinks and drugs; everything, an unquenchable lust. It's part of his genius.'

16

GIRL MISSING

After taking Gil to outpatient and a pharmacy, Sarah eased him out of her car. He was in a stupor, but she got him inside his apartment where he fell onto the sofa. She left him there to sleep it off.

He awoke the next day at noon to the memory of Tommy lying in a pool of blood. He got up, made coffee and lit a cigarette which, with his mouth still sore, was easier to smoke than his pipe. He knew the coffee was not going to do much to lift the blue funk he felt trapped in. He had gone from being operative to severe depression in just two days. On his kitchen table sat his rum and the prescriptions Sarah had bought. He was afraid to take the painkiller because he knew he couldn't stop drinking rum long enough to feel the effect. He spiked his second cup of coffee with rum, then drank a cup straight. The acid churning in his stomach told him it was high time he put something solid into it. He would go to the store for some groceries to take the antibiotic with. Then he would call Sarah like he promised.

At the convenience store he bought eggs, bread, orange juice and more cigarettes. Coming out, he encountered a black pimp.

"Goin' on, Gil?"

"Nada, Tony, jus' goin' on shit. How you doin'?"

"Goin' on shit, you got it."

As usual Tony looked like he just stepped out of Esquire Magazine; exquisite three-piece suit, hair slick, expensive watch and jewelry, his English Leather lending a sensual dimension to his presence. Gil winced when he remembered he had told Sarah he would talk to this very pimp to see if he knew anything. But Tony was in the store now and Gil felt he needed to feel more confident before approaching him with questions. He wanted more rum first. He wished he could just back out of trying to find Rachel. But he'd promised to try and help and he was indebted to Sarah now. She had begun to help them all with no hesitation and that was goddamn impressive! He had begun to like her. Her sweetness was like a breath of fresh air in the often cynical world around him.

# # #

Back at the apartment the phone was ringing. It was Sarah. Her mother gave her money for the search, could she bring it over? He'd said, sure. Before she came over, he scrambled some eggs, sat down and ate them with toast, washing down an antibiotic with orange juice.

Sarah arrived with what Gil considered a small fortune. He knew when he accepted it he'd have to use all the willpower he had to keep from blowing the family money on some drunken spree.

"Mom's at her wit's end because she doesn't know anything at all about what my little sister Rachel was into or who her friends are. I don't either, really. She's been in trouble for a long time, with Dad mainly. They didn't get along at all. He's dead now, but she's still rebelling."

Gil stifled an urge to drink some rum straight from the bottle. He stood up and paid attention, for Sarah was describing a situation much more serious than his own. Her family had a real emergency while his problem was mere drunkenness he'd brought on himself.

"Once when she tried to run away, I found her downtown with a pimp hitting on her. She got mad when I pulled her away. She tried to run, but I yelled at a cop to help me get her home. Now she doesn't trust me anymore. I knew she would run away again. I feel she's into something real serious. I feel sorry for her. Our father had a strong work ethic and I guess I do, too. She hates everything associated with him, our house; our religion-- hates St. Louis Park, even our money. The real trouble started last year when she had a heavy crush on a gentile boy named Steve. She had to sneak out to meet him."

"But that would only work for so long, right?" Gil asked.

"Well, she wasn't meeting him at night so my parents didn't suspect anything, but then one of Rachel's friends ratted on her and told my dad about Steve. Dad made Rachel bring Steve home so he and Mom could meet him, because he figured Rachel had lied about Steve being Jewish. Dad took one look at him and knew he wasn't a Jew. He asked Steve some questions just to be sure. Steve obviously knew nothing at all about Jews. So Dad told Steve to leave and told Rachel she could never go out with him again. From that day on, she hated Dad and quit talking to him unless forced to. She kept seeing Steve on the sly. When Dad found out, he grounded her for two weeks. That's when she started disappearing overnight. Dad got real mean to her then for disobeying him. Of course, then she rebelled all the more."

Sarah stopped her report on Rachel as she considered her role in the disappearance. "I tried to reach her, but she considers me a hypocrite, a phony because I used to appease Dad. She doesn't trust me, especially after I've stopped her several times from running away. She knows I smoke dope; yet everybody comes down on her for doing it. There's a few years between us---she's sixteen and I'm of age now at 21. When Dad died, Rachel really cut loose. Mom couldn't handle her at all. She went out the night before Dad's funeral and didn't come home 'til days after. We found the remains of her hair dye; she'd bleached her hair before she left. She also stole all of Mom's good jewelry. She slipped out during the night and was gone for good. We haven't heard a word. The police have no sightings of her. We knew Rachel was drinking and smoking dope. A lot of kids do, but I think she might have been into heavier stuff. I heard she was hanging with Steve and some pretty rough people around a bar downtown."

"Who did you hear that from?"

"I can't remember. I really don't know anyone in this new crowd she hung with. They weren't necessarily from her high school. They hung out downtown and considered anyone in the suburbs square."

"What bar did they hang at? What's the name?"

"I don't remember. I think I was told but it didn't register."

Gil assured Sarah he could handle the search of the night life and bar scene to find Rachel. She sighed and looked intently at him. She wondered if he really could do what he said He promised to call if he discovered anything at all.

As soon as Sarah left, Gil went to the liquor store for a supply of rum. When he got back he sipped some straight, listening to a Gene "Jug" Ammons record. The brashness of Jug's bold tenor sax gave him the push to get going. He took half the money Sarah gave him and hid the rest in a small metal box he kept under lock and key.

# # #

Tony the pimp was rarely seen on the street in the South, his own neighborhood. Due to the urgency of his quest, Gil would have to risk going to his door to get information. Tony usually had underlings run errands while he sat up in his crib playing chess with friends and guests. He was known to be a champion chess player. His house was brand new, a design of his own, a modern beauty in brick and oak-- inside and out-- the latest and best surveillance equipment monitored all activity.

Gil walked up and rang the bell on the big house. The door opened suddenly and a huge Doberman pinscher lunged at him, growling and straining at its leash, held by a tall, solidly built black man in a purple shirt, a massive silver crucifix around his neck.

"WHADAYAWANT?!"

"I, uh, I came here to see Tony."

"HE AIN'T HERE."

"Can you tell me where I can find him?"

"Who the hell are you?"

"I'm Gil Montgomery. I owe him money."

"Leave the money with me."

"I'd rather give it to him. I need to talk to him."

"He's at the bar, now BOOK, WHITEY!" The man was now hostile. He let the dog leash go enough so the dog could snap his teeth inches from Gil's leg.

"Which bar? Buster's?"

The big man pulled in the dog and slammed the door with such force it sounded like a cannon shot.

Downtown, off Hennepin, Buster's was packed for happy hour. Gil recognized several prostitutes and a pimp. Two provocatively dressed white girls were talking black. One was convincing but the other's mimicking was pathetic, lost to either race. Gil stepped to the bar and ordered a rum on the rocks, realizing he was already half drunk, too drunk for a mission.

"Have you seen Tony today?" he asked as he paid for his drink.

"Tony who?"

"Tony the pimp. You know. This is his home bar."

The bartender stiffened. "Let's see...," he said sarcastically, "do I know a pimp named Tony? I don't know, why?"

"'Cause I owe him money."

The bartender didn't reply. He turned and went on another round of filling drinks. Gil took a handful of twenties and shoved them into the trough of the bar. The barkeep returned. "Yeah, Tony. He left a half hour ago. Said he'd be over North. He's throwing a private party tonight. He's probably setting it up."

"Whereabouts in North?"

"I dunno. Ask her. She knows Tony." He pointed to the white girl who was hip compared to her companion. She was now at a table by herself near the bar and had been listening.

"What do you want with Tony?" she asked blatantly.

"You want another drink?"

"Sure, I'll take another drink. Without all your white bullshit, man."

Gil smiled. He got them both drinks. "I just need to talk to you for a second." The girl had a ripe young body under a tight short dress.

"What the fuck do you want?"

"I'm looking for Tony. You know him?"

"Sure. He ain't here."

"I hear he's throwing a party. Do you know where the party's at?"

"Who the fuck are you, man? Who the fuck do you think you are, comin' in from jump street askin' those kinds of questions?"

"I'm not a cop. I work on the railroad. My name is Gil. I owe Tony some money, that's all. An' I need to pay it soon."

"Only two reasons most white guys come in here. Either they're cops or they lookin' for pussy."

Her antagonism was becoming annoying. Gil took more twenties out of his billfold and set them in front of her. She stared at them, then back at him, but didn't speak. The other white girl, who had been coming on to a man, abruptly joined the table. "Mind if I join you? What yawl be talk''bout?"

"I just asked if she knew where Tony's party is tonight."

"Oh it's at his friend Jamie's crib next to the bar."

"What bar?"

"Stand Up Bill's. You can't miss Jamie's. It's the brown house next to the bar. It'll be swarming with spades, like cockroaches."

"Yeah, an' now that you finally know," said the first girl scooping up the money, "the party's by invite only so if he didn't invite you, you ain't getting in no way, 'specially if you ain't dressed no better," this said with a grin as if to indicate she was being less hostile.

"Okay, girl. I'll wear better threads. Now, I got some real bread for you if you can answer just one more thing. Do you know a girl named Rachel? Little Jewish girl who might've come in here or anywhere around."

"Why?"

"Because she disappeared."

"YOU A COP! I knew you were a cop 'cause you ain't here for pussy."

"No. No. I owe Tony some money, and Rachel is the sister of a friend of mine." People nearby began to stare at their table, thinking the girl was blowing Gil's cover as a cop. "Rachel's disappeared. Her mother is scared. You can dig that, can't you?" He signaled the bartender to bring drinks for them all, making a mental note to switch to coffee if he stayed much longer. He paid for the new drinks, then slipped the first girl a hundred dollar bill. Her expression became serious. In a lowered voice she got solemn, "I knew Rachel for a little while. We don't know where she is. She tried to hang around here like a second home. They let her for a while 'cause pimps were trying to cop her. She had a boyfriend. Both underage. I think a pimp got to her. I think she might've got shipped out east, man, New York City. That's what happens to a lot of young girls who just disappear."

"Thanks, girl."

"Name's Carol."

"Thanks, Carol. I thank you, and Rachel's mom and sister thank you, too."

Gil got up then and walked out. The bright sunshine hurt his eyes and the noise and exhaust from cars made him dizzy. He made it home, set his alarm and fell into bed.

# # #

When he awoke hours later, he realized he had shut the alarm off long before. It was already dark. He instantly remembered what he had to do and dreaded it. Coffee and rum again, heavy on the rum. He would need more food, too, or the rum would tear up his stomach. *Got to get my head on right and my ass over north*, he thought, as he put on his Zoot Sims album. Sipping rum, he sketched out a game plan. Then he shaved and put on his best formal wear, an old mismatched secondhand suit that looked very square but was all he had. He took out more of Sarah's money and stashed some of it in the bottom of one of his socks in case he got mugged. He put an ungodly amount of money into his billfold, then switched most of it to a pocket inside the suit. That girl had soul. She had gone into some very tight places with her new inner-city friends, and she was always helping someone out. He wished he hadn't drank as much earlier because he knew he was going to have to lay it on in order to have the guts to do what was coming. He did not want to blow her family money.

He stopped in at Little Tijuana Restaurant and ate two bowls of chili with onions and cheese, ignoring the time for a while. He swallowed two painkillers and an antibiotic. The party would go on all night long and Tony would be there. It was his gig. The goofy suit he wore, which he kept only for weddings and funerals, made him feel uncomfortable, stupid even, as he rode north on a city bus. The only place he knew in Near North was The Blue Note, which was situated on the edge of the ghetto. Now he was headed into the heart of the place to find a bar called Stand Up Bill's near Plymouth and Broadway. He felt like a buffoon riding a neon whale into the heart of darkness to find a black pimp who would consider him a fool for showing up. And he couldn't draw on rum too long to fuel his courage or he'd black out. All the money he was carrying looking like a tourist, a Tomfool tourist.

He got off the bus a few blocks before the bar, took out a pint of rum from inside his suit jacket, broke the seal and took two big swigs. A large brown shingled house next to the bar was rockin' wide open. The streets were lined solid with parked cars, and men were coming and going from the house. Jimmy Witherspoon's "Good Rockin' Tonight" blared out the door and open windows. Gil considered the house. Unlike the men inside who were all there to procure women and had been invited, he could be turned away. He started toward the house, then turned and walked into the bar instead.

It was all blacks. Most ignored him, but several gave him hostile looks. He was tempted to just go home, hoping to run into Tony again on his own turf. But Sarah and her mother didn't have that kind of time.

"GIL! How you doin' man?" It was Frankie, a waiter from the railroad. Gil relaxed. Frankie was dressed in a beautiful brown suit, wearing a brown derby, looking elegant in a rough neighborhood bar. "What you doin' way over here, Gil? Can I buy you a drink?"

"No, I'll buy you one, just for being here. It's really good to see you, man! I feel out of place around here, but I'm looking for somebody, a pimp named Tony, you know him?

"Sure. Most everybody knows that mother. He's next door at his gig. But it's private. You probably don't want to try to go in there without an invite. It's for clients, dig?"

"Yeah, just johns and pros I imagine. But I gotta talk to Tony. Would you consider going in there with me, at least going over there?" Frankie looked at Gil with mock seriousness, and then cracked a smile.

"Sure, why not. What are they gonna do besides throw us the fuck out?"

What a difference it made to be walking over to Tony's party with a black friend. With Frankie at his side, most of Gil's fear abated but he still felt sweat roll down his back. The ghetto of North Minneapolis was a place he never walked alone.

"You two got an invite?" asked a burley giant guarding the door.

"No, I just need to talk to Tony a minute or two."

"You need an invite, sorry, Jack."

"Hey, let 'em in, Jake," Tony said. Luckily he'd walked by and seen Gil and Frankie. Once again Gil was impressed by Tony's style. He wore a classic grey pinstriped suit with a pink tie and carnation.

"What's up, Gil? You sports looking for some action?"

"No thanks, Tony. I'd just like to talk to you for a moment in private, please; if I could… it's serious."

"Sure, man, follow me. Frankie, relax, grab a drink over there. On the house."

Tony led Gil into an office of sorts where another bodyguard stood by. This second solemn giant wore a red turban with a ruby-red jewel in the middle. He followed them into the room.

"You can leave, Sammy. Now Gil, I know you didn't come all the way over here without an invite just to socialize. Let's hear it; I got a house full of guys to take care of."

"Sure, Tony. Square biz, man. A sister of a friend of mine has disappeared."

"Yeah, so what's that got to do with me?"

"I just wanted to see if you've heard about any young girl copped by pimps lately? She was trying to hang around Buster's but she's only sixteen, little Jewish girl named Rachel. Her mother thinks she may have dyed her hair blonde. Do you know where she might be?" Gil took a grand out of his coat. "You can have this if you can help us locate her. Her mother is frantic."

"Yeah, I knew her. But I haven't had anything to do with her. I don't dig rich girls. They're too much trouble."

"I can dig it. But do you have any idea what happened to her?"

"I know where she probably is. I know who copped her too, but I ain't giving you no name. That's code, man."

"Yes, I respect that, but you said you probably know where she is. If you can tell me that, then this grand is yours. And if we find her, you get another grand, okay?"

"Who's we?"

"Me and her mother. This is her bread."

"You ain't got the man in on this, have you? 'Cause if you do, you can get the fuck out of here right now and take your fucking grand with you, stick it up your ass. I got my own bread."

"No, no. I ain't got no truck with the nabs, Tony. Rachel's mom, Ruth, is acting on her own. She gave up on the cops. There's nobody else involved."

"Uh-huh. But I really don't want to touch this, Gil. Look, I know you're okay, man. I know you from the hood we both be at, over in South. I trust you enough, but I ain't giving out the pimp's name. Tell you what, I'll take this grand and you forget about the other if you find her. Good luck. I don't like the pimp who copped her. He's from the Big Apple. Stone evil. I heard he took the girl out there, but she's probably up in Canada right now. They breakin' her in.

"Canada?"

"Yeah, up there somewhere, just over the border from New York."

"Somewhere?"

"Shit, I don't know. They break 'em in up there so the NYPD don't get wind of it. Probably use some shack out in the sticks, a cabin at a rundown resort, or property they own. Then they turn 'em loose right away on the streets in New York City. That's all I know."

"Alright, Tony. Thanks for taking time to talk."

"Sure. One more thing. If she's blonde now she'll end up on the Minnesota Strip. Those New York Johns really dig blondes!" Gil felt a pang of worry about her safety when her black hair started to grow out.

Frankie was going on to Road Buddy's and Gil wanted to go too, to keep drinking and stave off loneliness. But, Frankie wouldn't hear of it, and dropped him off at home with the rest of Sarah's money intact. Gil passed out before calling her.

# # #

The next morning, hung-over, coffee and rum in hand, he called Sarah. "New York City? Oh God! I don't understand. What do you mean? Why New York?" She was shocked.

"Because Tony thinks a local pimp sold her to one in New York City for prostitution."

"But I don't understand. She's still a girl, still in high school."

"They want young girls, Sarah. They're easier to steal and control."

"I've got to go to New York City then! Did he say where in New York?"

"Look, Sarah, you should NOT be going to New York. Not by yourself. Tony talked about something called the Minnesota Strip where they sell blondes from Minnesota. I don't know anything about it, but we can find out."

Sarah began to cry. "What can we do? Will the cops help?"

"You mean with New York? I don't know. Maybe through missing persons, but in New York City there's thousands of missing persons."

"I've got to go look for her, Gil. I can't just sit here and do nothing. Will you go with me?"

"You definitely should NOT go, Sarah. Your mother needs you here. Let's talk to Jim. He's not working, doesn't have a steady job. Maybe he'll go. I'm supposed to go out on the road or I'd go with him. He goes to a kung fu school. Maybe he can get one of those dudes to go with him. We'll work it out. He'll help you. I know he will."

"All right. But let's hurry! I'll be worried sick now, and I have no idea how to tell Mom this. Can we look for Jim tonight?"

"Sure, but let me get some rest, okay?" He hung up.

Stone evil? Gil remembered Tony said the pimps involved were "stone evil." It was chilling to think Rachel would probably never come back.

17

BRICKS AND BEAMS

Jim walked down Hennepin Avenue to the block where he turned west into the warehouse district to reach his studio. It was good to get off the big brash avenue. Its soulless bars and strip joints turned him off. It struck him as an oversized main street without the warmth and soul of those small towns. The only saving grace was the gigs jazz bands were allowed playing behind the strippers. Hard drinking was what it was really about, people coming for kicks but not looking happy. Jim thought about all the hard drinking Gil had slipped into. He's been fucking up, he thought. He'd be better off on grass.

A few blocks into the warehouse district and Jim's thoughts lightened. The evening streets were empty, the big buildings silent. No neon. But in this peace Jim felt a subtle excitement. He was going to his own studio to work alone without interruption. Other artists would also be working in their studies and bands could rent spaces to rehearse without restraint. By day there were galleries and a few bars and eateries where tourists spent money while gallery crawling. There would soon be trendy pseudo artsy places, but the district was big enough to retain its dominant feeling of a free zone, a new frontier for the soul.

Jim unlocked a warehouse side door and walked up a metal staircase to the third floor of the gigantic place. He loved the brick walls and huge ceiling beams and columns. Just being in such space made him feel good, and when he entered the intimate space of his studio, he could enjoy close up the colors of the bricks and the rough texture of the wood beams, their massive size and strength.

He'd kept the studio rent paid somehow. When he left art school he vowed not to take a job, but to paint, paint, paint until he knew, one way or another, if he could survive as an artist. The rent for the studio was cheap enough that he might be able to keep it going from the sales of his work, maybe take a part-time job at times. And, although it was against the warehouse rules, if he lived in the studio, he wouldn't have to rent a room, too. The warehouse wasn't zoned for living space. There was one toilet on the floor that all the artists used. Jim's studio had a small sink with cold water and electrical outlets for appliances.

The artist who used the studio before Jim was crazy wild. He had lived there breaking the rules but did so openly and brazenly. He was given two notices, and then evicted. In protest, the night before he left, he threw a wild party, then on his way out tossed whole open cans of paint onto the partition walls and studio floor. Management offered Jim a month's free rent for helping clean and repair the damage. Jim was grateful. He never before had space enough to work big canvases in and was eager to get started on one. Things really came together when Lance, a more established painter friend, arranged the sale of one of Jim's paintings to a big buyer for four hundred dollars. With this money Jim bought three very large canvases, a generous supply of paints, brushes and other supplies, plush a stash of reefer he liked to use while painting or playing his guitar.

The warehouse floor was silent. No one else seemed to be in their studios. Jim's eyes rested on the three giant canvases he intended to work on. He took one down to begin priming it, a canvas he could finally do for his own sake. It would depict a basketball player suspended in air, straining toward the hoop, his muscular being totally concentrated. This painting would take him deeper into his craft than the commissioned ones; more of himself would be invested. It would be enjoyable to work, yet challenging. He needed more knowledge of anatomy of the actual bones, tissues, nerves and muscles of the body, especially because every muscle of this basketball player's body would be straining to the extreme. He didn't know any models athletic enough to pose for him. Thus he felt incompetent to accurately portray the human physique, but his ability to see the picture in his mind realized as a painting would keep him working to render it as best he could.

He sat down to roll some joints. Light from a full moon was flooding over the nocturnal city through the big windows. He smiled remembering the rock musicians in a nearby warehouse who invited him over to share beer with them while they practiced. He switched off the lights, cracked a window to draw the smoke from his J, and sat in moonlight. Its glow transformed the studio with mystical luminosity. What a shame to eventually have to turn the lights back on to paint some more. He chose an Eric Dolphy album to work by and began a preparatory drawing on the canvas. He forgot time and the music. The records stopped. Hours passed. He stopped only to make coffee, and then resumed work.

# # #

Later that evening when Sarah arrived to pick up Gil to guide her to Jim's studio, she found him slobbering drunk, gurgling over a Gene Ammons record he was playing really loud. She was hurt and it stung. He looked too out of it to help at all. But he insisted he was ready to help her and staggered out to the car behind her. When they arrived at the warehouse district filled with buildings like the one that housed her father's main clothing store, the full moon cast huge shadows darkening the loading docks and alleys, shadows that swept across vast stretches of moonlight. She felt she was cruising Batman's turf but her Robin was dozing on and off. At a stoplight she examined him.

"Jesus, I need coffee!" he mumbled. "We'll have to park on the left side of the building where his big third windows are. I hope he's got some coffee. We have to toss stones at his window so he can come down and let us in. There's no buzzer." Then he passed out cold.

Around the left side, Sarah saw one light from a big third floor window. She got out and searched for pebbles to toss at Jim's window. Long throw, but she managed to hit his window once. He came and looked down at her standing in half-light.

He ran down the stairs to let her in the side door. "I wasn't sure I could find this place again, so I asked Gil to guide me. He's in the car passed out. I hope I can wake him up."

"Leave him there. He'll be okay. Come on up." Jim shook his head, "He's becoming a real stumble bum."

"I'm sorry if I'm interrupting you. I imagine you're painting." She enjoyed the inner sanctum of the warehouse and going up the stairwell to Jim's studio.

"Drawing, actually. It's okay. I've done enough tonight. Care to smoke a joint?" He opened the door and they stepped in.

"Sure. Your studio is really mellow. I'd love to live in a space like this!"

Jim put a Modern Jazz Quartet album on the turntable and turned the lights down. He handed her a J and as the marijuana took effect, it enhanced all Sarah's senses. The sound of Milt Jackson's vibraphone in Jim's MJQ record cascaded through her mind like a liquid symphony. She saw the moonlight lend a luminous, mystical intimacy to the studio and the touch of Jim's fingers as he passed the joint began to turn her on. She realized that the grass was not only making her more relaxed, it was also acting as an aphrodisiac. Jim looked very handsome in the moonlight, even though he wasn't her type. He was blonde with an athletic build and Sarah preferred dark-haired men with slight builds, but that distinction seemed frivolous now. While she still had control of herself, she came out with the reason for her visit. She asked if he could help find Rachel in New York City. Listening carefully, he agreed. She took his hand in both of hers and thanked him sincerely and he kissed her gently. She responded with a stronger kiss of her own.

Jim was feeling slightly guilty for having kissed her. He hoped she didn't think he was trying to take advantage of her. He hadn't been thinking of her romantically but she was becoming more interesting each time he saw her. She wasn't bad looking. Her breasts were fascinating, so ample, a gorgeous set of ripe fruit for some lucky chap to sample. Sarah was well practiced at reading the furtive glances many men gave her breasts, and she knew Jim was included. As they continued kissing, she stopped and lifted up her blouse. He responded by unfastening her bra. Soon he was fondling and kissing her breasts. She had never allowed anyone to go so far. The urge to undress completely came with a desire as overwhelming as a flood. She knew she'd have to stop immediately or lose her virginity to a man who was still, in many ways, a stranger.

"Jim, I've got to leave. I'm afraid if we go any further, I'll be here all night! I still have to get Gil back to his place and tell Mom you're helping us." Sarah put her bra and blouse back on. "I'm so pleased that you'll even go to New York to try and look for my sister. We'll pay you to find Rachel. Mom will be so grateful!"

"Sarah, you've been helping us jazz-babies out a lot. Now it's our turn. I know just the guy to help me, Chuck Wong, a friend of mine from my kung fu class. He's got a van too. I'll ask him tomorrow. We could probably leave in a day or two."

"Just call me when you're ready to go and I'll give you plenty of travel money, more than enough for everything you'll need. We can't thank you enough. Thank God at least there's a chance to do something to try to find her. God bless you!"

18

THE MINNESOTA CONNECTION

The next day Jim went to kung fu practice. He stopped to repeatedly thrust his hands into the big vat of dried corn, something students did upon entering and leaving the school. It toughened their hands. Master Jin-Chu was gone for the day and Jim's friend, Chuck Wong, was in charge of classes. Jim asked him right off if he would consider going with him to New York City to find Rachel. Chuck had a cool head and relaxed nature. Never one to go looking for trouble, he nonetheless enjoyed the proximity of danger and any kind of legal adventure. After hearing more of the details, he immediately agreed to go.

"But no drinks after class today. I have to be in shape for the next class. No drunken kung fu master…works in movie but not here!"

After class Jim stopped in front of Clancy's, the cop bar where he and Chuck had drinks after class. Because Chuck couldn't come, Jim was going to skip drinks this time. But through the window he noticed Dale, a cop he really liked, so he turned and went in. For a year Jim and Chuck had been stopping at Clancy's. A few of the other kung fu guys scoffed at this, but he and Chuck liked the challenge of getting to know the cops and listening to them share their private feelings about the pressures and situations they faced every day, how they coped and let off steam. Only cops and sympathizers drank there, giving Clancy's a rep as a serious watering hole where cops let their hair down. Getting to know these men hadn't been easy. They were served, of course, and Clancy was friendly, but it took a thick skin and many weeks before any cop would give them the time of day.

"What's up, Mantis?" Dale said, referring to the style of martial arts Jim practiced, Southern Praying Mantis Kung Fu. "Who are you preying on?"

"You. Just got some questions if you've got a minute?"

"Does it look like I'm going anywhere? Hey Clancy, give Jim a drink."

Dressed in off-duty street clothing, Dale looked more like a college professor than a cop. His graying hair was quite long. He wore dark trousers, a tweed jacket, and puffed on a pipe while composing his thoughts and listening. His expression became serious when Jim explained the mission he and Chuck were about to leave on.

"I wouldn't waste any time on Canada," Dale advised. "Looking for that girl up there would be like looking for a needle in a haystack. I'd just go right to New York City."

"But they could be beating her up."

"Yeah. They've probably already done that already. They don't waste time getting them to New York. They just break them in Canada; rent some old cabin out in the woods, in the middle of nowhere. You'd never find a place like that. They "game" her there, that's the expression pimps use for the brainwashing process the girls go through. Its total destruction of self-esteem and obliteration of all will through fear. Then they take them straight to New York City."

"Why do they start in Canada?"

"Because there's no one around up there, no New York cops to get hip. It's deserted. They pay off any Canadians who might be suspicious. No one sees the breaking-in process but the pimps. Then they bring them to the City, beaten down and enslaved, and put them out on the street. They know they'll be killed if they try to leave."

"How do they break them?"

"Fear and pain. They give them whippings with wire clothes hangers. They take a clothes hanger and twist it so it's just a long wire with the hook left at the end, and they beat them until they pass out. Then they revive them and beat them again – beat them all over their bodies with slashes and gouges from the hook. They beat, and then rape them repeatedly, submitting them to group sex until they are completely demoralized. Then they take them overnight across the border to the Big Apple and usually dump them right out on the street, beat up like that to go to work. When the girls cry about how their bodies look, they tell them use your mouth."

"Oh God! Holy shit! Where do we go, in New York, to look for her?"

"Right off Times Square, along 8th Avenue. You'll see. Its sin city, hookers and sex shops, porno movies all down that way."

"How do you know about all this, Dale? Have you worked it?"

"No. But, we've seen films generally outling their protocol. But I saw it up close when I was in New York City a few years ago. A friend of mine worked Vice, looking for a blonde from here that was shipped out there. The Minnesota Connection likes blondes because New York johns prefer them. They are in big demand and Minnesota's got a big supply."

"What's the Minnesota Connection?"

"It's a pipeline feeding hookers from Minnesota to New York, especially blondes. Pimps from here in Minneapolis connect with pimps in the Apple. They move in and out of the city when the heat's turned on and off. The "Minnesota Strip," as it's called, is where they station the blondes, along 8th Ave. from 42nd to 50th." Dale saw the look of utter shock on Jim's face.

"Tell you what, I'll go see Ed from Vice and get you a list of hangouts for pimps and pros in the Minnesota Strip area, their hotels and stuff. When are you going?"

"Monday morning."

"Okay. Meet me here tomorrow at this same time, and I'll have the list. Is this girl you're looking for blonde?"

"Not really. She's Jewish. But she dyed her hair blonde."

"You better hurry then, because when they find out she really isn't blonde she won't have the same value. They'll be even rougher."

# # #

Monday morning, Chuck Wong was excited about being able to see New York City; it was the first place his father had come to from China. Later he went on to live in Minnesota becoming one of the original cooks at the Nankin Cafe, the famous Chinese eatery. After a sound sleep Chuck got up to do exercises and a short meditation. He ate a breakfast of miso broth, rice cakes and a banana, packed a few things in an overnight bag: and then drove his VW van to pick up Jim. "Book city," he said. "Let's roll!"

They decided to take the route from St. Paul to Chicago and then take Interstate-90 through New York State, and enter Manhattan through the borough of the Bronx. Jim handled the maps, watched road signs and had money ready for the toll roads. It took them three days to get to New York City and another half a day to wend their way to 42nd Street.

When Chuck and Jim began to patrol streets around the Minnesota Strip, they reserved a room at one of the hotels on the list Dale got them, a hotel with active hooker traffic. But questioning girls in and around the hotel got them nowhere. The girls were immediately suspicious and soon refused to talk at all.

"You know what we're going to have to do," Jim said. "We're going to have to solicit the girls ourselves and then ask questions."

"You mean…."

"Yes, act like johns, pay for sex, I mean for their time, to start, so they're less suspicious."

"You do that. I'll stay and watch for Rachel. I've been studying her picture your friend gave us."

"Look, I didn't mean we have to go through with the sex, just get them in the room, pay them to do or not do something, and then ask questions."

"You do that. Maybe I'll start staking out some of the other hotels."

"Okay. I see you'd be uncomfortable. I don't dig this either. You just do what you think you should and I'll see what I can do."

Eventually Jim got girls into rooms but they all claimed no knowledge of Rachel. One accused Jim of being a vice cop, the very girl he was most tempted by. "The word's out on you, man," she said. As nervous as Chuck was, he often had better luck at talking to the girls around the lobby. They seemed to sense Chuck's genuine shyness and trusted him, but nobody knew Rachel.

As one girl undressed for Jim, she said she thought she knew where Rachel stayed. "Leave your clothes on. Here's the bread for your time, but I can pay you REALLY well if you take me to Rachel."

"How well?"

"A couple hundred, maybe more."

"Make it four and I'll take you." She led Jim several blocks to the Royal Hotel, second floor. "This is the floor. Pay me and I'll get her."

"No. You take me to her then I'll pay."

"You pay me now or the deals off. Pay me and stay back. I'll go to her door. She sees a stranger she'll freak."

Jim paid. The pro walked down three doors, pounded on a room and then bolted out the exit at the end of the hall. Jim let her go. An old black lady answered the door. She did not know any Rachel on her floor, or in the hotel. But Jim decided he and Chuck should check into the Royal just in case Rachel was there, rip-off or not. That night as they lay asleep in their cheap room, they were jolted awake by a furious pounding on the door. "POLICE! POLICE! OPEN UP!"

Jim jumped up and went to a peephole but it was blocked by a hand. "What do you want?"

"WE NEED TO TALK. OPEN UP! NOW!"

"Just a minute."

Jim turned to Chuck. "That's not police. They're after money. Let's go. Hurry!" He pointed to the fire escape. They grabbed their bags, lifted the window and hit the escape ladder just as the room door was broken in.

"What about my van," Chuck asked, "shall we take it?"

"No. Let's leave it for now. They may be watching it. Right now we just need to keep what's left of Sarah's money intact."

"Oh, you mean no kung fu practice on the bad guys?" Chuck joked.

"Not this time!"

They found a diner to wait out the rest of the night and ordered an early breakfast. The place was full of drag queens and female impersonators from the show at the bar next door. Several queen-types were too over the top for Chuck, who already felt the loss of sleep and was generally depressed by the raunchy world they had been searching, the porn shops and theatres, sex supermarkets and all the driven men and women hungry for illicit sex. "You know this sleazy, flesh-pit area is more than I can take right now," he said. "How about we take a day off tomorrow?"

"I hear you. Let's check out of that sleaze bag hotel, get your van and go get some good Chinese food and just relax for a day, maybe take in an art museum or find that kung fu center, our master's teacher founded."

But by afternoon of that next day, both Jim and Chuck felt guilty about not searching for Rachel, and they went to work again investigating the area around the last hotel on the list of hotels used by prostitutes. Two weeks had passed and no leads. They dreaded returning without any hope to bring the Jewish girl home. They started discussing giving up and going back to Minneapolis.

One day Chuck bought a martial arts magazine and asked the old man running the news stand if he'd heard of a young blonde prostitute named Rachel in the area.

"There are thousands of blondes in this city, young man, but I do see a little blonde who uses the hotel up the street there. Don't know her by name, but reason I noticed her is 'cause she's so young. I stand here all day and get a good view of the streets. Most people I keep seeing have regular routines. She goes up there to the Stanford." He pointed to a hotel not on their list.

"Thanks for the tip." Chuck handed him 2 twenties.

While Jim and Chuck were combing the streets, Rachel lay just blocks away in the Stanford Hotel. Chad, the New York pimp Reggie had turned her over to, had beaten her severely around midnight. He said she'd kept money from him. Pain kept her from sleeping. Worse than the intense pain was knowing Chad would return around noon. Rachel's body was covered with welts from a coat hanger beating. She had barely begun to heal from the beatings Chad's men gave her at his gaming camp. She couldn't find a position to lie in that didn't cause pain. He had even lashed the bottoms of her feet, which had bled. The soles of her feet were so sensitive that each lash sent a jolt of lightning behind her closed eyes. The pain was so excruciating she eventually passed out.

She was weak and feverish. Each passing hour increased fear and panic at the thought of Chad coming back. She was now more depressed than she'd ever been during the whole process of her abduction. Somehow, through the terror of it all, she had kept a spark of hope of escaping. Instinct was telling her to try, but to where? If he caught her trying to escape, he said he'd kill her. She was too weak to work the street, but he was sending her out anyway. Her will almost completely broken. Her absolute fear came from knowing if she became too weak, too sick to recover, Chad would have no qualms about killing her. Meat money, that's all she meant to him. She did have a two hundred dollar stash she got from an easy john, a timid old man who paid her just to strip. She was keeping that money for making a break. She had another hundred to bring to Chad, but he would expect two, the minimum daily take for each girl. The hundred for Chad was from a drunk who refused to pay. The slob had fallen asleep while she dressed, so she took what he owed her from his billfold. Feeling too weak, she turned down the next john who would've made her quota, and feeling too nauseous to walk, had sat out her time in a coffee shop.

She'd struggled back to the hotel early. She quickly hid the two hundred. When Chad called her on being a hundred short, she'd told him a john had stiffed her, which one had tried to do. Chad knew that a john did occasionally stiff his girls. Even though the other girls vouched for her, she paid dearly for this mistake. Chad beat her immediately just as he had on her first day out when she came back just fifty dollars short.

She hid the extra two hundred in a Band-Aid box in the bathroom until she could devise a better place. One slash to each wrist with a razor blade and it would be all over. She could fill the tub with warm water and faint away. Try to flee with the money stash or just take the razor bath? Either way she'd have to get on her feet. She knew how painful that would be. As she lay there trying to rally, the door opened. Fearing Chad, she bolted upright. But it was her roommate, Roberta.

"RACHEL, LISTEN!" Roberta said. "I heard them talking about you, Chad and a flunky of his. They said they're going to have to take you for a ride. You've got to get up RIGHT NOW! We've got to get you out of here!"

"Take me for a ride? What?"

"You know what that means. It means they're going to kill you. They noticed your real hair color coming back, that you're not a natural blonde. They've decided you're not worth keeping."

"Just like that? Just like that they're gonna kill me?"

"Just like that. You know how evil they are, and you know too much for them to just let you go. They won't take a chance on you turning them in. Have you got any money?"

"Yes. It's in the bathroom. In with the Band-Aids."

"Okay, I'll get it for you. Get some clothes on. HURRY!"

Rachel's feet began to bleed when she managed to get on her feet to get her money from Roberta. Just then, Chad burst through the door.

"WHAT'S THAT?" he yelled, eyeing the money. "Don't give that ho any money! Whose money is that?"

"It's mine," Roberta said fearfully.

"No, it's not. She's trying to protect me. It's mine," Rachel said.

"You held out on me, didn't you, you bitch!" He slapped Rachel so forcefully she gave way from the pain in her feet and fell. He grabbed the money from the floor. "You won't need this where you're going." He shoved Roberta out of the room and followed her out, slamming the door behind. He grabbed her by the neck. "You sneaking bitch! You're as sad as she is. You double your quota today or I'll whip you so bad you'll wish you were dead. Go on! Get your ass on the street!"

The fact that Chad had taken her money filled Rachel with rage. Anger overcame her fear and she got to her feet. FUCK YOU, she thought, I'm not taking this. Looking for her shoes, she realized all her clothes were still out in the main room where Chad had torn them off to beat her. Luckily her coat was still in the bedroom. She staggered to the window to reach the fire escape but, sealed by layers of paint, it wouldn't open. She left bloody footprints to the bathroom for a razor blade to slit open the paint around the window. Roberta's whiskey sat next to the tub so she could drink while taking her bath. Rachel grabbed it and drank deeply. She eyed the bathtub, razor in hand. It would be so easy. She took a step toward the tub to fill it, then turned and began slicing away at the seal on the bedroom window. The whiskey bolstered her resolve to escape, but the thin blade wasn't cutting the thick paint. She cut her finger. Again she thought of giving up, drawing water into the tub. But anger ruled her again. "I've got one chance, god damn it! I'm gonna take it!"

Fearing every second, knowing Chad was coming back to take her, it felt like an eternity to finally slice open the window and lift it up. She hobbled over for her coat, and then climbed out onto the fire escape. It was loose and shaky. It shifted from side to side as she stepped painfully down one step at a time, slowly, carefully descending to the end, still ten feet from the ground. She looked down the alley for help, but it was empty. She gripped the bottom and hung down in the air, watching for help until she had to let go. Her feet hit the ground and she screamed with pain, feeling an ankle crack. It would not support her when she tried to stand.

Chad leaned out from the window above, "YOU STUPID BITCH!" She knew he would be coming for her. Unable to walk, she began to crawl.

# # #

As Chuck and Jim approached the Stanford, Chuck glanced down the alley beside the hotel and noticed a young woman crawling along, moaning."

"Jim, let's check this out!" he swerved the van into the alley.

"What's your name, girl?" Jim called out; trying to match the girl's swollen, black-eyed face with the picture of Rachel they carried.

"Who are you?" Rachel asked.

"We're NOT cops," Chuck said. "We just want to help you. What's your name?" Realizing she was better off with these two strangers, she said, "its Rachel… Rachel Rosen."

"LEAVE THAT BITCH ALONE! SHE'S MINE!" Chad entered the alley waving a gun. "Get the fuck out of here!" Chad demanded. "MOVE!"

Chuck slid out of the van and faced off with Chad. But then he suddenly focused his eyes intently toward the street behind Chad as if seeing someone approach. He made a motion as if to call them in. Chad turned for a second to see who Chuck had motioned. In that second, Chuck jumped up, twirled, and performed a kung fu high kick in the stomach that sent Chad flying, his gun clattering as it rolled away. Chad started to get up, but Jim stepped in and sent a power punch into his face, breaking his nose and causing a stream of blood to cover his face and chest. Chad scrambled to get away as fast as he could.

They both lifted Rachel up and gently carried her to the van.

Rachel was very frightened. Who were these new men? How could they fight like that? Were they taking her to safety as they claimed, or to more torture? What were they going to do? They said her mother sent them to find her, but men were liars. They seemed kind, but so did her boyfriend who betrayed her and so did Reggie. Trust in him ended in multiple rape and beatings. Regardless, whoever these men were, she could not run from them with a broken ankle, and the wounds on the bottoms of her feet from the lashing by Chad had reopened when she dropped from the fire escape.

The oriental man opened a first-aid kit from his van and disinfected her feet, wrapping them with gauze. The one named Jim said they were taking her to an emergency room to have a splint put on her broken ankle. The pain was so great from that ankle she thought she would faint, and she screamed when any weight was accidently put on it. She lay on the cot in the van, cold, shivering and whimpering, curled up in the fetal position. It began to rain and soon became a downpour so heavy Chuck had to pull over as he couldn't see the street. It was dark outside, darker inside the van, darker yet in Rachel's mind. Panic still possessed her and a depression so deep she did not want to live. Even if these men were setting her free, if they were taking her back to a place she had run away from, it wouldn't matter. Her self-esteem was destroyed. She just wanted to hide. If only she had taken that razor blade and slit her wrists then and there to let her blood rain into warm bathwater. Death would be so welcome.

Jim and Chuck carried Rachel into the hospital. She made sure her coat was completely buttoned, for she was still naked underneath, having to leave her clothes behind when fleeing from Chad. A sense of dignity had been beaten out of her long ago, but shame hadn't. Now there were harsh lights and people working on her body. Then it was over and she was out on the parking lot pavement on crutches wearing the new sweatshirt, sweatpants and slippers the hospital provided. Her ankle now had a splint and boot to protect it. Jim paid the bill in cash and picked up her pain pill prescription. But for a moment they thought they might be detained by police because the doctor who treated Rachel couldn't get her to talk and he was suspicious of Jim and Chuck.

"I think the police should know about this girl's situation. She's been horribly abused," he said.

"Doctor, let's put in a collect call to her mother and you can talk to her," Jim said. "I need to do that now anyway. Her name is Ruth Rosen. I gave you all her information when we registered."

The doctor agreed.

"Hello," he said, "Mrs. Rosen? Mrs. Rosen, I have a Jim K. Jensen and a Chuck Wong here who brought a girl named Rachel Rosen into the hospital here in New York City. Is she your daughter? I see. And did you send these men to bring her home? Okay, thank you. One of them wants to talk to you, here he is."

Jim had to hold the phone away from his ear. Ruth was screaming, crying, and laughing all at once. "Oh Jim, we are so happy you found her. Oh, God bless you two wonderful men."

On the road out of New York State they stopped for food and bought Rachel chicken soup, a sandwich and milk. She took two pain pills and fell into a deep sleep, the first real rest she'd had in months. They covered her with a blanket and she did not move as they drove day and night to return Rachel to her mother and her home in St. Louis Park.

# # #

When Ruth saw her daughter come through the door on crutches, tears came to her eyes. Rachel allowed her a brief hug, but dodged a hug from Sarah as she made her way to her room. She did not say a word.

"Go with her, Sarah," Ruth said, "see what she needs while I thank these two gentlemen." Jim explained how they had found Rachel with a broken ankle, how she had fled the pimp who imprisoned her.

"She's very shut down." Jim said. "She's been through hell and she's still in shock."

"Well, I can't thank you enough for being so kind and getting her to that hospital. When you called from there, I was so relieved to know she was with you that I wanted to run out in the streets and dance for joy! It took such a weight off me. Can you stay for a cup of coffee? I want to know more about you two. You should get a hero's welcome with a parade and tickertape! Please sit down a minute. I'll be right back with coffee."

The comfortable living room chairs nearly put Jim and Chuck to sleep, as they were exhausted from driving straight through from New York. Jim looked around. A proper home. Family obviously central. There was a painting Ruth must've done of the man who perhaps was her husband. There was also a photo of them together and photos of their daughters, Rachel as a little girl and Sarah as a teenager.

A feeling of stark horror struck Jim as he viewed Rachel's innocent face in the photo, and the thought of the evil men who had stalked and almost killed her. He felt a tinge of guilt as he looked at the photo of Sarah again, remembering how intimate they had been the night she came to his studio to ask for help finding Rachel. He had rushed her. He shouldn't have gone that far so soon with her. Sitting in her proper home made him realize she was a proper girl, the marrying kind actually, not like some of the easy girls he had seduced and been seduced by around art school.

He thought of Ruth, a real lady, a nice person; and of the dead father in the photo who would no doubt want a Jewish husband for Sarah. He would've thrown Jim out of the house if he'd known he'd fondled his daughter's breasts after offering her grass. Maybe he should back off until he could be certain what his real intentions were with Sarah. Or maybe he should take a clue from her.

When Ruth returned with coffee, Jim took out the money left from the trip to New York and tried to return it to her.

"Oh no. You two keep that."

"But there's three thousand dollars here."

"You keep it and split that. I've got another thousand here for each of you."

"We can't accept that much, Ruth. We were just glad to be able to help."

"Look, son, you deserve much more. Take it. Both of you. You guys did a miraculous job and we will be forever grateful to you."

"Okay, Ruth, I'll take this but I'm gonna give a lot of it to our kung fu school. Half of that is enough for my needs."

"I'm giving some of mine to the school, too," Chuck said. "The rest is going for repairs on my van."

"Ah, it sounds like you both think as highly of your school as I do of you. So Jim, tell me a little bit about yourself. I know you are a good artist from when we were in that show together. How did you get so good?"

"Oh, I'm not really that good. I just like to draw and paint. I started doodling around drawing when I was a kid, carrying little tablets around to sketch bugs, frogs, snakes, cats and dogs, anything that fascinated me. I had color crayons and those cheap watercolor sets. Then I took art class in high school and hung out with the teacher. I learned more from that guy than I did in art school really. I played basketball in high school, too."

"Yeah, Jim's an ace at basketball," Chuck said. "He plays with the black guys. He's the only white guy that can keep up to them at this court they play at."

"I truly love basketball," said Jim, " but I had to make a choice. I knew I'd be doing art long after I got too old to play basketball and I wanted to learn more ways to express myself through art."

"Where is your family?

"My dad was a foreman in a steel mill in Gary Indiana. He was killed in an accident. My mother died of cancer last year."

" How's your painting going?" Ruth asked. "Do you make a living with it?"

"Not yet." I work part time as a guard at the Minneapolis Institute of Art.

"FANTASTIC! You are a REAL artist!"

"How about you, Ruth, how are your painting going?"

"Well, I was doing a lot of painting before Rachel disappeared. When my husband died I found that painting kept my mind off losing him, but when Rachel was gone, too, I couldn't concentrate anymore. Thank God when you said you'd help us by going to New York City I had some kind of hope.

 But now I'd like to know something about you, Chuck--what do you do for a living?"

"I work for the City of Minneapolis. My father came here from China to work at the Nankin Cafe as a cook and retired from there. I study kung fu."

"He's damn good at it, too," Jim said. "He's next in line to be a teacher at the school."

"Thank you for letting me get acquainted with you both. You two gentlemen and that other guy, Gil, are part of this family now. If you ever need anything, you let us know. Our door is always open to you. So now I shall say good night or Aleikhem Shalom."

# # #

Upstairs Rachel sobbed uncontrollably. With Sarah holding her, Rachel remembered how Sarah had stopped Reggie the first time he'd hit on her. Sarah could see he was a pimp and protected her, but Rachel had resented her for it. Between sobs Rachel mumbled, "I'm so sorry."

"Don't be sorry," Sarah answered. "Don't be sorry. You were innocent. You didn't know about evil. God will punish those men who did this to you. They are living in darkness."

Rachel finally fell asleep. She looked weak and bruised, but in time she'd physically recover. But would her mind ever heal?

Sarah got up from the bed and looked out the window. Seeing Jim and Chuck leaving, she knew she should go down there and thank them before they left.

Instead she turned out the light and sat in the darkened bedroom. The thought of talking to Jim made her uncomfortable. She had taken the initiative that night in his studio when she let him fondle her breasts, and now she felt embarrassed and not sure how else to feel about him, so she waited until she saw the van tail lights before joining her mother.

Two days later Rachel began bleeding severely. Ruth rushed her to St Louis Park Hospital where she had a miscarriage. She was under the care of Ruth's personal physician. She remained there for several days and care was also given to her lacerated feet. Ruth called in one of Minneapolis's top psychiatrists to talk to Rachel while she was hospitalized.

"She's suicidal," Ruth told Sarah. "The psychiatrist could hardly get two words out of her, but he diagnosed her as suicidal. He thinks we should put her in a mental ward so they can watch her all the time."

"Oh my God! You don't want that, do you?"

"Well if we don't, you and I will have to watch her constantly, or she could take her own life. The psychiatrist is willing to come to the house to try and treat her, but we have to make sure she doesn't get out of the house alone."

Several days later Ruth approached Sarah, "This isn't working out very well, is it?"

"No," said Sarah.

"We're both suffering loss of sleep from watching Rachel day and night, and she's just getting more morose. She's not responding to psychiatric treatment either."

"I know," Sarah replied. "We're becoming almost as depressed as she is."

"Not quite. But it's awfully gloomy in the house. And I know you're skipping classes at the university so you can get more sleep. I hate to see your studies suffer like that. Listen, I feel pretty good today. I want you to take the day off from watching your sister and go do something fun. Go ahead, go now. I don't want to see you back here until tonight. Then you can take the first watch and I'll spell you at midnight. GO! Go and have fun."

# # #

Sarah grabbed her purse, left the house, and jumped into her Jaguar. There was a jazz concert that afternoon on campus at Coffman Union, so she drove to Dinkytown, the little commercial area that catered to students. She stopped at McCosh's Bookstore where old Mr. McCosh located used copies of all the titles she needed for a course she was taking called The American Novel. She could well afford to buy all those books brand new at the university store, but she got a good feeling from giving the money to this bearded old man who made his living handling books. She was amazed at how he knew just where to look for each one in the random piles of books and high shelves.

She took some lunch at Bridgeman's before crossing over to the campus to the student union just as the jazz concert began. All the seats were taken except one in the last row; next to it sat Jim. Sarah decided to simply stand on the side but it was too late. Jim spotted her and motioned for her to take the seat next to him. She gave in, joined him and managed to smile. She was grateful the music was playing so she didn't have to talk right off. She knew there was an unwritten rule amongst the hip that when jazz was being played you completely shut up and listened. One talked only between numbers.

"Who are these guys?" Sarah asked when the first number ended.

"The Cray Brothers," Jim replied. "The two guys in black suits are the Cray's--on piano and sax. They're local guys; their family owns a liquor store in St. Paul."

"Ooooh, they look so serious in those black hats and shades!"

"Yeah. They look like gangsters. They never smile, seems like. Play some serious jazz. I dig them."

Neither Sarah nor Jim spoke much between numbers after that. Sarah was conflicted. Half of her wanted to reconnect with Jim; the half that sought romance. She also needed to score some more grass, which would insure seeing him at least once again. Her other half resented his smug silence. It seemed to indicate he had the upper hand and could force her to speak first. When the concert was over Sarah remained silent and when Jim didn't say anything she mumbled, "See ya," and got up to leave.

"Hey, where you going so fast?" Jim asked. "We've hardly said hi to each other."

"I know. I don't know where I'm going. Where are you going?"

"Well, I could use some coffee."

"So could I. Let's get some here."

"How's your sister Rachel?"

"She's really hurting, Jim. On top of everything she had a miscarriage. She's really shut down, closed off. And she's full of anger inside. She looks so miserable and cries so much her eyes are puffy. She can't sleep at night without having a light on in her room."

"Does she talk to you?"

"No, not to us, and not to the psychiatrist, either. Whenever any of us tries to ask what happened to her in New York, she screams at us. The psychiatrist says she's suicidal. Mom thinks so too. It's depressing because it seems like there's nothing we can do to reach her. But one thing really surprised me."

"What's that?"

"She wanted to know about your kung fu classes and asked me if I knew where your kung fu school was. Rachel wanted me to take her there. I was glad to. Overjoyed in fact, because we couldn't get her out of the house for anything else. I drove her over to the Southern Style Praying Mantis School of Kung Fu, over the Market Bar-B-Que. We stood there and watched the men practice, saw them jam their open fists into that big vat of dried corn by the door to toughen then up."

"WOW! That's cool that you both went there."

"And you know what she did? She took that mantis symbol for your school that's on the pamphlets and put it above her bed like a poster."

"Wow."

"That was such a relief for me, you know? Because I figured she'd be a man hater for the rest of her life. But there's three men at least, you, Chuck, and Gil, that she seems to be grateful for. Mom could end up putting her in a hospital mental ward just out of desperation. Rachel's at a stalemate now, just stagnating, and it's dangerous. We've got to be able to get her out of the house and into some kind of normal life."

"Yeah, what she's been through is too much for her to carry around for the rest of her life. She's so young. Listen, I've got an idea. We should talk to Dale. He's the cop who helped Chuck and I know where to look in New York. He told me he knows an ex-cop who set up a safe house to get girls off the street and into a safe zone. Let me call him. He could talk to your mom."

19

LUCY AND MARY: WITHOUT A SONG

"I been chasin'jazz down all my life, Cassie. I grew up on Lady Day and Satch. That was my pabulum. My parents had jazz cookin' on the player all the time. When I was a little girl, I could sing every note of Billie Holiday's records and, hum, all of Prez's solos right along with him. I know Lady Day was from Philly. Folks say she from Baltimore, but she came up in Philly."

Lucy was talking to the other waitress at the Club during a break."Round Philly I closed the clubs, hung in the after-hours joints and reefer pads 'til dawn with all the musicians. I'm a dancer but music's my thang too. I be out there day and night, sometimes more than the musicians. They be askin' me what's goin' on 'cause I usually knew more that was goin' down—who was playin'with who and where—than most of them did. But this little white-assed town doesn't have much music, not my kind anyway. I want to blow this hick place, but Boris seems to like I here." She sighed. "I could use a girlfriend, too, if I have to stay here much longer, someone to do girl thangs with. Women 'round here, their idea of fun is to join a sewing circle."

The other waitress looked at her with concern. "It's just different here, honey, you'll get used to it. You'll find a woman friend too. Patience, honey."

# # #

Lucy made her first visit to Pan's Pipes coffeehouse to meet Boris. She went to their jukebox and it surprised her-- it was all jazz, the hippest box in town outside of the black joints. She punched selections then sat down to be served. A disinterest-ed waitress brought her coffee and Lucy listened to the cuts she had played: Sarah Vaughan singing, "You're Mine You," and Cal Tjader's version of "Green Dolphin Street," with Paul Horn on flute.

Then Boris showed up with keyboard virtuoso Marcus Lyle! They sat down with Lucy, and introduced him. Lucy noticed that it must be the first time Lyle had ever been in the place as people began falling out over him, smiling and staring, all except the square waitress who obviously didn't know who he was. Lucy observed the waitress treat Marcus without and interest, as she had treated her. For some reason she was almost rude. Marcus responded kindly and politely as he always did with everyone, but the beats in the place were mortified! So was Boris.

Lorenzo, the owner, was watching through the kitchen service window, getting angrier by the minute at the so-called waitress. Marcus just drank his coffee. He had to ask for cream, but the whole scene didn't matter to him. He looked happy enough. He played a cut on the box by Charlie Parker, and then had to leave. Lorenzo rushed right out of the kitchen to confront the waitress.

"You dumbo! Don't you know who that was?"

"No, I don't."

"That was Marcus Lyle!"

"So what? Who's he?"

Lorenzo's Italian face was contorted with anger and disbelief. "So what? He's only the best musician in the Twin Cities, That's what! 'Who's he?'" he said, mimicking her. Marcus Lyle is God."

"I don't care if he's Santa Claus."

"YOU'RE FIRED!"

The waitress took off her apron and walked out.

"I never should've hired her. I knew she wasn't gonna work out."

"Yeah," Boris said, "she'll be better off with her own kind."

"She got her paycheck today so she won't be back."

# # #

A dark, Italian-looking woman entered the coffeehouse and went to the kitchen.

"That's my little sis," Lorenzo said. "She's come for her paycheck. Excuse me."

"That's who should've waited on Marcus Lyle," said Boris. "Mary, Lorenzo's sister, she's a boss waitress. She's gonna be disappointed when she finds out she just missed seeing Marcus."

"She's an interesting looking person," said Lucy. "What else does she do besides work here?"

"Well, she loves jazz, and when she's isn't playing pool at The Mixers Bar up the street, she either writes poetry or chases Marcus Lyle."

"So her thang is poetry then. That's what I like to know, what people are really about. For me the rest is all secondary."

"Oh," Boris replied, "so if I read you right, you got me second fiddle to your dancing then, right?"

"Come on, honey, nothing can cop your place in my heart, not even dance. So this Mary's a poet?"

"Yeah, she runs the open mic poetry readings here. She's a good poet, been around, New York, San Francisco. She's had some heavy poet boys, but she's dropped 'em all when she got hip to Marcus. But he's got no eyes for her. Sad tale. He's got his pick of women. Everybody really digs Marcus, but women move 'round him all the time, like schools of fish, all trying to get his attention. Mary's just another one of them, prettier than most, but she ain't got a backstage pass. It's sad. Here she comes, I'll introduce you."

The beautiful woman came over to the table. She gave Lucy the immediate impression of being down to earth, with her long, glossy, black hair, faded jeans and brown leather vest over a denim shirt. She wore a gold necklace with a five-point star.

"Mary, I'd like you to meet my girl, Lucy. Lucy, this is Mary, the poet laureate of Pan's Pipes."

"Oh my, that's so fancy. I'm just a local poet. You're the lucky girl, Lucy, having Boris. He's our bandleader. He puts the real soul in this place. We poets just fool around with words; Boris sends us on soul excursions every time he plays."

"Uh-huh, he sends me too!"

"I can't believe I just missed Marcus Lyle!" She looked at Lucy. "I'm going over to The Mixers to cash my paycheck. I could use a drink. If you'd like to come with, Lucy, I'll buy you a couple. That is, if it's okay with Boris?"

"Lead on, sister. Boris trusts me."

# # #

"I hear you gotta thang for Marcus Lyle," Lucy said as they walked up to Seven Corners and The Mixers Bar.

"Yeah, I do. That cat stands out like the hope diamond in a bin of coal. I guess you could say that it's more like I'm obsessed. They all talk about how spiritual he is, that's fine, I know that. But I'd like to jump his bones."

Several musicians and painters greeted Mary as they entered the bar. She cashed her check, bought drinks and then went to the box and punched Bobby Blue Bland's "Blind Man."

Bland's raw voice filled the place with blues and Lucy felt good. She watched Mary engage a pair of pool hustlers and hold her own. A crack shot, she slammed balls into pockets, making them crack like little cannon balls. Lucy saw the men defer to her with respect. *There's something about this Italian I really like. Maybe she's the friend I been needin'.*

20

BLUES AT THE TORRID ZONE

Watusi Lucy was UP and sashaying down Hennepin Avenue doing dance show steps from the days when her sinuous body and Olympian leaps had earned her the nickname "Watusi." Life was sweet when you had money and a man to meet. Lucy was totally unconcerned with people who stared, as she danced by them with the prowess of a cheetah.

She was determined to rescue Boris from the blues he often got from playing in the pit band that backed strippers at the strip club Torrid Zone. After his gig there she would sweep him away to buy drinks for them with her tip money at an after-hours, then buy breakfast at the all night diner on Lake Street.

Dean, drummer in the house band Boris led at Pan's Pipes, rounded a corner onto Hennepin and spotted Lucy immediately, the beautiful, strikingly tall afroed sister steadily dancing everyone by.

Dean himself was on his way to meet Boris to tell him about a possible gig. He kept Lucy in sight for a while. Suddenly she broke from her dance stride into a full run, for just ahead a thief had stolen an old lady's purse and was fleeing. In seconds Lucy caught up and tackled him. In the ensuing struggle the purse fell. Lucy reached for it, but recoiled in shock when the male thief stabbed her in the side. The man grabbed the purse and ran while Lucy clutched at her side to stop the gushing blood. Dean reached her and then a policeman.

"Help her, Mister!" he said. " Put pressure on that wound. Use both hands! I'm calling an ambulance."

"That poor lady!" exclaimed Lucy. 'I tried to save her purse!"

"We'll help her," the policeman said, "get her to the station and help her sort things out. But right now I've got an ambulance coming for you. That wound is serious." He turned to Dean. Thank you for your help, sir. I'll need a statement from you as a witness to this crime."

"BORIS!" Lucy blurted out. "Boris! He won't know where I am. He's expecting me!" She began to sob.

"I'll tell him what happened, Lucy," Dean said. "I'm going there right now. We'll come to you, at the hospital."

At The Torrid Zone, Boris ran his sax through the changes of the last bump and grind number for the strippers. Two old bleached-blonde strippers were executing the grand finale the club was noted for. Each dancer had swivels attached to the nipples of their breasts from which golden bangles swung on strings. Without the use of their hands, by deft body movement only they made those bangles rotate in airy circles, a different direction for each breast.

Boris was sick of the general atmosphere of lust in the place, the drunks, their howling and leering, the simplistic music he had to play. There were times when he could admire a beautiful young stripper who could dance without shame, making art out of tease. That brought everybody up. But older, more pathetic dancers were easier to keep on the club payroll and worked for less pay.

The lame music they had to play behind the strippers was the hardest thing to stomach. It killed Boris's spirit night after night having to play the same inane bump and grind numbers like David Rose's "The Stripper," all that thump, thump, athump, boom, boom aboom shit. He was desperate for a real gig, somewhere but places that booked jazz in the Twin Cities were dwindling. You could damn near count them on the fingers of one hand. Jazz bookings were short and gigs were rare. Thank God for the gig at Pan's Pipes, the beatnik coffeehouse. It didn't pay much, but he could play whatever he pleased there and it was keeping his spirit alive. The guys in his band loved the freedom and the customers really dug the scene, were loyal fans. They talked about jazz as art. Boris knew it was art. He also knew that jazz and money didn't necessarily mix, but musicians had to make a living.

Outside, the sidewalks were filling up with people leaving clubs near closing time. Dean rushed along through the buzzed up, raucous crowd until he reached the T-Zone Club and dashed up to the bar to order a double whiskey. "And give him what he's drinking too," he said, pointing to Boris.

"Lucy was hurt, man, just a little while ago."

"SHE WHAT?"

"Easy, man, I think she's okay. She tried to stop an asshole who stole an old lady's purse. Lucy tackled the guy but he stabbed her and got away. A cop got her to the hospital."

"OH GOD, NO!"

"The cop thinks she'll be okay once they treat her at the hospital. She's not gonna die. She's at General. I told her we'd come there."

"LET'S BOOK! DRINK UP!" They slammed down their drinks and started toward the door.

"HOLD IT! Where do you think you're going?" the bar owner yelled.

"My girl's hurt. I gotta go to her. It's an emergency."

"You ain't going nowhere 'til you finish the last number."

"Fuck that, I'm going!"

"You go and you're fired, you and the whole band. I got customers waiting for that last number and you're gonna play it."

Boris realized how badly the musicians needed the gig.

"All right, you cheap son of a bitch, I'll play. But I should just walk!" Boris went on stage, snapped on his sax and began a slow intense blues. The other musicians, who had been waiting to play something previously agreed upon, held back in surprise.

The panic Boris felt over Lucy and all the frustration he was carrying, the cold, blind-alley system of the white city he felt trapped in, all that emotion began coming out of his horn, first in rushes, then torrents, a blues so strong, so raw and powerful that the people all looked up. They stopped what they had been doing. The girls quit hustling and all the jabbering, horny-fool men shut up. The bartenders stood still as statues. The musicians were keenly alert. They were almost afraid to touch what Boris was playing, but the drummer began a simple, tentative beat. The bassist joined and then the piano, all of them holding down for Boris to blow strong and heavy.

Blues now poured through him with the power of a great river, blues which he used to ignore, pay lip service to only while he emulated John Coltrane and explored modern jazz. He had taken for granted the blues that lay like bedrock in the collective subconscious, taken for granted blues truth which he always recognized and felt deeply when he heard it, and was now pouring out of him with the fury of an unleashed dam.

Boris came down off the mountaintop that night in the sweat, the funk of that flesh-pot club. He sensed a new power in the blues and kept them in his style from then on, if only a tinge of it like Bird always kept, a blue edge to his wings that sang like Kansas City. Boris had finally begun to fuse his own style, opened the door to let the blues in. He emerged from Coltrane's shadow with his own voice, an axe, a sword newly sharpened with a razor sharp blue edge.

21

AT WIRTH PARK

Later that night, Sarah got a call from Gil. He sounded sober and wanted to know how Rachel was doing. He'd talked to Jim and was worried. He had an idea for Rachel's recovery and wanted to get together with her to talk about it.

"Yes, I want to see you, too. Gil, how about I pick you up tomorrow? Let me take you somewhere for lunch, or to a museum? Where would you like to go?"

"I'd like to go to Wirth Park," said Gil. "It's close to where you live, too. I'll be ready at ten. See ya."

Sarah picked Gil up in front of his apartment building. She noticed how shabby he looked. He hadn't shaved that morning, either. She wondered if he was hung over.

"Good morning, Gil. Say, I'd like to stop at the Lincoln Deli and get some sandwiches and dessert before we hit Wirth Park."

As Sarah drove Gil along Olson Memorial Highway toward Theodore Wirth Park she felt repulsed by Gil's sloppy dress and drunken behavior. She knew she had a compulsion to help people who were needy. Could she help him? Maybe he was worth it? Or maybe she should nip this in the bud.

But she knew how Ruth felt about Gil: "We owe that man something more. By God, we should put up a monument to those men, you know? Gil and his friends Jim and Chuck."

Soon, they pulled into the parking lot and could see the lake. Black people were fishing along the shore of little Lake Wirth, and a friendly mix of blacks and whites were enjoying the small beach. They just sat in the car for a while sipping coffee. Someone's beach radio was playing "Our Day Will Come" by

Ruby and The Romantics. The song made each of them wonder if their hopes and dreams would find fulfillment or some kind of expression in their lifetimes. The little park was so quiet and laid back compared to the fancier beaches around the Lake of the Isles that it almost felt like being out in the country and one should hush up and just be for a while. But they were going to have to talk. It was time to acknowledge each other, and for Sarah to thank Gil again for finding Rachel, as her mother wished.

Neither one knew what to say. They just sat there as if washed up upon a neutral shore. Gil had settled into his old habit wondering what he had in common with such a rich girl beyond her love for jazz, and Sarah felt he had closed himself off again. For a moment she felt like snapping at him to jolt him out of moroseness. Ridiculous that they shouldn't talk after all the things they had gone through. They were not strangers. There should be some level of comfort in their being together.

In the silence Sarah was unexpectedly overcome with emotion. It was so overwhelming it kept her from speaking while she tried to sort it out. Foremost was a growing attraction to Gil bordering on lust, which completely disarmed her. This mixed with a genuine compassion, not only compassion but respect, for what he was and what he dealt with. She remained quiet, subdued, until he spoke. "Are you okay, Sarah? You look like you're going to cry?"

"I'm fine," she lied. "I was just thinking about what could have happened to Rachel and how you helped us."

"I didn't do anything. Jim and Chuck did it all."

"You set it up by talking to that pimp. That got us pointed to New York City. Without you finding out what you did it was like searching for a needle in a haystack."

"It still was like that, Sarah. They just got lucky they found her when they did—maybe it was destiny?"

"Gil, we will always remember you because of how you helped

us. Don't try to diminish it. It was huge, HUGE, just like, well… like jazz is to me now. Did I tell you my uncle gave me boxes full of jazz records? You might like to come over and hear them someday?"

"Sure would. Sounds like a groove."

"Are you hungry?"

"Not yet. But I can show you a good spot for a picnic up the hill. There's also a little flower garden up there with herbs and flowers, all labeled. It's very quaint."

"Okay, let's go. I've got the sandwiches."

The thought of being up there alone with Gil was thrilling. Less than an hour ago she was going to cut ties with him, and now she was ready to follow him anywhere, to be there for him no matter what. "Those records my uncle gave me are amazing. Jazz is so expressive, so vibrant. Why can't we hear more of it? Why don't they book it in the clubs here more often?"

"Because it's not part of the dominant culture. Because the people who enjoy it, blacks, minorities, and people like you and me are not part of the dominant culture." Gil actually had three years of college, Sarah remembered Jim telling her that. Underneath that street-tough exterior he was actually well read. In his apartment she'd seen novels by Hesse and Baldwin.

The walk along Cedar Lake Trail turned into countryside. All traces of the city were gone—only the birdcalls and leaves rustling in the breeze were heard. The little flower garden was enchanting. They met plants as new friends. They found a spot for their picnic and Sarah laid out a small blanket on which she place the basket of pastrami sandwiches and baklava pastries for dessert.

They sat near a spot where a little stream of water, not more than a trickle, was pouring down a bank at the edge of the trail. The sound it made was so pure and pleasant. They were both charmed and fell silent. Sarah was thinking about her friend Mira, thinking maybe meditation was like this -- hearing this beautiful sound. She closed her eyes.

"Sarah," Gil whispered. "There's a deer over there."

Sarah leaned towards him to have a look, forgetting how close they were to the edge of the trail. A rock gave way, and she lurched to avoid falling over, and fell into his arms. For a moment they held each other with smiles of surprise, and then he released his grip. But she held on, arms still tight around him, and they kissed. The kiss was mutual. She knew it. They kissed again and held each other in silence until another couple came along and they let go to say hello to them.

22

CONTRETEMPS

Sarah was on Gil's mind every day after their visit to Wirth Park and the kiss that surprised and thrilled them both. But along with the pleasure it brought to think about her came a troubling reality: if he couldn't quit drinking he knew he wouldn't stand a chance with her. Someone, he couldn't remember who, had warned him not to take alcohol for his lover. He winced whenever he thought it over; as he knew he didn't have the strength or the will to sober up.

In fact, it was ironic that actually his obsession with alcohol was the result of a love affair with a beautiful woman. One who left a scar deep in his subconscious.

He'd wanted to take a graduate course in the contemporary novel at the University of Minnesota and his advisor agreed. It was there that he met Juliette, a lovely Parisian woman. She was in her early thirties, older than other girls on the campus. With her long blonde hair and robust body, she was a natural and down-to-earth woman, who never wore a bra or nylons. She dressed casually with a Parisian flair and exuded a confidence she could achieve whatever she set out to do. Gil admired her and the way she lived life so fully, appreciated wine, the nightlife, and jazz. Gil really fell hard for her.

Juliette was attracted by Gil's unaffected naiveté and touch of rebellion. A mutual chemistry developed between them and everything seemed more natural when they were together-- as if the life-force, always looking for ways to flow more fully, had brought them together.

Gil accompanied Juliette when she made the rounds of St. Paul haunts because she was writing her thesis on F. Scott Fitzgerald. She'd introduced him to French poets Rimbaud and Apollinaire and artists like Maurice Utrillo and Alberto

Giacometti. She knew a lot about the French New Wave filmmakers, too. Gil was amused by her ambition to see all of James Dean's movies "now that she was in America." He took her around with him to the clubs to listen to jazz and she was fascinated by his collection of jazz records.

They were compatible and excited to merge their worlds. Gil felt he'd found the perfect partner and they become engaged to marry after graduation.

One night, as he arrived to pick her up, he found Juliette in tears, she was hysterical. She'd received a phone call a little earlier that her father was dying and she was packing, ready to catch the first flight out of Minneapolis back to Paris. She promised to write and said she'd be back.

But eventually the letters stopped, her mother was ill, too, it seemed. Coming back was not in the plans anymore and he knew it was over. Gil could never find out why. Perhaps if he had gone over to France he may have had some closure. In a way, he was afraid of what he may have found. Instead he drank more alcohol to numb himself for the loss of Juliette.

She had used the French word *contretemps* to describe her need to depart; for the sudden disruption of their love affair. Gil would never forget how she pronounced that wretched word. The sound of it kept haunting him. It meant an unexpected and unfortunate occurrence, among other things.

For Gil *contretemps* would forever be a symbol for the disaster against time with Juliette; of the blues so deep it felt like it could kill him. This rupture in his psyche left him with a cynical mistrust. He began drinking solely to forget her. It was hard to stop drinking as the jazz world was a sister to alcohol and he began living with it on a daily basis.

# # #

As alcohol eroded Gil's morals and continued to make inroads into his life and self-esteem, denial still shielded him from reality and the mess his life had become. To him it was simple: Gil against the world, a world which kept dealing him a rotten hand; or was it Gil and other alcoholics against the world, for he felt alkies were the only people he could really communicate with, for only they really knew the score. As healthy people began to shun him, he got lonelier and his desire for company grew. He was driven from the warmth of his room out into the cold to reach crazy bars to talk to people until he had spent his last dollar. He was often mugged, ripped off, beaten by bouncers. Cops did him favors more often than not, but one beat him badly after Gil insulted him. His life became a round of hospitals, jails, detox centers, poverty, and depression. Finally he lost his job with the railroad and he was being evicted. Jim told Sarah about Gil's situation and she called him. "What are you going to do?" she asked. Gil felt a mixture of shame and pride, shame that the girl he deeply admired and desired should know his true condition, and pride which made him want to reject any help she might offer.

"I don't know what I'm gonna do. I have to be out of here by tomorrow night. I don't know what to do with all my stuff."

"You could put it in storage. I'll pay for it. Don't hock your typewriter. You haven't done that yet, have you?"

"No. Not yet."

"Don't. Let's put your stuff in storage. I'm sorry, but I'm not going to give you any money for rent until you get some help for your drinking. It hurts me to say this, but I know if I give you money for rent, you will just drink it up. It's happened before."

Gil was silent and it made Sarah feel awkward. "I'd better hang up," she said, "or I'll start crying."

"Sarah, I don't need storage. I can get my stuff down to a suitcase, backpack, and my typewriter. Goodwill's coming for the rest. I'll ask Dean if I can stay there for a night or two, or ask Jim maybe. But I want to thank you for your concern. I know I don't deserve it."

"Gil, all you've been doing is getting loaded. You're wasting your talent as a writer. I want you to try and get help. Call me when you want a ride to AA."

# # #

Jim called Sarah the next day and she asked him if he'd seen Gil.

"No. Why?"

"He's homeless, Jim, as of today. He was going to try to stay with Dean."

"I heard he lost his job, too. He's going down."

"That poor guy. He needs help."

"Listen, Sarah, I've seen you try to help him. He's not ready for help from anyone yet. He'll just keep using people to get more booze until he hits bottom or dies. Look, I think I know how you feel about him. You're falling for him, aren't you?"

When she didn't speak, Jim continued, "I'd hate to see you get hurt by him. He's my friend too, but to be honest, he's turning into a loser. Until he kicks booze he's no good to anybody. I think you should think about it, Sarah, or you're gonna get burned."

# # #

The driver of the Goodwill van gave Gil some cash for two rare jazz records. Gil bought rum and tobacco and the next day he was on the street with seven cents to his name. He hadn't been able to reach Dean by phone so he walked four miles carrying his heavy belongings, hoping to find him home. Carl answered the door, his face contorted and hostile.

"Carl, how are you? Is Dean home?"

"HE AIN'T HERE! He's playin' a gig." Carl just glared, "What? Are you homeless, man?"

"Yeah, I lost my crib."

"Cold! That's cold as a white man's heart. Come on in then."

The blues coming from the box in the music room became more audible. It was Bessie Smith singing, "Backwater Blues." The sound of the blues made Gil feel better. In that very room Dean had introduced him to a lot of great jazz records, music of all kinds. Dean always had real good records, strong and solid. Gil deeply appreciated this, and the excitement of hearing new artists.

"Man, those blues sound good to me today!"

"Oh yeah? That's not blues, that's THE… B…L…U…E…S! You fucking white people wouldn't know the blues if they snuck up and shit on you! SHE died. Bessie died because white people wouldn't let her in their fucking white hospital when she was bleeding to death from a car accident."

Carl grabbed his 151, drank deeply from the bottle, and extending it to Gil, then snatching it back. He moved his angry face toward Gil's and howled with rage. Gil jumped back, turned, and started to leave. Carl laughed insanely: "Sit down, you fool! I've got to take a leak." Gil hesitated, wavering between flight or sticking it out; deeply hurt by Carl's rage.

Carl was very special, as were all jazz musicians. He'd been hoping Carl could make a comeback, but his behavior was like a kick in the teeth. Noticing a brown paper bag near Carl's chair, he picked it up and peered into it. Hundreds of pills in various cases and many loose, all mixed up. Seeing them, his own problems felt petty. Carl's tranquilizers were for coping with the loss of his wife, but now he lived in a nightmare of twin addiction to tranks and alcohol. The sadness and compassion he felt for Carl was added to his own desperation, and put him over the edge. He began to cry. The record player had switched off, but Carl kept singing. *"Something's wrong with this scene. When do we get help for our people? When do we come clean?"*

He stopped and looked over at Gil. "Hey! I'm sorry for getting all up in your face an' all. Here, you want some of this, man?" He passed the rum. "I'll get you a clean glass. You look like you could use a good drink. So you lost your crib. An' you're probably busted too, right?"

"Yeah, I feel like I'm totally fucked."

"Oh no, no. Don't say that! You ain't that fucked. You still got all your faculties." Gil nodded, overwhelmed thinking of Carl's condition, now crying in silence.

"Well," Carl said, "Let's not just sit here, wallowing in the blues. I know some chicks who are throwing a party and I'm invited. You can come too. Kill that rum if you want and forget your troubles for a while. These chicks are stone foxes." Gil drank the remaining rum, forgetting it was 151 and it sent a punch from behind like a sledge-hammer.

They left the apartment and started walking down LaSalle Avenue at a rapid pace, Gil trying to keep up as the 151 set in. Carl was strongly motivated: It was always music or women with him and money a third.

"Come on, man, it's only a few more blocks." He hurried on again as Gil tripped on a hole in the sidewalk and went down. A squad car happened to be passing by and pulled over to the sidewalk next to him. Gil yelled ahead for Carl to keep moving as two officers came up to him.

"You all right?" When Gil failed to walk a straight line, they loaded him up and took him to the 4800 Columbus Avenue detox center.

# # #

Detox was routine for Gil. Better there than waking up in a padded cell or a hospital.

"You again!" said Tom, the afternoon attendant. "You might as well move in here, save yourself rent." He knew Gil was a writer and they kidded about it. "How's your writing problem?" he asked. It was their joke that Gil's writing problem interfered with his drinking.

That afternoon Gil witnessed a man stricken with a seizure from withdrawal. At night he went to an AA meeting just to get an extra cup of coffee.

On the morning of the third day when his vitals were normal he was released. He stood outside the door for a moment in the cold morning air, thinking of the walk over to Dean's. A young Indian who'd given him several cigarettes was released just behind him. Right out of the blue he turned to Gil and said,

"You gonna make it this time, man?" The directness was surprising and effective.

"I don't know," Gil answered. The Indian smiled. He understood.

"Well, good luck, man."

"Thanks. Good luck to you, too."

As he stepped out into a world filled with alcohol, Gil realized he had never seriously considered quitting. He headed back to Dean's house and hopefully a roof over his head for a few days.

Dean met him at the door. "Welcome back, Gil. Carl told me you wanted to stay here a few days."

"Yeah, I do. Thanks, man."

"You want coffee or rum or both?" Dean asked.

"Both please."

But Dean just poured him some coffee, sans rum.

"I got some rum up in this top cupboard for company. Carl hasn't found it yet. I hear he freaked out on you the other day?"

"Yeah. He got all up in my face and yelled. He scared me. I thought he might take me apart."

"He can get weird. I don't know what to do with him sometimes. But I know he can't make it on his own anymore, all those meds he's on. I know he can't hold a job. Hard enough for him to keep gigs."

"And now you're stuck with me here, too. Carl's got an excuse. I'm just a falling down, piss on myself, drunk."

"Don't worry. Carl told me you needed a place to crash for a while. You're always welcome here. I know you've had some hard times. Look, I've got to get to work. I'm usually on my way by now."

Dean reached into his pocket and pulled out a few bills. "Here's some scratch money. I'll get an extra key made for you on my way home. Help yourself to any food. I'll be back around six."

After Dean left, the apartment seemed too quiet. Gil could hear Carl snoring in his bedroom. He didn't want to face Carl when he woke up. He wanted some rum but wouldn't steal from Dean's stash. He thought about getting another job; and that he'd have to score some rum to get him through all this.

He picked up the few dollars Dean left him and headed out to get coffee. Maybe later he could catch a meal at St. Stephens Church where they fed the homeless. After three refills of coffee, Gil went on a hyper walk. But he couldn't walk off the depression that was setting in. Being homeless wasn't the only source of his depression, withdrawal was. He was used to being high on rum by this time of the day, and he was feeling sick already from lack of a fix.

23

WOODSHEDDING

In the intense heat of early September, the inner city felt like one vast concrete prison, an oven from which there was no escape. Everywhere Gil went hot winds drove relentlessly through the vacuum of the wind-tunnel streets. He saw the rich business people dressed in uncomfortable hot suits, but they only had to descend from their air-conditioned offices to their expensive air-conditioned cars and ride in cool comfort to safe air-conditioned suburban homes. All summer long people who had money were taking vacations at lake homes up north, or at resorts on cool lakes, while the poor remained behind trapped in the squalor and crime that increased with the frustrations and passions aggravated by the heat.

Gil had no interest in fishing, water skiing, or swimming. The only thing he liked about lakes was watching the boats sail like poetry in action. For the first time in his life he began to think about the lakes up north. Maybe somehow he could hole up in a cabin by a lake and try to write again-- a fantasy at best. All he could do was try to wait for autumn to cool the streets. Besides wasn't up north the realm of rednecks?

Then one day when he went to Jim's studio to try and borrow money, Jim confronted him. "I think you need to get away from here for a while, Gil, and sort things out. My friend Eric Finn is coming down to the Cities from Bemidji to bring some of his paintings to a gallery. I took the liberty of asking him if you could go back with him to woodshed for a while, to think over your drinking problem. He said he'd talk it over with you when he gets here. What do you say?"

"Hell, no! What am I going to do in Hicksville?"

"What are you doing here, man? You're hitting on nothing right now...you won't even wash dishes. You were offered a dish washing job and you blew it. It's just a suggestion, but I know Dean is going to ask you to leave soon because his landlord says one of you two has to go. He wanted Carl out because he causes a lot of trouble, but Dean will never kick Carl out unless he's forced to. He hasn't the heart to ask you to leave yet, but he told me if he has to, he will." Jim moved his new painting over to a corner of the studio. "You could be on the streets with winter coming on. Sarah thinks it would be good for you to go up north. I told her you were coming here today and she's coming over to talk to you about it. Do me a favor. Stay here and let her in. I have to get to kung fu class." He stepped out the door, "Promise me you'll at least talk to her, okay?"

Resolved that he was not going to be pushed into going north with an agenda, Sarah meant only one thing: A possible source of booze money. At the sound of a little rock hitting the window, he went down and let her in. She was reserved, like they all were with him now, and when he flat out refused to consider going north, she started to cry. He then said maybe he'd go, just to stop her crying, because she was starting to soften his anger. Her concern was upsetting him.

"Look at you," she said; wiping tears from her big liquid eyes, "you don't even eat right."

"I get one good meal a day at St. Stephens."

"Yeah, right. If you promise you'll go with Eric Finn, I'll give you a little cash to take with you so you won't be totally broke going up north. You can get a few things you need. But if you spend it on booze, I'm through with you." She dried her tears. "Every time I try to help you, you just go on a jag. You helped get my sister back, but you weren't so far gone then. What can you lose by going up there? At least up there you can rest and start to think straight."

Knowing money was forthcoming, he lied. "Yeah, I'll go. Guess I have to."

When she finally left, after sincerely wishing him the best, he headed straight to the nearest liquor store. He brought back a half gallon of rum which he proceeded to drink straight and then mixed more of it with the cold water from the single studio faucet. Halfway through the bottle he found Jim's Nina Simone album. He stood listening to her rendition of "I Loves You, Porgy," which always entranced him, as he sipped from the rum bottle. He drank until he passed out; falling sideways into a long painting Jim had placed between two sawhorses while adjusting the finished painting's frame. It was the basketball painting Jim had done for himself; the one he had great pride in. He'd hope to enter it in an art expo competition that spring.

The frame broke as Gil's inert body crashed through it. The rum bottle was smashed between him and the canvas, the rum spilled all across it. The jolt of impact woke Gil instantly. He staggered to his feet. His first concern was the rum. Seeing the rum gone, he picked up the broken neck of the bottle and hurled it into the mess. Then he noticed what had happened to the painting, he knelt down to look, lost his balance and fell into the canvas, cutting his hand on the glass.He staggered over to the basin, oozing blood, and grabbed a towel to wrap his hand with, sat down, and passed out again.

Jim returned to his studio on a natural kung fu high, happy, at peace. But seeing his work destroyed, his first impulse was to kick Gil as hard as he could. But then he saw the blood in the mess and the sight of it stopped him. He grabbed Gil and shook him: "You fucking fool! That's it, man you're outta here! Wake up and clean yourself up. You gotta go, boy…you're outta here. Right now."

# # #

"You still want to take this sad son of a bitch with you?" Jim asked Eric, who'd arrived just after Gil's cut hand was bandaged. Eric looked at the destroyed painting in disbelief. He was silent a while then said sternly, "Look, Gil, I'll take you up there on one condition only…that you try to dry out. Otherwise you might as well just stay here. You wanna dry out?"

"Yeah, I guess I'll try," Gil mumbled.

"Whaddya mean I guess? Look me in the eyes, man, YES or NO?"

"Yes."

"Okay. Get ready, take what you want and do it as quickly as possible, because I need to get going."

"My stuff's not here, it's over at my friend Dean's place."

"Okay, then we'll have to go get it. Let's go."

Jim thanked Eric for helping Gil, and said goodbye without a word to Gil; turned and began cleaning up the bloody mess he'd made.

# # #

Gil slept during most of the long car trip up north, waking only briefly to catch a glimpse of the white statue of the Blessed Virgin Mary outside a convent in Little Falls. The statue's purity moved him profoundly. How peaceful, he thought, forever unattainable. Stricken with sadness, he felt like he was being hauled off to a Siberian prison. He wanted to run the next time Eric stopped the car, but it would be a long overnight hitchhike in the cold to get back to Minneapolis.

Eric Finn and his wife Carrie were originally in the same circle of artist friends Gil knew in the city, but they became "back to the land" people when they spent an inheritance on a down payment on a place near Bemidji, Minnesota, and were paying the hard dues it took to make the mortgage payments on it. Both worked hard, Eric at sign painting and doing odd jobs, and Carrie as a waitress while waiting for a hospital job.

Knowing that Eric was an artist made it easier for Gil to think he should be able to get along with him as long as he might have to. Eric seemed kinder than his hard, lean appearance suggested. He obviously worked very hard to keep their place going. But Gil decided if Eric should assume a macho role and try to push him around, he would simply flee.

While Eric was blonde and angular, Carrie was a dark-haired brunette with soft features and a warm personality. Gil took the vitamin pill she gave him with the valerian herb tea she said would calm him down, and relax his nerves. He was to keep the bottle of vitamins and take one daily. The two children of the family, boy and girl, watched Gil curiously until told to go to bed.

Eric put Gil up in the heated garage he had made into an apartment and a studio for painting and stretching his canvasses, which occasionally he sold in galleries. He was also gaining a reputation in town as an excellent portrait and sign painter. The studio was very basic, a cot for sleeping, electricity for the light, a small refrigerator and coffeemaker; and small sink with hot and cold water. There was an outhouse in the back which would be freezing in winter. But Gil would have his privacy. Eric gave him times when he could come in to use the house bathroom to shave and shower. He showed Gil how to make coffee for himself in the morning and invited him to join the family for breakfast.

"I went through the same thing you're going to go through, Gil," he said. "I came up here to start a new life. I was severely alcoholic, had the DTs, the whole bit. I joined AA up here. You are welcome to come to meetings with me if you like, but only if you want to go for yourself and not just for me or anyone else." He paused for emphasis, "Meantime, no drinking on my property. And best stay away from ole Harvey up in that shack in the cornfield. He's an alkie too, but he has no intention of quitting. I let him have beer because he gets it no matter what I do and he can't handle hard stuff."

Gil didn't understand who Harvey was and he didn't ask. When Eric left, he looked around the studio and tried to picture himself being there for any length of time. The pain of withdrawal had already given him a bad headache and he felt nauseous. It came with every detox. Why had he agreed to leave the city? What a fool to think it was an easy way out. He remembered Sarah. That dear girl had given him money for the trip, money he could have lived on. Instead, he'd bought rum and ruined

Jim's painting. For weeks now the thought came to him that if he could quit drinking he might have some luck with Sarah. She could be a really hip companion and good for him, too. But it seemed like a dream now.

One day at a time. Eric was talking about one day at a time, how it was done, staying sober. Maybe he could do it for her. But Eric said to do it for yourself. Right then he wanted to go out and walk to a liquor store and beg for money, but Eric said town was ten miles away. A bar would do, he knew how to bum drinks, had become an expert. But bars were probably that far too.

That night he couldn't sleep. The next day he was very sick. Carrie had him take a hot bath and gave him more tea. He slept that night. The following day he was beside himself for lack of something to do. It was so quiet here out in the woods. The constant sound of traffic and buzz of people moving about was absent and it made him nervous. Eric told him when he felt better he could help him find some work and that would help him keep his mind quiet. The third day he took out his old journal and decided to jot down some thoughts. Maybe a poem would come. He had also saved some of the notes he had kept for starting a novel.

He went for walks on the land. The family had fifty acres, including the cornfield. The rest was wooded with a creek and trails for hiking. Walking helped. Up on the field he spotted the shack where Eric said old man Harvey lived. He kept a distance from it, knowing if he met Harvey he would get drunk somehow. He now had four days of painful sobriety, and he was going to try to quit for Sarah, for a chance with a real quality girl. He did not know how to quit for himself. He had never thought about it that way. Was it lack of self-esteem? He didn't care. He hated the pop psychology crap that was going around, coming from California, using little catch phrases like I'm okay, you're okay. It was NOT OKAY!

Soon after Eric Finn moved his family up north from Minneapolis, he received a lot of help and advice from a neighbor named Harvey O'Brien, a famous stonemason with a reputation for heavy drinking. When his wife died of cancer last year, he lost his will to live. He let his masonry business go, along with his employees. On a night of heavy drinking and smoking, he'd passed out with a lit cigarette and burned his house down. A young musician, Joe Citro, whom Harvey had adopted as a surrogate son, had driven up to visit, found the house afire and pulled the old man out just in time to save his life.

Eric took Harvey into his family home, but his drinking was a problem there. Carrie said he was endangering the family and had to go, so Eric put Harvey up in a cabin, more like a shack, that he built out on the cornfield.

"You could sell your land, Harvey, and buy a house in town where you could pay a maid to help you with housekeeping and meals, even an apartment would be easy to take care of. It's too cold to stay out in the shack this winter." Eric added, "That wood heater isn't going to be warm enough and is hard to keep going especially at night. If I could afford it, I'd get a propane stove put in."

"No. I'm okay with renting from you. That property of mine is already in my will. It goes to my adopted son, Joe. He's down there in the Cities following his dream to be a musician, but the land will be his when he's ready for it."

Every day Eric worried about what to do with Harvey. No one else wanted to take him in. Joe wanted him to come to Minneapolis, but Harvey wouldn't budge.

Halloween had come and gone, and Eric and Gil left tracks in thin snow walking Harvey's mail across the big field toward the cabin with smoke rising above. Harvey's Social Security check arrived and he wanted it cashed so he could buy some booze. But Eric resolved to let him have beer only. Harvey's love of whiskey would surely call death to his door.

"Hello Pops, how ya doin'?" Eric looked around the shack. "Say hello to Gil, he's visiting us for awhile."

Harvey ignored him. "You got my check?"

"Yeah."

"Well…you gonna make a run for me?"

"Yeah, I can do that. You got a grocery list?"

"Nope. Ain't made one. Just get me the usual stuff, okay? An' whiskey. Get me some whiskey…five or six bottles, okay?"

"No, Harvey, I'll get you a case of beer. An' listen, you gotta make it on that, old man…make it last. I'm not gonna buy you any hard booze. You'd kill yourself with whiskey."

"Holy Jesus, Eric, I need that whiskey or I'll get real sick. Please? You don't get it, I'll get real sick. You know if you don't get it for me, I'll get it myself…somehow…you know that."

"Here. Just sign your check and I'll get you some beer and food."

"Goddammit you whippersnapper you!"

"Calm down, Harvey. You know we love you like a grandpa, you know, me, Carrie, and the kids. We wanna keep you around for awhile."

When Eric and Gil returned with Harvey's groceries and a case of beer, he ignored the food, leaving the box on the floor, and opened a beer right away. After his second bottle he realized he felt the same as he had when he picked up the first one, only a little sicker. "Goddamn you, Finn. You fucking moralist!" He shouted.

He picked up a full bottle of beer and threw it through a window— glass flew all over the floor. His mind was fixed on getting whiskey any way possible. He knew no one would go to town for it, but maybe he could find a way to get some from Log Jam Bar a few miles away. "I'm really gonna be sick now. They want to deny me the only thing I've got left in this rotten world—whiskey."

Then he remembered the young guy, Gil, who came along with Eric. He was supposed to be drying out but, by God, he could always use some money, couldn't he? Harvey got up, put on his shoes and a thin jacket, and hobbled out the door, leaving it open, dragging his one bad leg along in the snow. He found his way to the studio door and started knocking.

Gil had stoked up the wood heater and had settled down to read one of Eric's books by Henry Miller, the only book in the studio that interested him. In the Cities he would have jazz playing. But here he'd quickly tired of the jazz collection Eric kept to work by, stuff he heard too often, classic stuff. He longed for something new to hear and missed the excitement of live jazz. He had just settled in with Miller's novel when a loud BANG made him jump in his chair, making him realize how bad his nerves were.

"Open up, Youngblood, open up!" Gil rushed to the door, opening it to see an old man standing there shivering and shaking from the cold.

"Jesus! Jumpin' Jesus Joseph Je-Hose-E-Fat. I damn near froze out there, Youngblood," he said, pushing past Gil toward the heat of the stove. "Guess you don't remember me. I'm Harvey. Look kid, I need you to do me a favor. I'll pay you for it. I want you to make a run to the Log Jam Bar—out by the gas station-- two miles away and get me some whiskey. I'll give you ten bucks for yourself. Here," he said without waiting for an answer, shoving money into Gil's hand, "get me three quarts of whiskey and keep ten bucks for yourself."

"Whoa! I don't know. I'd do it but Eric told me he won't buy you any hard stuff."

"Ah, come on, kid, what Eric doesn't know won't hurt him."

"Yeah, but I don't know if I want to see the inside of a bar right now. I'm trying to dry out. That's what I came up here for, or so they tell me."

"You don't have to drink there, kid…just get me the three jugs and get the hell out and keep ten bucks, okay?"

"All right," Gil answered, knowing if he thought too long he'd miss a chance to score some run, which he still wanted more than sobriety, and he didn't want to give his conscience a chance to work. "Sit down, Harvey. You want any coffee while you wait? I can make some."

"No, no. No, you go on ahead. I got all the coffee I want at home. I need me some hooch, pronto! An' looks…don't tell Adam, the owner, it's for me. He doesn't know you yet so he won't say anything to Eric."

Gil tried to walk so Eric couldn't tell where his tracks would be heading. "If you don't want to slip, stay away from slippery places." He'd had heard that at an AA meeting and he pushed it out of his mind. Here goes my three weeks of sobriety. One more week and I could get my thirty days medallion. He didn't dare think about Harvey, what three bottles of whiskey would do to him. I'll only get him one, he reasoned, tell him that's all the bar had to spare.

When Gil got back, he found Harvey asleep in the studio chair. He let him sleep awhile he opened his own bottle of Bacardi, drinking half of it straight. The rum took him to the place his old minimum daily ration of grog used to, only this time it hit him faster, harder, numbing his conscience and the gnawing guilt he felt about what the booze could do to the old man who looked so frail and vulnerable. When Gil nudged him it startled him awake. "You got my whiskey?"

"Yeah, here it is."

"You only got one here. Where's the other two?"

"He only had one he could sell. Said he needed the other two for the bar trade. Here's your change, Harvey. Come on, I'll walk you back to your place."

# # #

The door to the shack was open, swinging in the cold November wind and Gil noticed a box of groceries sitting on the floor and two empty beer bottles.

"Do me one favor, will you, kid? The fire…will you light it for me?" Harvey was drinking whiskey straight from an old coffee cup. Gil noticed the wood heater and lit it. The fire began to warm the shack somewhat, but a cold draft came through the window Harvey had smashed with a bottle of beer. Gil took the cardboard from the grocery box and patched up the window and swept up the glass.

He quickly said goodbye-- he was in a hurry to get back to the studio and his rum. But the full realization of what he had just done to the pathetic old man hit him with devastating guilt. It wrecked his high, but he knew he'd finish the bottle of rum anyway.

In the morning, Gil had a royal hangover and someone was knocking at the door again. They had knocked earlier too.

"You want lunch, Gil? You missed breakfast." It was Carrie.

"Okay. Thank you," Gil replied. His head was throbbing. The word breakfast and the thought of food made him sick to his stomach. For a few days he had remained sober, free from hangovers. How could he have blown his sobriety for the miserable hell he now faced? He wanted to race over to the shack to check on Harvey. Surely he was all right or Carrie would have said otherwise. Or would she?

Gil decided he'd better make a showing at lunch, but fear and remorse made him dread every step he took toward the house. There were lots of long faces at the lunch table. Eric didn't say a word so no one else did either until Carrie spoke. "Harvey's dead, Gil. Maurice, our son, found him this morning. He'd frozen to death. The door was standing open. Someone got him whiskey and now he's dead."

All that day Eric would not speak to Gil or even look at him. This left Gil feeling like an enemy in his host's house. Now there was no one to talk to. Just when he had stopped feeling like a prisoner and had really wanted to try to stop drinking so he'd have a chance with Sarah, he had slipped back into his old behavior, making a mistake that cost an old man his life. Now he was isolated and the guilt was crushing. That afternoon the family avoided him; even the children who had been so friendly to him looked at him with fear. He declined supper, saying he felt sick.

After a guilt-ridden night with very little sleep he got dressed early and watched for Eric, knowing he came out at six o'clock every morning to feed and water the horses. He saw Eric draw pails of water and carry them to the corral. He followed with his nerves raw with emotion. Eric saw Gil approach but didn't speak. In the morning stillness Gil heard the horses drink and then the swishing of their tails, but neither man spoke. Finally Gil said, "Good morning."

"Morning."

"I did it."

"Harvey, you mean?"

"Yes. I did it. I got him the whiskey."

"I know you did. I've been waiting for you to admit it. Now that you have, I'm trying like hell to forgive you, but to be honest, I don't know if I'll be able to. It will take time."

"I understand."

"No, you don't. How could you? Harvey was like family. The kids have been crying. They don't have grandparents up here and he was like their grandfather. But we need to think about you. I've got to forgive and you will have to learn how to deal with the guilt you're now carrying. For another thing, you've got to start talking at AA meetings. You can't just pass anymore, you've got to open up and talk, get things off your chest."

# # #

Two days later Eric asked Gil if he wanted to go in town with him to pick up supplies and catch a morning AA meeting. Gil was in the process of trying to write his feelings in a journal and declined. That made Eric angry. "Oh, so you want to sit here and sink in your own funk, huh?"

"Jesus. Leave me alone!"

"Look, Gil. Your moping around is just feeling sorry for yourself. Either you get to a meeting and start talking or you'll never get out of your shell. You're not unique. Every one of us drunks hit a bottom as low or lower than yours, but we found the courage, the guts to at least talk about it and share with others. We began to open up and live again."

Eric stared at Gil," If you don't try to work for your freedom, man, you may as well go back to Minneapolis and drink. You stay pissed off and you'll go off the wagon anyway– hit the skids again."

Gil didn't reply. It was painful to hear Eric accuse him of simply feeling sorry for himself when he was already carrying more sorrow than he could bear over what he had done to Harvey and to his folks, too. But he was right about the meetings. Still he felt too hurt to speak.

"You make up your mind. I'll give you a few more meetings but you ain't going to just sit here and stew all winter, man. You can do that back in the Cities. I dig you, Gil, you know that. And I really don't like the tough love thing, but it's all I got left with you--to be frank."

Gil knew Eric was trying to help him. He stood by the studio window and watched Carrie come out of the house and hand Eric the list of supplies before he got into his truck and headed for town.

Somehow something shifted in him. He decided to go out and try chopping wood like he saw Eric do. He split the wood with a vengeance once he caught on. Each blow to the wood was an outlet for his frustration, and it flew in pieces around him. He looked at one of the oak logs he had just split in two and realized it was just like his mind, split equally, one half still wanting to return to the Cities and drink; the other half, trying to work the Twelve Steps. Jazz was in the balance. No jazz up here and for him where there was no jazz, there wasn't any life.

# # #

A week later Gil finally talked at AA:

"I'm Gil, I'm an alcoholic. I met a Sioux Indian once on Franklin Avenue. He was standing by the Anchor Inn Bar, said he'd been asked to leave there. I was already looped from the bar at the other end of the avenue. 'I got a stash,' he says, and he pulled a pint out of his vest. He'd been crying. He took the bandana off his head to wipe the tears. He said, 'We Sioux are warriors, man, we don't cry. I come from a warrior tradition. But I just lost my wife. She got killed in an accident and I miss her. I can't go back to the Dakotas like this, I miss her too much.' He kept wiping his tears. We drank most of the pint, and I thanked him and wished him well and turned and started across the street and passed out. He ran out in the street and dragged me back. He stayed with me, said he'd take me where he was staying if I couldn't make it home.

When we got there they were partying. They set me on a couch on the porch and I passed out. I woke up towards the end of the party, early in the morning. A drunken woman was going to bash my skull in with an iron she'd grabbed from an ironing board. I didn't see it coming but the big Sioux, who'd came out to look for me, grabbed her arm just in time and she slammed the iron into the couch instead. 'You leave my bro alone, you Witch!' he shouted at her. She was probably in a blackout and wouldn't remember it at all. He saved me twice that day."

It was the beginning. Gil started to open up at AA meetings. He was starting to trust them. They were all united in one cause, even though he thought some were rednecks.

# # #

"Do you want to go dig the band at the Log Jam Bar?" Eric asked one night. "I know you miss jazz. The band there—Cliff and the Boys— are good, maybe not as exciting as your Minneapolis jazz, but they play good music and it's not polka. We can drink coffee."

Adam made them feel at home, giving them free refills of coffee. They even had a table near the bandstand. Gil was touched by the local quartet playing standards. Two young blacks arrived to share their table. Gil fell into a comfortable rap with them, realizing how much he missed being among blacks. The two tall slim boys were athletes from Minneapolis on scholarship at the College of Bemidji. Gil could tell the boys were aware of a couple pretty girls who were flirting with them, but they didn't ask them to dance.

"We date a little at the college," the boy named Nate said, "but we aren't looking for anything heavy up here unless it really happens. We got girls back home. They'll wait for us 'til spring."

"Do you like the band?" Eric asked. Both blacks were thinking of one of their favorite Twin Cities band, but, like Gil, they were amused by this local band and enjoying the live music.

"Oh it's cool. These guys are all right."

"They be doin' it," Marvin said, "tellin' their stories. I like that."

Instinctively, Gil felt eyes trained on their table. Looking around, he noticed two redneck types scowling at them across the floor. The two blondes beside them seemed to be trying to engage or distract them."

"Are those two guys from the college?"

"Oh yeah," said Nate, who had noticed them long before. "Those jokers are from school, they're football jocks. They're on scholarship from Georgia. They've got a big Confederate flag on the wall in their dorm room and they're real proud of it."

"Hey, here they come," Eric said. The big Southern boys strode up to the table. One of them knocked over Nate's beer, spilling it in his lap.

"Oh gosh, what a shame," the jock said with a sneer.

"You Niggers are out of place here," the other jock said. "You oughta go back to Minneapolis to shantytown with the rest of your scum."

Gil got up, adrenaline rushing through his veins, ready for a fight.

"It's okay, man," said Nate. "Sit down, it's okay."

Gil sat down, resolving to try and restrain himself. He looked over at Eric, who was also angry. No one spoke until they knocked over Marvin's beer, then the two jocks yelled "Pussies! All of you," and sauntered back to their own table.

"I'm glad you guys stayed cool," Nate said. "We're not afraid of them. They do shit like that at the dorm, too, but we're the first two blacks to ever enroll at this college and we don't want no trouble. We want other blacks to be able to follow us up here. We can eat some crow for that."

The coffee he drank at the bar kept Gil awake back at the studio. He stepped out into below-zero air to relieve himself and was startled by the sound of wolves howling, an eerie thing to hear while alone in the middle of the night. It was fascinating, not unlike the lonesome sound of the train whistle at night, out on the road, in the middle of nowhere. The wolves sounded close enough to have a look, so he stepped back inside to put on his heavy coat and Sorrel boots, and set out on the path the horses made to the meadow flanking Eric's property. The wolves howled again and the supernatural sound echoed and reverberated in the emptiness he felt deep inside. The wolves were across the meadow at wood's edge. They watched him enter the meadow snow, then turned and trotted back into the woods.

Then he was startled again-- by light! The meadow opened up to a clear view of a sky completely ablaze with a sublime, pulsing white light. It was not only spread in glowing gossamer curtains across the entire sky, but also swirled from the zenith… a cascading celestial light show enriched by a spectrum of blue, red, and green. It was so intensely awesome that he had to look away at times, down at his feet in the snow. The wolves had reassembled farther off and resumed howling. He looked up again. It was a sight to humble anyone, make them believe in talk about the fear of God or that Higher Power by the AA people. That very power was now breathing upon the window of the sky, condensing spirit waves of ethereal light; moving mysteriously in an electric theater of silence.

He took it as a sign. It awakened a little hope amid the blackness of guilt he felt about Harvey, and as difficult as it might be for him to ever forgive himself and live a sober life; he had just experienced a baptism of light which he knew would never leave him. On the way back to the studio he realized how impoverished the night sky was in the inner city. The sky was always obscured at night. One never saw stars, not even the gift of one clear bright star; never the miraculous light he had just witnessed, the aurora Borealis.

# # #

The next morning when Eric asked him if he'd like to ride along over to his neighbor Arnie Johnson's place to buy some hay for the horses, Gil said, "Sure!" without hesitation. He knew his willing response surprised Eric.

When they turned into Arnie's place, Gil looked out over a field where huge, shaggy, brown beasts resembling the wooly mammoths of prehistoric past were grazing. The breath from their nostrils rose like white smoke in the cold air.

"Are those buffalos?" Gil was astounded.

Eric nodded, "Yeah, Arnie's got a whole herd of them."

"Really? What does he do with them?"

"Nothing. Just lets them be. He likes them. He might trade one or sell one once in a while to other folks who keep them."

After introductions, parking the truck, and a tour of the barn and stables, Arnie said, "I'll load you up some hay, then I gotta feed my buffalo. You're welcome to come along if you'd like. I reckon you don't see many buffalo in Minneapolis, Gil."

"Yeah, that would be great!"

When the hay was loaded Gil and Eric hopped up onto a flatbed truck, loaded with the feed for the buffalo, and Arnie drove it out to where they roamed. The big beasts moved slowly toward the truck and stood in anticipation. The horns on the bulls looked fearful but their smoky, liquid eyes were soft, placid, and peaceful. Arnie jumped right down in amongst the buffalo and spread out the bales of hay as Eric shoved them off; then spread out the dried corn from the buckets.

"Jesus, look how calmly he walks around among them," Gil said.

"Yeah, they're tame--to him, but I wouldn't want to try it. You want to?"

"No thanks, man! I'll just watch from up here. Each one of those buffalo looks like they weigh at least a ton." Gil was fascinated.

"See the little buffalo, or the calves? He's got three of them now, haven't you, Arnie?"

"No, there's four, actually. The fourth one's over there with his mother. The wolves have been coming out a lot again this winter, to the edge of the field to watch the calves. Whenever the wolves show up the buffalo form a circle around their calves and keep them inside."

"Just like in the movies," Eric said. "The settlers made a circle of their covered wagons when the Indians attacked."

"That's the idea. Last winter it was so cold, the snow so deep, that a lot of the deer died and the wolves were hard up for food. They came right out in the field here to eat the undigested corn out of the buffalo dung--dug the kernels right out."

After finishing the feeding, Eric and Gil decided to head for home. "Was it really that cold here last winter?" Gil asked.

"Yeah, you go through a winter like that, you know you've been through something."

"Sounds like survival of the fittest; the wolves, the deer, the buffalo and their babies."

"Yeah, it's survival but I never did cotton much to that survival of the fittest jibe. It's too cold and scientific for me. At least some of us humans believe in tender mercy, of giving a helping hand to helpless ones and cripples. A lot of people have never been down and out. We didn't know a goddamn thing about surviving up here when we first got here from the city. Thank God I made some friends through AA who helped me out or we might have had to give up and go back to the jungle. Do you believe there's more to life than just survival?"

"Shit, I don't know, man."

"Well, I do. There's more to life than just survival. You stay sober, work the program, and someday you'll be living a peaceful life."

"Yeah, I guess. To tell you the truth, I just can't shake my guilt…about Harvey. If I hadn't bought him that booze he'd still be alive."

"You didn't kill him, Gil. He killed himself. He was gonna do it, one way or another. He wanted to die. It was just a matter of time. After Myrtle died he just gave up. He made his choices. He wanted to follow her, I guess. He could be with her now, maybe. But you, you got a long life ahead of you. You have a choice too. Read, *The Promises in the Big Book*. They'll come true for you, too, if you stay sober. There is life after booze."

As Christmas neared, Eric asked Gil if he'd like to accompany him and his son Maurice on a Christmas tree hunt. They took an axe and toboggan and trudged into the woods, scaring up squirrels and several rabbits in white winter coats. They were heralded by crows and scolded by jays. There were many stories left in the snow in the form of tracks by the birds and critters if one could read them. Eric let Maurice select the tree, then he felled it with the axe and they placed it on the toboggan to haul back to the house. That night Gil was invited to stay after supper while they trimmed the tree. Carrie served hot apple cider and eggnog and there was plenty of popcorn left from batches made to thread and string around the tree.

Eric gave Gil a chance to earn some spending money before Christmas. Gil had enough to pay his way back to the Cities but it would be nice to buy some Christmas presents. Eric paid Gil to do the chores around the place while he finished up two road signs. He also paid Gil to help him put the signs up. Gil even took a week's job at the sawmill when the foreman asked Eric if he'd fill in for a sick worker. Eric sent Gil. The weather was freezing and it was tough work, but the pay was more money than Gil had received since leaving the railroad. He did some shopping in Bemidji and spent most of the money he'd earned on simple gifts for Eric and his family.

They splurged on Gil. Knowing it was his first Christmas in a new place, they bought him all the things they thought he needed: more warm clothes, tobacco, coffee, two jazz records Eric had Joe bring from Minneapolis, and some new books to read-- Henry Miller classics, The Air-Conditioned Nightmare and Black Spring, knowing Gil liked the author. The children, too, each gave him little gifts, which really touched him. They had accepted him from the very beginning, knowing nothing of his past. Like most children, they were not prone to judging people and had accepted him as if he were a new family member. Gil was overwhelmed. It was the first Christmas in years he'd spent with a family and he was given an abundance of gifts and love.

# # #

Back in Minneapolis, Sarah had the midwinter blahs. The weather was often below zero, and Gil, whom she longed to see again, was salted away up north. So when Jim called one day she was glad for his offer. "I think you could use some cheering up, girl. I have two women friends who said they'd like to meet you. Their thing is going out to dig live jazz, and they'd like to take you along sometime. Can you dig it?"

"By all means!"

"Okay, I'll give them your phone number. Their names are Lucy and Mary. Lucy's a dancer. She's married to Boris, a sax player. Mary is a poet--a beat poet. They really know the scene. They'll take you to some good jazz joints."

The next day Lucy called and introduced herself. After suggesting an evening of listening to jazz she ended up her chat with Sarah: "Cool," she said, "we'll have us some fun. Listen, can I ask you a favor? Can you pick me up on the way? I gotta square with you. Jim says you drive an XKE. I'd LOVE to ride in an XKE! Can I ride with you?"

Later that evening when Sarah drove up to her address, Lucy ran down the steps and gawked. She was tall and thin and in her younger days friend called her "String Bean," but when she became a professional dancer she earned the tagline "Watusi Lucy" for her ability to jump and prance. She was wearing a short skirt that showed off her long, muscular legs. She had no use for jewelry, it was cumbersome when she danced, but on off work nights she wore a necklace of plain rich-brown colored wood beads, a gift from Madam Celeste, the North Minneapolis fortuneteller who foretold her meeting Boris, the man in her life.

"Oooooooh my GAWD," she exclaimed. "Talk about class! This short is right out of the Riviera or something! Who's your sugar daddy?"

"Well, believe it or not—my sugar daddy was my father, whom I lost last year—I miss him a lot."

"Sorry, girl." Lucy looked sad. Sarah then told her a little about her family as they drove over to meet Mary.

"There's Mary."

She was waiting on the sidewalk in front of Big Al's, a club near Seven Corners that had music on two levels. "WOW!" said Mary. "I haven't seen a car this cool since I dug the Ferraris and Maseratis in Italy."

She was an Italian beauty everyone fell in love with. Black hair, and dressed in black, wearing a black beret, she had an air of authority about her, a street cred boldness which broadcast the fact she'd been on the scene in both America and Europe, with Rome, Italy as her birthplace. She proudly wore a gold astrological symbol of Leo the Lion; as a beatnik still carrying the banner of bohemianism.

Sarah felt good entering a club with such strong women. At Big Al's it was their custom to grab drinks and stand for a while directly in front of the bandstand so they could trade quips with the musicians. A hot, funky band led by Boe Bailey, a young trombone player, was kicking and bucking with rhythm. "BLOW, PREACHER, BLOW," Lucy yelled.

"We call him Preacher," Mary explained, "'cause his solos are like soul sermons." A sax player was adding blues responses to Boe's doctrine. When the sermon was over people yelled their amen's and Boe greeted Lucy and Mary. He was about to begin a new number when a black girl in a sleek red dress and short fur coat walked in. Boe caught sight of her and motioned for her to come up on stage. She walked right up to the mic and began to sing:

"When the blues tried the front door

they got whipped an' sent away.

When the blues tried the front door

they got whipped an' sent away.

Treated like a mongrel, scorned like a whore,

that was long ago but it's true to this day.

Sarah had never heard anyone sing with such intensity. She was hearing live blues sung for the first time. When she asked Lucy who the singer was, Lucy didn't know her name, only that Boe was encouraging the woman to sing.

Next a singer by the name of Shirley Witherspoon, a cousin of the great jump blues singer, Jimmy Witherspoon, began to sing. While Sarah listened intently, she didn't notice that Lucy and Mary had slipped into a booth with friends. There was no room for Sarah, who felt uncomfortable and vulnerable to the many men cruising by, looking for a woman to hit on. Lucy grabbed Sarah's coat. "Don't worry, honey, we're going upstairs in a minute, we ain't gonna let the wolves grab ya." Sarah hadn't noticed that the crowd was a little rough until then. She was fending off a man who was being insistent when Mary noticed and yelled out: "Keep moving, motherfucker! Leave that sister alone or we'll all kick you in the balls!" The man quickly stepped away.

The upstairs jazz room was decorated with a seaside motif: Fish nets, wharf posts, life preservers, seagulls in flight, and a large sign reading BEYOND THE REEF. Lighting was dim. Rum drinks were featured. Between sets Duke Ellington's recording of "Flamingo" with Herb Jeffries was playing on the sound system.

"Lucy, Jim tells me you're a dancer. Are you dancing somewhere now?"

"Not 'til I can cop another gig. I got stranded here last year. I was dancing with an R&B revue from Philly. The leader was hitting on me to put out, but I wouldn't. His main punch got jealous anyway and had somebody slip me a Mickey. I passed out and missed the bus. So here I am, stranded in this little white-assed place with no money an' no work. I been working as a cocktail waitress ever since. Can't find a dance gig nohow."

"Lucy's from Philly," Mary said. "We're like Hicksville."

"That ain't right. This town is, not you all. You're hip but this dead-ass town is a drag, so hoity-toity. Like a small town, with little cliques all into polka music and sewing circles and ah, racism too, plenty racism hidden like, like the nicer variety. I shoulda left long ago but Boris snagged me. He thinks this place is the best thing since popcorn."

"What do you think, Sarah?" Mary asked.

"I think it's clean, quiet and peaceful compared to other places. My dad took me to New York once. His dad came there from Russia. Lots of Jews like me there but it's too rude. People are too fast and cold. It is loaded with culture, though."

"You should go to San Francisco. It's hip but it's mellow."

"Yeah," said Lucy, "you should a stayed there with those beatniks, Mary. That's your scene. Lots of jazz there, huh?"

"Mary, do you know of any beat coffeehouse here in Minneapolis?" Sarah asked.

"Does she! Her brother runs it. Pan's Pipes Coffeehouse. And my husband has the house band. We'll go there sometime. They got an old black singer plays piano an' sings blues on Monday night's name of Lazy Bill."

The musicians in the upper room were older men dressed in elegant suits and played with a refined style. They opened their next set with "One Note Samba," a bossa nova song by Antonio Carlos Jobim.

Then an aristocratically handsome older silver-haired man stepped forth to sing "My Foolish Heart."

"Oh, Richie, you are SO SMOOOOTH!" Mary said.

"What's his name?" Sarah asked.

"Richie Mayes."

"He's a silver fox, alright," said Lucy. And I must admit he can sing like Billy Eckstine. I hope Boris looks that good when he's that age."

"He will," Mary said. "Lucy's got herself a good man. Damn fine sax player, too. And he only has eyes for Lucy."

"How about you?" Sarah asked. "Who's your man?"

"She's in love with a band leader. Bad case too. She's way gone over him and he doesn't even notice. I keep telling her, stone fox she is, she can have any man she desires but she's stuck on him."

"I can see why. I saw him play once at Road Buddy's. He's gorgeous. And his band's the best I've ever heard."

"What about you, Sarah, you must have a boyfriend, a sexy co-ed stashed somewhere."

"No, girls, no one on the horizon yet, either. There's one guy I got my eye on but he's treating me like a sister, though we did kiss once."

"Get on him, girl! Sometimes they need a nudge, a shove, dig?"

# # #

As Christmas approached in Minneapolis Dean and Boris were relaxing at the bar in Road Buddy's. "I'm worried about Carl," Dean said, "his relatives are all going to Omaha for Christmas to be with the grandparents, and they didn't invite him to go with."

"His relatives don't like him?"

"They don't want to deal with what he might do, how he might act. He hasn't had much to do with them since he's been sick, but he still feels hurt that they are leaving him out. And when he's alone at holidays, he thinks about his wife too much."

"His dead wife?"

"Yeah, and then he really loses it."

"He's got you, doesn't he?"

"Sure, but I don't count when he goes into his blue funk bag. He'll mope and then go on a real bender."

"So let him drink and pass out."

"That would be all right if he just passed out, but he might start smashing things up again."

"Well, shit, let's get drunk with him--all of us--let's have a Christmas party and we'll keep him company. With all of us around, we should be able to control him. If he acts up we'll all sit on him!"

At Christmas, out of goodwill, they all went to Dean's: Boris and Lucy, Jim, Sarah--even Gypsy, who had nowhere to go--and usually spent Christmas Eve in a bar.

They began by sampling the booze in the kitchen, all except Lucy, who seemed subdued and insisted on drinking eggnog without the dark rum. No Tom & Jerry's for her.

"What do you want to hear?" Dean asked Sarah. "And don't say Christmas jazz. We don't do that shit. Don't do Bing Crosby either."

"Well, I don't know…Put on some soul music. You know best. Maybe Lucy will do the shing-a-ling."

Lucy looked indignant. She shook her big Afro in distain. "Lucy ain't gonna shing-a-ling. Frankly you people disappoint me. You way outta line. You're supposed to be concerned about Carl. But you proceed to get blasted and get him blasted. You all be numb and dumb on the Nazarene's Birthday. Child, that ain't right. I wouldn't even be here if Boris hadn't drug me."

"Don't be so uppity," Boris said. "You got no better place to be 'cept church an' you don't go to church, so just cool out. You can be the designated driver."

"Yeah. Somebody's got to do it, and I'll have to watch yawl get stupid."

Carl entered the kitchen wearing a Santa hat, carrying his last-minute supplies.

"Ho-ho-ho! What it be like, Santa?" Boris asked.

"What it be different from?" Carl replied.

"What it be likened to?" Sarah offered.

"What it be more different than?" Jim asked.

"Better git it in yer soul." Carl smiled. "What yawl drinkin'? You got any 151?"

"No, no. We got you some dark Bacardi. Help yourself."

"Well, hand it over then. If I can't have no 151, Boris can't have no codeine cough syrup neither."

"Oh ha-ha, Carl, I gave that up long, long ago. You wanna gig before we get too blasted? You want to play?"

Carl poured himself a glass of rum then removed the cover from his bass while Boris took out his sax and blew some warm-ups. He began toying with a melody he liked. Dean, whose drums were set up in their usual spot, added rhythm at a jaunty pace. "Choose something," he said to Boris, who kept on with the melody he was remembering fully.

"What's the name of that tune?" Sarah asked Gypsy.

"Oh, it's "In a Shanty in Old Shantytown"-- maybe he's playing it as a reference to the humble birth of the Naz?"

Sarah picked up her chianti bottle and went to sit by Lucy, but since she was so morose, she turned to Jim. "I wonder how Gil's doing. Do you think he's sober?"

"I hope so. Eric's probably got him in AA by now. Eric doesn't mess around. Its woodshedding and tough love with him…just what Gil needs."

"What do you mean--woodshedding?"

"Um, it's a jazz term," said Jim. It means to go off and be completely alone to get in touch with yourself and your axe, your instrument, to search your soul, playing, playing, playing, reaching for the deep well of creativity, for inspiration, to find new ideas, new expression, new ways to improve your chops, your playing."

Then he thoughtfully added, "but in Gil's case he's digging into sobriety. Let's hope he gets his head on straight."

"Say, I like that phrase 'woodshedding'! I guess being up North is a great place for that—it takes a quiet place for that, like you need for meditation, away from the distraction of people--so you can come back and join the living. But I miss him… I'd like to see him back on Green Dolphin Street again." Sarah was referring to her favorite cut of all, a version of "On Green Dolphin Street" by Cal Tjader with Paul Horn on flute. It was on the box at Pan's Pipes, and she always played it there. "Say, who's in the kitchen cookin'?" The smell of chili and roasting chicken permeated the apartment.

"Lucy…Carl put her to work and she got a hold of the Ken Davis Barbeque Sauce," said Boris. He began to play the opening lines of "Parker's Mood" and soon Gypsy joined him at the mic.

Someone began to bang on the floor of the apartment above and yell, "Knock it off," from the hall. Most of the renters were out of the building for the night, but a few were protesting the noise. "We got chili, barbeque chicken, biscuits with honey and butter, and great slaw from the deli--let's grease," said Carl. Boris decided to quit playing and they all sat down to eat.

Carl went back to his bass when he'd finished eating and played a beautiful acoustic version of "Solitude," then sat down to talk to Sarah. But he soon leaned into the couch and began nodding off. *I'm dreaming of a white cop car,* he sang, *just like the ones I used to know,"* then fell fast asleep.

"Come on, Boris," Lucy said urgently. "Carl's safe now, asleep and harmless. Let's go home before I get too tired to drive. Gypsy's rollin' reefer and I be tempted to stay for one if we don't get movin'. You folks sure juiced up your Christmas."

"Don't be so righteous, Watusi," Boris said.

"Well, it ain't right. Come on, let's round trip. Oh…I better say thank you. Thanks, Dean, for the good chili and chicken. God bless yawl and the little Naz too."

"God bless the child," Dean said.

"Amen," Jim said, blessing everyone with the sign of the cross.

"Peace," Gypsy added.

A joint passed between Gypsy, Dean and Jim. Sarah declined. Then Dean fell asleep. "Come on, Jim, before I get too tired to drive, too," said Sarah. "Gypsy, I'll give you a lift. Where you going?"

"Selby-Dale. But you don't gotta go out of your way."

"It's not out of my way. It's my mission, ferrying you jazz babies around. Let's book!"

WOODSHEDDING – PART TWO

January and February were months of solitude. Temperatures could drop as low as forty below zero and the two months were the longest Gil had ever known. Outside of having supper with the family and the AA meetings in town, he was completely alone. The loneliness was so palpable he felt he could cut it with a knife. Memories from his drunkenness, the remorse and guilt, all flooded into this chasm devoid of human warmth. It was terrifying to feel himself on the edge of an abyss of fear that had the potential to completely paralyze him. He swallowed his pride enough to ask Eric if he would be his sponsor and Eric agreed. "Start a journal--you're a writer. Put anything and everything in it...write down your feelings. It will help you vent your emotions until you feel you're ready to do a fourth and fifth step. Your guilt will begin to dissolve, especially when you can forgive yourself. Ask for grace from the Higher Power."

Journaling did prove therapeutic and led to outlines for a novel. Then poems came, some culled from what he could remember from originals lost in his drunken past; others inspired by his new environment, clean as snowflakes, and crystal clear as icicles. Others were sparse, stark and as honest as the animals domestic and wild; whose presence he valued as company. It was encouraging to find that when he put the new poems together with the few he had saved from the Cities and those he could recall enough to rewrite, he had enough for a modest chapbook. In two months he wrote more than he had ever written in his entire life.

Writing relieved some of his loneliness, and occasionally there was another blessing, a great luxury really, a letter from Sarah. She knew how starved he must be for any news from "Green Dolphin Street," their nickname for the scene. Her kindness made him wish he had shown her how much he really appreciated her friendship back when he had the chance. He had taken her for granted. Up North now, and alone, it was clear as a bell what a beautiful, sensitive soul she was.

The mail was a connection with the outside world for the family. They got a lot of things they needed and wanted from mail order catalogs, and the postman's arrival was a daily event. This excitement wasn't an option for Gil, but once in a while Eric brought him a letter from Sarah, and Gil would read it over and over, fascinated by news of what seemed so far away. Sarah, he thought, oh Sarah, Sarah so formidable, clever, benevolent Sarah, merciful, generous, female. Warm Sarah, hip Sarah, oh Lady Sarah, how lucky I am that anyone remembers me, and that I have you: a Jewish goddess to boot! Thank you for being my jazz baby friend!

By winter's end he was actually thankful that up North there was nowhere to run. He had reached the end of his leash, like the iguana in the play Night of the Iguana by Tennessee Williams. Once he sincerely appealed for help from the Higher Power, to slake this thirst, and remove the powerful craving for alcohol; his bitterness dissolved. He welcomed exchange with anything alive, relished conversation. He talked at meetings, sharing with and trusting people he once suspected as redneck, people he had liked to call 'Jack Pine Savages.' They were all just people like him now, with a common compassion and goal: To find freedom and help each other stay free of alcohol. When spring arrived Gil felt the healing power of the land begin to swell, especially up in the big field which Eric called "Freedom Field." The family went there for picnics and any other reason they had to celebrate. The glorious green grass, splendid in sunlight; the energetic spring winds; the earth, sky and sun were all singing to anyone who came upon the big field. One wanted to fill their lungs, breathe deeply, and sing along with the field.

One day Eric brought kites back from town for the kids, but was too busy to help them assemble and fly them. Excited, the kids brought the kites to Gil. He showed them how to make tails for their kites. Maurice got his airborne by himself, but little Suzanne, the four-year-old, lost hold of her kite string when Gil handed it to her and the kite got away, rapidly diminishing the string, tugging the spool away across the grass. Gil tried to grab it, caught the spool and steadied the kite. He handed the kite back to the little girl, who did all she could do to keep from being pulled forward with it.

Gil had never enjoyed anything more than the simple joy of being with these children, happy with their kites. In the summer ahead, the kids would spend hours crisscrossing the place on horseback, and when winter came again would slide downhill on their sleds from field to valley below. Eric could afford to buy them expensive toys now and then, but when he did the kids often ignored them and rushed outside, to be in nature instead.

When Gil sat down on a large rock to remove a pebble that had lodged in his shoe, Suzanne said, "Why don't you go barefoot? We always do. It's fun." So he did. He had never gone barefoot, not even as a child. His feet were tender so he walked more carefully than the kids with calloused feet, but he enjoyed the grass, feeling connected to the field. He even sensed how the invigorating spring wind was cleansing the land as the sun warmed it while seeds began to germinate.

# # #

That spring Eric took on a house painting job and asked for Gil's help. Gil put aside most of the money he got for the eventual trip to Minneapolis. The job only lasted a week and soon he was back up in the big field days, this time playing Eric's conga drum. This gave him another pastime besides writing. It was a novelty to be able to drum as long and as loudly as he pleased without disturbing anyone. One day while playing, a dark woman with long, black hair came walking gracefully toward him, as if out of a vision. As she came closer, he saw she was Native American, and he was so surprised he stopped playing.

"Don't stop. Keep playing. It sounds good."

But he was transfixed by her beauty, unable to play. She stood completely erect yet relaxed, as if rooted to the land, belonging to it as if she alone owned it and all others only had visitor passes.

"I like that Latino drumming, man. You must be Gil, huh? Carrie told me you are staying with them. I'm Heart Song. I'll be here for a while, too, visiting and resting before going back on the road. Me and Eric go way back…we met at art school in Minneapolis."

"I'm from Minneapolis, the inner city. I've lived around 26th and Nicollet a lot, around the art school area. I knew Eric from there, too. He hung with some other artist friends of mine before he came up here."

"Well, nice to meet you. I'm going back to my sweat lodge now. I'm building one down there, for Carrie. She wants me to show her how to do sweats. Keep up your drumming, man; it will be nice to work by down there. My people use drums too, but our rhythm we feel from the heart, from the earth." She smiled and turned to leave.

"Nice to meet you, too," Gil said, concentrating more on her as she strode from the field to descend to the valley than on his drumming, which he had lost interest in. He soon gave it up and followed his curiosity to the edge of the hill. He saw her down valley fashioning a mound-like structure of bent saplings whose bark she had peeled, leaving them skeletally white in the sun.

"Oh good," she said as he approached. "Can you give me a hand, Gil? I'm going to drape these tarps over the frame."

"Sure. What kind of wood is that?"

"They're willow saplings. I got them from the grove in that low-lying area over there. They bend well and they hold up in the steam without cracking when dry. There," she said when they had the last tarp in place, "it's almost ready for Carrie's first sweat. We just have to select some big and holy rocks for the fire. You wanna try a sweat?"

"Oh I don't know. Forgive my ignorance, but what's it for?"

"Purification. A physical and spiritual cleansing. A way to pray and get closer to The Great Spirit. It sweats the impurities out of you while you pray for guidance."

"Okay, I'll try it. You take off all your clothes like a sauna?"

Heart Song smiled. "For sure. You go in naked like you were born, from the womb of The Mother. The heat gets pretty intense. Don't worry, I don't do co-ed sweats. I just conduct them for other women. I'll get my cousin Buckwheat to do one for you. He's coming back soon. He dropped me off, and then took off for a rez in Wisconsin where his brother lives. Can you help him put up my teepee poles when he gets back? I can't stand staying in houses when I don't have to. I got enough of that in the city. I'm a land-based person. I like the feel of Mother Earth under my moccasins. The sweat lodge here is a symbol of the Earth Mother. See how it swells like bread in the oven or the womb of a woman about to give birth? It's also like a tomb, like a burial mound…from the womb to the tomb…the Mother holds it all, gives it and takes it away…then gives it again. Oh look!" Heart Song pointed out a huge carrion bird passing above. "A turkey vulture. It's an omen. The vulture is a symbol of the Mother, too. Anyway, if you do some sweats you will see that each time you go back into the womb of the Earth Mother, she lets you be born again through purification, through revelation, giving you new life each time."

Gil felt humbled in the native woman's presence. The poet in him found her talk of symbols refreshing. Whenever anyone spoke about what's real, about what really matters instead of the usual trivial chatter, it was refreshing. It made him want to get back to the real essence of things himself. Gil was just trying out baby steps on his wobbly alcoholic sea legs, and he knew she had worked long and hard on herself spiritually to possess the kind of power she carried. He sensed that she was the kind of person you rarely ever met in a lifetime, maybe once or twice at best.

What he sensed was correct, for she had been studying medicine with various medicine people all across the states, had medicine people in her heritage and hoped to become a powerful activist and medicine woman herself. He took his leave from her, saying he was glad to meet her, and she thanked him for his help. As he walked to the studio, he remembered he had left his drum up on the field, so he changed direction. You could do that, he thought, in the country, leave things out and when you came back for them they'd be right where you left them. You could never do that in the city. They'd be gone in five minutes.

When Heart Son's cousin, Darrel, or "Buckwheat" arrived, Gil found him to be a friendly Ojibwe in his early thirties. He said very little, but Gil sensed that in his quiet dignity he had a deep understanding of all that went on around him. And there would be much to learn from him if he opened up.

Darrel prepared a sweat for Gil soon after his arrival. Using a big forked stick, he carried hot rocks from the fire outside to the center of the lodge, placing them in a circle. He chanted prayers and sprinkled sage on the rocks to purify the air, then dipped water to pour in small amounts over the rocks. The lodge quickly filled with steam.

Darrel had assured Gil that a sweat was not an ordeal but a cleansing, and he was careful not to overheat the lodge.

Gil was not used to praying. The only praying he'd done was hangover praying, like "Lord, if you help me out of this jam, I promise I'll never drink that much again." Of course, those promises were always broken. This time he prayed humbly and sincerely, asking the Higher Power, whom Darrel called The Great Spirit, to remove his craving for alcohol and some of the guilt he still felt over Harvey's death.

After the sweat they went swimming in the nearest lake, driving there in Darrel's old beat up Ford pick-up. The cool water felt great on his now heated skin.

"So why do they call you, Buckwheat?"

"Because I like it. I eat a lot of it-- like buckwheat pancakes-- ever try them? And kasha, a Russian recipe for buckwheat. My spiritual name is Bows to Crows, but Heart Song likes to call me Buckwheat, and so most everybody else calls me that. She knows Bows to Crows too, and uses that when she's talking serious to me."

"May I ask why 'Bows to Crows?'"

"Because crows are spirit messengers from the other world. To me they are symbols of the Great Mother. They are holy birds and I bow to them whenever I hear or see one."

On the return ride, Darrel turned to Gil in earnest. "There's something that happened during your sweat that I saved to tell you later so you might remember it better. Your spirit guide talked to me in the sweat."

"My what?"

"Your spirit guide, like the guardian angel the Christians talk about. We all have one. Yours was a female spirit, a very strong, fierce one. She said she is watching over you until you are healed."

Gil wanted to know more about the spirit guide but didn't know how to ask, and Darrel's demeanor suggested that in his economical way he had told Gil all there was to say about it.

"I know what you are going through, you know. I heard you quit the bottle. I did too. I go to a lot of AA. I speak at meetings. Just remember how you felt when you came out of that sweat today. You don't want to lose that new life. You were born anew. The Great Spirit gives us new songs to sing."

That terrible urge for a drink, for his old daily fix of at least a half pint to get him through a day had long been removed after Gil had sincerely done his AA Third Step work. But he still had to be vigilant, and the sweat lodge experience helped him want to keep that clean and sober feeling and stay focused.

Then, when he was no longer driven to get alcohol, he had plenty of chances to cop it if he wanted. Eric trusted him then they went to town, let him wander here and there, for coffee or to shop. Once that winter he had dodged Eric in town long enough to get to the liquor store for pint of rum which he hid in his jacket. But when he helped Finn unload feed sacks back at the farm, the pint fell out and broke on a rock in front of them. Finn didn't say a word.

Three things had helped him endure that long, bleak winter: AA meetings, reading Henry Miller, and writing, putting his feelings in a journal, making sketches for a future novel. Occasionally a poem would come. Now with the snow gone and things growing green there was much to do, and he could take long nature walks enjoying the solitude and the beauty in wild things. Whenever he felt restless or a slight depressed he knew his best defense was to stay busy.

With that in mind, after coffee on a beautiful early June morning, he went out to the family garden to pull weeds. He had never worked in a garden. It felt good to have his hands in the soil. The sun had begun warming the earth and the birds were singing. He heard a screen door slam. Heart Song had come out of the house with her coffee. He now thought of her as a half-breed. In a talk they'd had she told him she was half French Canadian, and that Madeline was a name she was given from that world. He was sure she gave the Native side of her heritage more importance in her outlook, and having a perspective of both cultures, intimidated by neither, her attitude seemed to say, "Look here, I already know all the monkey business you whites have been putting down, but the Ojibwe is better and I'll identify with that." She had a degree from the art school in Minneapolis and an earlier education on the street. They had tried to de-culture her in a white boarding school, but she came out determined to study Native medicine and become a medicine woman.

Madeline walked slowly up, sipping her coffee, her plain cotton dress and black hair gently undulating in the wind.

"Father of the sun and Mother earth," she said, smiling.

"Good morning," Gil replied. "I felt like pulling some weeds today."

"There's no such thing as weeds. That's a word white people invented for plants they're ignorant of. 'Weed' connotes undesirability. There's nothing undesirable in nature, everything has its place, a reason. Everything is part of the circle of life, take out one part and the wheel doesn't roll right."

"But Heart Song, if Eric doesn't take these weeds out, eventually they will take over."

"That's because they're strong, way stronger, than those domestic plants. Weeds are survivors…they have real strength. Sure you've got to take some out, but you don't have to dump poison on them. That's one thing Eric knows. He knows you don't have to use insecticides and weed killer chemicals. They kill the organic life in the soil and end up in the water system. The whole point is you don't kill life to get life. They didn't have to split the atom. That was wrong from jump street!" Heart Song looked directly at Gil and continued:

"That's another violent approach…how can anything good come from an act of destruction, smashing atoms? Those egghead scientists, if they had any common sense they'd quit tampering with everything and just work with it. Look over there." She pointed to the yard. "Those dandelions. See how strong they are. No one will ever eliminate them totally. They're like us Natives, genocide cut us drastically, but we keep coming back. So will the buffalo. I came to talk to you about what Buckwheat told me. He saw your spirit guide during that sweat you guys took. Did he tell you about it?"

"Yeah. He didn't say much but he was real serious."

"That's why I want to talk to you. He never says much. Doesn't explain enough sometimes. He's seen these things before. Spirits often come to the sweat lodge to heal or bring messages. And sometimes evil ones are sweated out of people. He said your spirit guide told him she will help you get well. Did you feel anything special?"

"No. Just real clean afterward. But I believed what he told me about her.

"Seriously, Gil, it's rare when someone gets help like this. You should always remember your spirit guide when you're tempted to drink. Buckwheat should have told you that. He needs to be more of a big mouth like me. I've heard he really speaks out at AA though. He goes to speaker meetings around Wisconsin and sometimes in Minnesota and the Turtle Mountain Rez in North Dakota. They like his talks."

"He left, didn't he?"

"Yeah, he pulled out yesterday…went back to the rez in Wisconsin where my cousins live."

"Are you going to stay on for a while?"

"No. I changed my mind. I'm hitting the road. I was going to kick back here for a while but now the road is calling me again."

"Where are you going?"

"To Hopi Land to see Grandfather David."

"Who is he?"

"He's one of the Hopi elders, a spokesperson for them. I want to learn some medicine from them. All the tribes look to the Hopis as keepers of ancient spiritual teachings and prophecy for Turtle Island. I travel all over to study medicine. Last year I was at Crow Dog's place on the Rose Bud Rez in Lakota land studying with Henry Crow Dog. This year I will learn some of the Hopi ways and visit the Navajo too. I've got some wampum, some stuff to trade for some of their turquoise and silver. I'll use some of that on the way back to finance the trip. How about you? How much longer will you stay here?"

"Well, I guess until I feel I can make it back in the city without drinking. I'd go back now but Eric said to stay a while longer."

"Yeah, you take your time. This is a good time to be on the land… summer…beautiful here too. You can't get this in the city. The city will wait for you, it ain't going anywhere. And stay off that firewater. It does nothing for people but knock them on their ass. How's your writing going? I heard you write."

"Yeah, I write poetry mostly. It's loosening up now that I'm not drinking. I just wrote a poem about the kids flying kites up there in the field. I'm going to start a novel."

"I read a lot in art school after I settled down. The first year I was angry. I drank a lot of wine and took it out in street fights. It was too much trouble and too much anger so I switched to coffee and hung out wherever there was music. I've seen too many natives go down the firewater path and never come back."

That afternoon when the rural mail car came there was a letter from Sarah, more news from the jazz world and at the end of the letter, "I miss you." The three words reverberated like a mantra. Her letters, more than anything else, had kept his morale alive during the long, lonely winter. The thought that she could see and even believe in a better side of him was beginning to make him believe in it himself. Gil felt like taking the next bus to the city, but Heart Song's advice, not to rush things, was wise. He knew the city could turn a man inside out. But by fall he would have spent one year woodshedding in recovery. Maybe he'd wait a while longer and return when he was really sure of himself.

24

THE SUPREME IDENTITY

On the afternoon of her twenty-third birthday, Sarah stood in front of the Buddha in the oriental wing of the Minneapolis Institute of Art. She had never seen anything so arresting and unique. How could this mute figure speak so loudly to her across the centuries? In Buddha's countenance the world was held at bay. His serenity indicated enlightenment, the Supreme Identity. Fascinated by the statue, and reflecting on its meaning, she had a startling thought. Buddha's victory was totally revolutionary! Normally everything in one's life, the body, the senses, mind are all directed outward in active involvement for gain, but here was a man with eyes closed, completely motionless, a pioneer on an inward journey with no guide, but himself.

And I had no guide when I tried meditating, she thought. In New York, Mira had a teacher; but all I've have is the book she sent me. It will have to do. It gives a simple form of meditation for beginners. But there's a catch—no drugs or alcohol. Alcohol wouldn't be a problem but giving up grass might not be easy.

Sarah had come to rely on marijuana as a stress reliever. And now that she loved jazz, the smoke allowed her inside the music in a deeper way. Great sacrifice was necessary if one wanted freedom and peace of mind.

It was a struggle, a long hard one. Sarah had cut her use of grass way down but she couldn't quit completely. She started meditation, got it going but was bothered by guilt. Then one day during a conversation with a Quaker girl she met in a psychology class, a moment of clarity allowed her to definitely make up her mind.

"I don't know if I really want to quit smoke, or if I'll ever be able to," Sarah said.

"Of course, you can--and of course, you want to," the Quaker said. "If you keep changing your moods with grass, you'll never find your real self. 'Know thyself' is what the Buddha said. If you want to get free and stay free, you can't depend on a drug." Sarah immediately thought of Gil.

# # #

"Sarah, you had a caller today," Ruth said.

"Caller? What kind of caller?"

"A gentleman caller."

"Oh, come on, what are you talking about?"

"A handsome young man named Mark Hamilton. I believe he said he was in high school with you?"

"I don't believe you. If it was him, it must be for something else, he wouldn't have any interest in me. Maybe a class reunion or something."

"Well, it hasn't been long enough for a class reunion. He said he'd call again, so I gave him your private number-- he wants to take you out."

"He wouldn't even look at me in school. He was going with a cheerleader and then he went to some Ivy League college. I bet he dropped out. He's really good-looking though, and he thinks he's a charmer."

The next day Hamilton called to ask Sarah if she'd like to go out for coffee or a drink. "It would be nice just to talk and get caught up," he said. She almost said "what for" but realized it would be impolite, so she agreed. When he came to the door late that afternoon, she was struck by his charming smile, wavy brown hair and slim, solid body. He wore an Eastern style collarless shirt and sharp looking slacks and shiny loafers. They took his Corvette an American sports car that didn't have the authenticity, Sarah felt, of her English made XKE.

He asked her where she wanted to go, and rather than guide him to a hip bar in the city, which he would probably consider shabby, she said, "Oh, anywhere you like."

Let him show his true colors, she thought. She was sure she already had him pegged as spoiled and shallow. He drove her to a trendy bar on Hennepin Avenue. He ordered whiskey and she ordered coffee.

"Why just the coffee?" he asked, swishing his drink.

"I hang out with jazz people and I can't keep up to their drinking, so I just do coffee. I'm meditating now so no drugs or alcohol!" There, she thought, I just dropped the two main interests of my life --jazz and meditation-- they'll both probably pass right by him. To her surprise he commented on both of her interests. "Oh, yeah, I dig jazz, too… especially Miles Davis "Kind of Blue." But Sarah knew a lot of college boys might buy that album because college girls considered it cool make-out music. Then he said, "Buddhism? Yes, I know a little about the Buddha. Have you seen *Siddhartha*?" he asked.

"The movie? No, but I've read the book by Hermann Hesse," she said.

So, Sarah thought, he wasn't a total square and he was so damn pretty. She kept losing herself staring at his good-looks. Then he popped a line that really stood out: "You know, I always wanted to ask you out back in school. I thought you were deeper and more interesting than the other girls in the crowd I was with. I guess I didn't because I didn't think you'd go for a guy like me."

Sarah smiled, "I'd have gone out with you." She remembered the buzz among all the boys, how big her "tits" were, as they vulgarly put it. Guys wanted to date her for the size of her breasts, as if they were first prize in a competition. It disgusted her.

Mark Hamilton conducted himself well, held his drink, and was very polite, could even be fascinating at times. But she felt guilty, thinking of Gil, and what he was going through trying to dry out.

He deserved more time. But despite her feelings, she agreed to a second date with Mark.

With things stable at home, Rachel safe, and Ruth calmer, Sarah found her the apartment her father said she could have when she graduated. She rented a duplex in the Cedar-Riverside neighborhood which included a garage for the XKE. She chose the area because it was attracting a nucleus of bohemians, including her poet friend Mary.

The first box she unpacked was the one labeled "Coffee." She took out the French Press and opened a can of French Market Coffee and brewed a pot. After she'd had a cup, she opened a box that was labeled "Books" lifting out a paperback on top, *Think on These Things,* a book by J. Krishnamurti that had changed her life.

Just then there was a knock on the door. Her first visitor, Mary, stood in the doorway with a bottle of Chianti and a book of Chinese poetry. Sarah had already meditated and now it was an occasion to celebrate with her friend. The wine got them really talking while they played some of the jazz records Uncle Saul had given her. When the conversation settled on Mary's frustrated obsession with the band leader, Sarah was relieved to be able to discuss her own dilemma, having to choose between her feelings for Mark Hamilton and her loyalty to Gil, who now seemed to be recovering and writing her regularly.

"Who is this guy anyway, this Hamilton? Where'd he come from? Is he a rich boy."

"He's from St. Louis Park. Went to college out East for a while but said he didn't like it."

"Well what's his thing? Is he into the arts?"

"I don't think so. He likes sports and rock and roll. He likes going Up North to his parent's lake cabin to go fishing."

"And chase women? He sounds like a superficial guy…a preppy. Are you sure you want him for any reason other than his looks?"

"Well, he's nice."

"Nice? So much for nice. Does he have any backbone? I bet he likes your XKE!"

"Mary, that's not fair."

"What about Gil? He sounds for real. You aren't ditching him yet, are you?"

"Oh no! I'm really fond of him. The guy's been through so much and he's so talented--if he can just stay off the booze. That's why I'm so confused. I like them both– I want them both."

"You know that wouldn't work, girl. Men think they can have two or more women but God forbid us having anything on the side. Let me ask you this, what does your heart tell you?"

"I don't know yet. I feel like I owe Gil. He really helped us get my sister back."

"NO, NO, NO. Don't decide with this 'owe' business, decide from your heart."

"I'm trying to, Mary, I'm trying."

25

SENT FOR YOU YESTERDAY

"Sent for you yesterday, here you come today," sang a man coming down the hall as Joe was leaving his apartment. The stranger was dressed all in black and had long, black hair. He read the number on Joe's door and stopped.

"Are you Joe Citro?"

"Yeah."

"Well, I'm Gypsy. Boris sent me. Can we talk? Inside, I mean."

With the door shut behind him Gypsy said, "Boris tells me he thinks you need to slow down, learn how to relax. I brought some reefer that could help you with that if you'd like to try.

"I don't know. I don't dig drugs or alcohol. My parents both messed up their lives with alcohol."

"Whoa…this is not like alcohol, and it's not a drug, dig. It's a natural substance. It wasn't made in a lab. It's an herb that grows natural, like comfrey or sage. It actually has medicinal properties and you don't get hooked on it like you do on booze and hard drugs."

"I still don't know."

"Well, dig, I'm not a pusher. I don't go after people. I got all I can do to service the ones that come to me. I jus' stopped by 'cause Boris said you needed to peace-out, man, and I personally don't like to see creative people uptight. I hear you're a horn player."

"Yeah, I play trumpet."

"Cool. My father played clarinet in Ellington's orchestra. He had lots of stories about jazz and life on the road. I really dig jazz too. Look, tell you what, man. About the reefer, give it some thought. I'll lay a nickel matchbox on you for free, and' you can try it and make up your own mind about it. The stuff is free, in nature, grows like a weed. But people in the city like this don't have access, dig, so there's a little service charge!"

Gypsy gave Joe one of the smaller size matchboxes that hold wooden kitchen matches which he sold for a "nickel," or five dollars. It held enough cleaned grass for two or three joints. He showed Joe how to roll a joint, and then brought out a pre-rolled joint of his own to share with Joe, telling him how to inhale deeply and hold the smoke in.

In a matter of minutes the man Joe had regarded as a black-clad intruder felt like a lifelong friend in a world held together by love and brotherhood, and Joe felt as though released from a straight-jacket into a brave new world, slowed down, profound, a feast of sight, sound and tactile delight. But Gypsy was leaving. "I'd love to stay and talk jazz with you, bro," he said, "but I gotta book. I have more people to see yet. Plant you now, dig you later!"

Joe watched as Gypsy seemed to glide down the hallway, his long black hair swaying. He turned to give Joe the peace sign, saying, "Goodwill to all men!" Joe wanted to follow him, but already he seemed to be a mile away down the endless hallway, where at the end a red exit sign glowed as if from another world. Gypsy was singing:

She's a little low

and built up from the ground,

just awhile before day

she'll make your love come down."

"Hush, he said, and pointed to his nose. "Shut your door—the smell, your neighbors." He continued:

"Sent for you yesterday,

here you come today..."

This struck Joe as funny and he began to giggle. He made it back into his place, shut the door and exploded in a fit of laughter. Something about Gypsy's song had released a tide of mirth. He realized he was voraciously hungry, went to the kitchen, made a peanut butter and jelly sandwich and got lost in it all – all the creamy voluptuousness of it. Then he went to his record player and put on a blues record by Lightning Hopkins, the most profound thing he had ever heard!

When Gypsy told Boris he had laid some reefer on Joe, Boris schooled Joe on how not to get busted. He didn't make it real obvious, but ever since the day he saw Joe make it at The Blue Note jam, Boris decided to look out for him. He had never bonded with a white kid in that kind of commitment, but color didn't matter. Not only did Boris think Joe's talent was special and needed nurturing, but he sensed Joe was too tender inside. The world could find that soft spot and rip him open with it until he somehow weathered enough blows to form the scars that could cover and protect him. It was a male thing —like the loyalty of soldiers in battle. The risks a jazz musician constantly takes were stressful, treacherous at times, and no one else looked out for you but fellow musicians. Boris, used to being kicked around Colorado, felt nothing they did in Minnesota could surprise him. Gigs were scarce as hens' teeth, but that couldn't kill his spirit.

Once when he'd been drinking a lot, Boris told Joe he was too soft and knew he had hurt the boy. "I'm not soft! I've been doing construction work all my life. I'm no sissy!"

Boris apologized and never brought it up again, knowing there was nothing but time, time and friends who could temper Joe. He was still wet behind the ears in the ways a city could con you, and Boris would school him as anonymously as possible until Joe could hard-scrabble and sing in adversity.

# # #

Joe received a postcard from his mother. He hadn't heard from her in a long while and was considering driving north on his next days off to check on her. The card read: *Joe, we sold the house and we're headed to Los Angeles. I left your things with Harvey. Don't worry about me. I'll write. Love, Mom.*

That postcard was from Reno, Nevada and she never wrote again. He was afraid her boyfriend Frank would help her squander the money from the sale of the house and then dump her.

But now Joe had more money than ever and was putting it in a bank. After years of helping support his mother from his own jobs, he now felt guilty about keeping it all. Outside of bare living expenses, the only money he spent on himself was for some "smoke," as he called the reefer from Gypsy, and buying record albums. To dig live jazz, he only paid the cover charges, stayed sober on coffee, and always tipped.

"Look, man, you only live once," Boris told him, "so lighten up, spend some of that money on yourself. You earned it. Buy yourself some sharp threads. You don't have to go around shabby anymore. You're a talented, unique dude; you ought to dress like it."

So Joe learned to buy a variety of clothes, which, to Boris's dismay, were still conservative. Then Boris talked him into buying an expensive stereo set. "Music is your life, man, what better investment can you make?" The salesman at Sears sold him a beautiful set with a cabinet of rich reddish-brown mahogany. He also suggested a set of earphones so Joe could listen to his music as loud and long as he wished without disturbing others in his apartment building. The new stereo became the centerpiece of Joe's apartment. He put a rack next to it filled with his new records and kept his two favorite Clifford Brown albums prominently displayed.

# # #

One Friday after a hard week's work, Joe came home expecting to bathe, eat and relax by playing some records before a gig with Boris was shocked to find his stereo and most of his records, gone. A draft of cold air was poured in from an open window. Shattered glass lay on the floor below. Joe felt as though all the wind had been just knocked out of his life. He could not understand who did this. No one but Boris had ever seen his apartment. He began to feel sick to his stomach. He sat down and began to cry. For the first time in his life he wanted to drink, to get drunk, as drunk as possible. Without one thought of his personal vow never to drink, he got up to find a liquor store. Then he remembered the gig with Boris. This made him more depressed, as he didn't think he could play, as emotionally shattered as he was. He took a hot bath to try and calm his nerves some. Maybe he could stay sober until after the gig.

"JESUS!" Boris said. "Who the hell knew you had that stereo?"

"I don't know. Nobody."

"Well, somebody had to know. Could they see it through the window?"

"No. I always keep the shades down."

"Think, man, who else besides me has been in there? Does Sam know where you live?"

"Sam?"

"The drummer. Coke head Sam."

"Oh wait, there was a drummer here. But I don't remember his name. I got hired with some musicians who were picked up at the last minute to play for a private party. We all rode in the same car and I asked the driver if he'd stop at my place here so I could get my trumpet. The drummer said he had to take a leak and asked if he could come in with me. After the gig when we got paid, he acted like the leader so the guy would pay him and he would pay us. He took a whole half the bread and let us divide up the rest. That's why I can't remember his name, I didn't like him.

He was the same drummer who was in the band at The Blue Note when I sat in there and you filled in for Earl."

"That was Sam. He was casing your place an' he came back an' stole your stuff. He's been breaking into everyone's place, stealing whatever he can, to feed his cocaine habit. The word on the street is don't ever give him your address or he'll clean you out."

He continued. "The son of a bitch is crazy. He was a good drummer but coke has copped him and he'll do anything for it now. You better not buy another expensive stereo unless you move, 'cause he'll just break in again. I'm glad you called me. After the gig you come over and stay the night with Lucy and me. We'll pop corn, play us some sides, maybe watch the tube a bit."

26

BORIS'S BID

Many creative people have an aversion to mathematics, but Boris loved the subject. While nearly flunking most of his subjects in high school, he got A's in math and band. He enjoyed music notation, loved writing out his own musical ideas and sight-reading new music. Other musicians came to him for help with difficult parts. He wrote out scores and did arrangements for bandleaders, acting as assistant. Composing and writing out music were as important and natural to Boris as breathing. He wrote as a poet, laying out notes on paper instead of words.

He kept a folder of his original music for his dream: To record an album. It would feature the crowd-pleasing pieces audiences loved and a few new things, including one Joe had written called "Mardi Gras," a joyous, colorful piece for trumpet. When Boris finally had the entire album planned out and ready to record, the opportunity fell right into his hands. Herb Davis, the owner of the only recording studio around that did records, was in the audience one night when Boris's band was playing at Road Buddy's. Davis was excited and offered Boris his card and a recording deal. Boris accepted, Davis booked sessions and the band paid for it by pooling every cent they could among them all, including a nest egg of Lucy's. This gave them only a quarter of the needed sum. The balance came from a new player in their circle, a generous Jewish girl named Sarah Rosen who offered it interest free. The recording was done in two sessions, producing two masters, one kept by Davis on file, the other given to Boris to keep until he could get backers to raise the extra money for production and distribution, possibly under a bigger label. Boris's plan was to take the master to a Chicago record company in person, hoping for a wider market and exposure and more profit.

Then came another break. One fan of the band, a railroad porter persuaded a "rail," or big shot railroad executive, himself a jazz lover, to give Boris two free passes round trip to Chicago on the Northern Pacific. Boris asked Lucy along and was ready to depart when Joe got ripped off, and he stayed back to console him. When they were finally ready to travel again to Chicago, Boris went to place the master recording into his suitcase, but it was gone!

Boris searched in vain, then remembered that the day Joe was ripped off, Boris had ran right to Joe, forgetting to close the window he had opened for fresh air. SAM! It had to have been Sam, ripping them both off in the same day!

Boris was filled with rage and panic. There was still another master that Davis kept, but panic gripped Boris when he thought of what Sam would do with the stolen copy, and rage filled him at the thought that their hope and dreams had been hijacked.

Lucy also was severely depressed and angry. She had been looking forward to Chicago jazz and maybe a dance show. The nest egg savings she had invested in the project seemed to have gone to a coke-head. Boris dropped everything to run all over town hunting down Sam, but he and his bass player cohort Lou had disappeared.

In the meantime, Davis offered to press and release the album locally at a minimal cost, but everyone's morale was too low to raise money so soon again.

Then, a week later, Joe ran up to Boris. "What the hell is going on, man? I just heard our album on the radio today on the local jazz station. They said it was by the Sam Cooper Quintet, off a label from Chicago!"

"Oh Jesus, NO!"

"Yeah. They played a whole side. Said it's been getting a lot of air play in Chicago and New York, too. It's really hitting big."

"Sam! I knew it was him ripped us off. Took it to Chi Town. That's where he's from. Wait 'til I catch that motherfucker, man, I'm gonna kick that funky mother's ass sideways into next week. I'm gonna cut his balls off!"

27

BACK ON GREEN DOLPHIN STREET

By July Gil felt ready to return to the City. He knew the real test would come from all the temptations and pressures of city life. Eric invited him to remain as long as he wanted, but Gil felt ready to leave. He told Eric he wanted to send some money up to him after he got work to help pay for all the family had done for him, but Eric refused saying, "Just send us a copy of your book when it's published."

Stepping off the Greyhound Bus in the Minneapolis depot, Gil felt fear and got real shaky. He searched for a pay phone. He had to try to line up a place to sleep by nightfall. He dialed Dean's number and when there was no answer he couldn't think of anyone else to call, and this frightened him. He had assumed Dean would be there.

Don't assume anything, he thought, *especially in the city. Just accept.* He didn't have the nerve to ask Jim to stay at his studio, not after the way he'd trashed the painting Jim had put so much work into. He'd sent Jim a letter of apology, best leave it at that. He had some savings for a modest month's rent, and he didn't want to squander a huge chunk of it just to rent an overnight room. Not knowing what to do made him jumpy and he started to sweat. The city already felt more formidable than he thought it would be. He wanted to get out on the street immediately but so far he had no destination.

He grabbed his luggage and left the depot. A block up the street he paused to light his pipe. Hefting his luggage and typewriter, he felt awkward, out of place, like a hick or a soldier on leave. The discomfort made him angry. The anger produced an overwhelming desire to hit the first bar he saw for a few stiff drinks. The urge panicked him. This urge had vanished long ago Up North. How could it reappear so intensely? He hadn't expected an easy time of it, but he'd started out without fear. Now he wondered if he could cope. The city could test you to the max. If you had any weaknesses it would find them with all its tentacles. It was seething with incidents that could uncover and implicate, trap and expose.

He walked on, desperate to keep his mind occupied and off alcohol, avoiding the fact he had no idea where to go. Before long another bar appeared. Don't think, Walk! Walk; walk into a future that's REAL, undistorted by alcohol. He crossed Hennepin Avenue, his avenue of misdemeanors, walking quickly to shed its pall. Nicollet Mall was only two blocks ahead. The bus shelters were there and he could set the luggage down until he could think of somewhere to go. People of all races were moving about and their diversity sparked his spirit. He had missed this ethnic richness, missed music too-- live music. With that thought he realized he was near the bus line that could take him to Road Buddy's. That's it! That was his connection. This IS my city, he affirmed. MY city and I WILL find my place in it again.

Setting his luggage down by a barstool at Road Buddy's, he looked up to find himself staring at a bottle of Meyers dark rum at eye level behind the bar, shelved with Bacardi and various other rums. Meyers had once been the most desirable drink in the world for him, everything about it--the rich taste and smell of it--a whiff of island paradise. Oh! It was so perfect and so lethal, ecstasy and then oblivion. But, it was no longer an option. Don't think, he restated, your mind is full of tricks if you let it run away with you. Don't think! Look away, too many times you lost everything by taking that first drink. Your savings for rent you worked so hard for Up North will disappear like water swirling down a drain and you'll wake up in some unfamiliar part of the city, hung-over, beat up, to face another season in hell, lucky to be alive.

"Hey! Captain Bacardi! Where have you been?" It was Doug the bartender and the smile on his face was heartwarming.

"Hey, Doug! I've been Up North, drying out."

"You mean you quit drinking? You?"

"Yeah, I'm off the sauce, or trying to stay off."

"Well, how 'bout some java? I keep a pot of that good black stuff for myself. Nobody else drinks it, jus' me and you, Gil."

Musicians were assembling onstage for some afternoon sets followed by free food and free drinks. Gil saw Boris pick up his sax and begin playing runs and some soulful phrases to warm up. The sound was deeply pleasing. It touched something deep inside Gil that had been locked away for too long. Once again he felt that rich anticipation of a jazz set just beginning.

"Boris tells me he's going Up North, to woodshed," Doug said.

"Yeah, he's going to where I just came from-- Finn's farm near Bemidji."

The band began "Green Dolphin Street" with Boris playing flute. The tune had a transporting effect on Gil and it took him to a marvelously transcendent place, akin to travel, and adventure. Suddenly he had an epiphany: He realized he was listening to live music in a bar without having alcohol, that enjoying coffee with music was enough, that he could do this for the rest of his life. He only had to remain vigilant.

The band's second number began with a Latin tinge, and Gil immediately recognized the start of Horace Silver's "Señor Blues."

Then he saw Dean whose face was full of emotion, "Pin Boris, man. He's got that one down, doesn't he? Welcome back Gil!"

"I'm hip. He's tight. Always was."

"He's really been kickin' lately. Raw! He finally dropped that Trane bag and has come into his own. Here comes another cat that's really come out." Dean pointed to Joe Citro who had just walked in with his trumpet. Joe waved to acknowledge them at the bar, and then joined the other musicians on stage.

A jolt of guilt unsettled Gil. The security and comfort he'd been feeling was eclipsed by the memory of Harvey freezing to death on the booze he'd got him. This guilt was like a cancerous wound that would not heal even after he'd confessed it to another member of AA. If he couldn't forgive himself, how could he expect Joe to forgive him for what happened to Harvey?

"So how did it go up there?" Dean asked. "You sure look a lot better."

"Well, at first there was nothing to do. When you quit booze there's all this time you used to piss away in bars and you have to start listening to yourself, learn to live with yourself. It was spooky up there at first; no noise, no traffic, no jazz. It was so quiet I couldn't sleep at night. The music on the radio was all country or top 40 shit, most of which was worthless. I could talk to Finn and his family once in a while, but they were so busy most of the time with their own lives. I had so much time on my hands that I began to remember all the bad shit I did drunk. Finally Eric got me into AA. I started reading his Henry Miller and James Baldwin novels and then I started to write."

"Righteous, man. I was hoping you'd start to write again. I wish I could cut down on booze. I got a DUI while you were gone. Had a helluva time trying to get my drums to gigs with my license revoked. Had to get people to drive me or pay cabs. Just yesterday got my license back. You know, many is the time I've wished I could just hole up in a room somewhere and kick booze. But on this scene there's booze everywhere I go. I'm constantly working around booze heads and strung-out people." He looked at Gil and realized he was just back in town.

"Say, forgive me; have you got a place to stay? You can stay at my place. Carl's still there but we got room."

"I was gonna ask if I could stay the night then look for a place to rent tomorrow. I wanna see if I can get back on the railroad. You say Carl's still there? How is he?"

"Spooky. He's goin' down slow. You'll be okay, though. He really likes you, just doesn't know how to show it very well. He's full of pain."

"Oh yeah?"

"Say, have you called Sarah? She's finished college and got an inheritance from her dad. She's got long green, real long; fact is she's loaded. Maybe get a loan from her? Got herself a nice new crib and out on her own."

"I wrote her I was coming but I won't ask her for any bread. I want to set myself up. But God bless her."

"I think she loves you, man. You should at least call her and tell her you're back."

# # #

Over on Cedar-Riverside, Gypsy stood at the bar of The Centurion, upscale place preppies gathered while slumming around the bohemian neighborhood. The atmosphere was stifling to Gypsy, but he nursed a beer while waiting for one of his steady customers. Two young preppies took the only stools left at the crowded bar and regarded Gypsy with disdain. They ordered trendy mixed drinks. Waiting in such a place made Gypsy nervous, knowing he stuck out for any nark who might have a reason to be watching. The two squares talked louder with each round of drinks and Gypsy began to listen.

"I've got that rich Jewish bitch wrapped around my finger!" one said.

"Is she a good fuck?"

"I don't know yet. Her face isn't much but she's built like a brick shit house! Man is she stacked!"

"Yeah, I know. I saw her when you took her to that joint downtown."

"Yeah, she really digs me."

"Ah, Mark--I know you, boy-- you're after something besides that Jewish cunt. You marry her, you'll be in line for all that dough—and you can be using it in the meantime. Pretty smart for a guy who flunked out of Harvard!"

"Fuck you. See if I give you a ride in her XKE."

Gypsy's client showed and held their transaction in the men's room. He then left and took a bus over to see Jim, his next customer. After concluding their transaction, Gypsy told him what he'd overheard from the preppies at the bar. Jim thought it had to be Sarah they were going on about. He wondered how to tell her?

28

EARL

"You better go over to St. Paul where Earl lives," said Tommy the owner of the Blue Note. "He wants you to call him, Dean, to set up a time to rehearse before you start the gig here with the house band. Ah, if he takes you on, you're in, dig?"

Dean and Carl arrived a half hour early, having somehow located the house right away. A well-kept 1960 Cadillac was the giveaway. News about Earl and his Cadillac traveled fast when he first got to town. They all heard that he listened to special music as he cruised around in his Caddy. Long before the invention of eight-track or cassette tapes he had rigged a way to battery power a big heavy tape recorder he'd taken into Kansas City clubs to record jazz royalty then carried back to his car, where he strapped it in the passenger seat with a box of the big tape reels to choose from.

Dean rang the doorbell. No answer. They heard a saxophone playing and it seemed to be coming from across the street. Crossing over a hill to follow the sound, they spotted Earl, walking slowly in the cemetery, and blowing toward various grave markers. Then he turned upward to the sun. He was blowing long beautiful phrases and original melody lines. Dean and Carl stopped to listen.

"Gentlemen-- thought I'd warm up before you got here. Guess I got carried away and forgot the time. Nobody ever visits these graves so I had a good time playing for these souls." He made a sweeping motion with his sax. "I play for them every now and then. They don't say much about my squawking, but I like to think they might like some of it. And I enjoy it, you dig?"

They walked back to the house to talk and relax a bit and see if they could work some things out.

Carl was really impressed. "Why did you end up here in the Twin Cities, Earl? You could be in New York."

"I came here one time with Lester Young," said Earl as he brought Carl's drink. "Prez had a relative here. I've like it here ever since. Had it in the back of my mind to end up here if I could. The Cities are nice and quiet. I like that now. Kansas City was NOT quiet. It swung all day and all night, never stopped. There was so much action, so much music you couldn't stop to sleep for fear you'd miss something. Real jumping town, wide open."

James, Earl's piano man, had arrived and the session began with a couple of standards--"All the Things You Are," and "Someone to Watch Over Me." They fell in together easily enough and Dean began to relax.

"There's one thing I insist on," Earl said while they had more drinks on a break, "and that's melody. I've got to be true to the melody. You can fool around with chords of harmonic progressions to some extent, but I don't want to change the character of the song. People love melody. You can embellish it somewhat, but you'll lose them when they can't recognize it. If I can't improve on it, I just leave it be."

He looked at them. "You play just fine for me. Next rehearsal we do at the club. I'll get you the repertoire. Can you dig it?"

"Groovy," said Dean.

"Righteous!" said Carl. "This is gonna be better than New York!"

29

BACK ON THE ROAD

Cooking jobs were always open in the city, but Gil was reluctant to take one. He wished he could go back to his old job on the railroad. He missed the excitement of the road. He was even willing to start over as a third cook because the road wasn't just a cooking job for Gil; it was a way of life. There were the layovers in Chi-Town and Seattle and the four and a half days off between runs. He'd missed the camaraderie with the railroad men, especially the blacks whom he felt closer to than most of the whites he knew. He decided to honor his feelings and at least go over to the St. Paul office and talk to the dining car department to see if it was possible to get on there again.

"Well, well," said the assistant superintendent, "where you been, Gil? We missed you. Are you ready to go back to work?"

"I really want to-- if you'll have me. I'm dry now and I intend to stay that way."

"We heard that. Tell you the truth; we just kept your job open, put you down on medical leave in case you came back. So if you want to go out next week, I'll put you on with Cliff. His second cook got drafted."

"Yeah. Okay. I'd really like that."

"So, welcome back. You stock the car next Friday and go out Saturday morning."

Saturday Gil started work and because it was summer; the train was carrying more tourists than usual. The dining car kitchen was hotter and the hours longer. Many trainmen drank between shifts in the bunk car and on layovers, but Gil now sober, had no trouble adjusting to the heavier work load. Two of the most militant waiters had quit before the run, drove out to

Oakland, California and joined the Black Panthers. Gil remembered a run-in he'd had with one of them. It started over something simple but quickly flared up into a confrontation. It ended in a standoff without a fight, but the unpleasant encounter gave Gil a sense of their deep emotional resentment and frustration.

One afternoon, as Gil worked against time preparing food for a dinner meal that would last through three full capacity seating's of forty eight passengers each, an old black porter came into the pantry while the waiters were setting up. He had come to fill his thermos with coffee. When the porters came in for their coffee, they usually joked around with the waiters. But this old fellow just smiled mysteriously and said, "I am the spirit, man," just out of the blue, then turned and left. The other black waiters continued their work without comment, as if what the porter said was matter-of-fact. But Gil was touched. Their music was like that, too, he thought. Black music came on without apology, breathing life into a troubled world, and then was gone, until you could find it again.

# # #

With his first paycheck Gil rented a small apartment a couple of blocks from Road Buddy's. He'd now be closer to work than he'd been in South. Road Buddy's could become his living room where he could socialize and listen to jazz. That evening, he ran into Dean who was seated at the bar. Gil told him about his job and his new crib nearby.

"You could buy a car now," Dean said, "and get around easier."

"Nah! What would I want with one of those goddamn things? All they do is pollute the air and kill people. I'll ride a bike."

Dean's face got serious. Then he told him what they'd all feared: Carl had cracked up. "He really went off the deep end this time. When I got home last night after work there were cops all over the place. They were dragging Carl out of the crib and he was screaming 'I'll kill you, you fucking pigs!' He'd been drinking all day on top of his meds and had the box turned up as loud as it would go. Lots of people who couldn't get the landlord on the phone called the cops."

He took a breath and continued, "Carl was smashing furniture, slamming it into walls. When one of my next door neighbors pounded on the door, Carl opened it and started to chase the guy with a broken rum bottle. Fortunately cops grabbed Carl in the hallway and were able to cuff him and haul him down to the squad car."

Gil was shocked. "Yeah, really crazy. Sounds liked he trashed your crib, man!"

"Yeah, and it gets worse. Carl tried to smash the windows out of the squad car with his feet. They took him straight to the mental ward at St. Mary's Hospital. Normally they would've taken him to Hennepin General because he'd cut his hand; but the captain said, 'No, he's crazy! Take him to a mental ward where a shrink can examine him.' He's on a 5150 lock down there."

# # #

Why hasn't he called? Sarah had sent Gil her new telephone number as soon as she moved. She's heard that he'd been back for over two weeks now. Was he all right? She worried that he'd taken to drink again. Then the thought came to her that he might be dumping her and fear began to seize her. Soon a depression made her begin to withdraw socially. On the morning she was supposed to meet Mary at Pan's Pipes, she could hardly make herself get out of bed. Mary had offered to go over Sarah's poetry and maybe edit some of it, and Sarah had been thrilled at the opportunity. But by that morning she'd begun to think Gil had met someone else.

I can't believe it-- after how devoted I've been to him when everyone told me to drop him. All those letters I wrote him to support him getting sober. Why didn't he at least have the decency to be honest with me? Let me know what he's doing and how things are going?

Sarah looked at the clock. It was 10:00 a.m. and she was supposed to meet Mary in an hour. It took all the willpower she could summon just to get dressed, but she finally grabbed a travel mug full of coffee and got into her XKE and took off for Pan's Pipes Coffeehouse.

# # #

Gil wanted to wait until he was set up with a crib and secure in his job before calling Sarah. He didn't want to borrow any money from her because he wanted to show her he could lead a sober, responsible life. During the five day trip to Seattle he'd worried about her and as soon as he got back to his crib and his own phone he called her right away, but she wasn't home. He realized then that he'd probably waited too long and should have called her sooner. Disappointed by not reaching her, he wanted to get out and be with people. Just then he remembered the invite from Boris: "I hear you kicked the juice, man. You ought to come see us at Pan's Pipes. We be doin' it! We got jazz as good as or better than any club in the whole Twin Cities. I got the house band there, it's my band and we cut loose, we cook! There's poetry, too. They do an open mic thing every Thursday night. I know you can dig that!" Gil decided that's where he'd go today for coffee and conversation—just what he needed.

Gil caught a bus a few blocks away and headed to the coffeehouse. Upon reaching Pan's Pipes around 11:00 a.m. he paused at the front window to gaze at the only object on display, a green ceramic statue of Pan, the nature god, playing his pipes. The sly grin on Pan's face made Gil smile. He guessed that at night the heavy curtain behind Pan was rolled away and you could see the upstairs band on a stage right in front of the window. *Why didn't I come here more often? I guess I never went anywhere that didn't have booze.*

Gil opened the door and straight ahead of him was—wonder of wonders—Sarah! She was sitting with the cool Italian beat poetess named Mary. When Sarah saw Gil, she jumped up and come running over to him to give him a big hug. He grabbed her and kissed her on the lips and felt his heart beat faster. Soon they were sitting together at a large table catching up on Gil's job, his crib, poetry, jazz, and Gil's woodshedding adventures.

Sarah said she had to leave soon and Gil quickly asked her for and secured a dinner date. He'd been holding her hand tightly since their kiss, finding it hard to let her go.

30

AT THE FUJI-YA

For their first date after Gil's return, he took her to the Fuji-Ya, a Japanese restaurant. Gil enjoyed riding in the XKE he once considered bourgeois. Even in his bitter alcoholic days the car's design and color pleased him. It held the potential excitement of beauty frozen in form just like jazz. Sarah parked near the restaurant and they walked hand in hand for half a block to enter another world.

They were seated immediately. Sitting Japanese style on cushions, they sipped green tea which neither had tried before. Because they liked the taste of it and the lift it gave them, it would be imprinted on their sense of Japan and the oriental aesthetic in general. Everything about the Fuji-Ya appealed to that aesthetic, its austere beauty, the Japanese waitress in a gorgeous kimono, the Koto music, simple flowers, and Ukiyo-e woodblock prints of their history and folk tales. Gil was grateful that he could appreciate the evening sober with all his senses in balance and calmly enjoy the atmosphere.

The woman facing him was so special. She had a beauty that emanated from her many good qualities. Her long dark hair glistened in the mellow light of the restaurant. He knew she loved jazz and poetry like he did and also supported musicians with money and with praise. She had integrity, was loyal, hip, and trustworthy and by God he was enjoying her presence.

"I want to know about you? How are you doing, Gil?" She looked at him with admiration, "You seem like a new person."

"Oh, yeah, and I feel like a new person, too. Most importantly I am still sober. I'm renting a little crib over by Road Buddy's so I'm close to jazz and getting over to St. Paul for my job with the railroad. I got my old job back and its going well. And I'm writing, working on a book. I don't know how many times I tried to get a book going when I was drinking. Now I'm actually working on it every day and I like the way it's going. It's like…"

"Don't tell me," she said, joining in, "It's like Jelly Roll Morton singing 'Doctor Jazz.' Say, how's Carl? I heard he's really in a bad way, some place where I can't get in to help him."

"Yeah, they got him locked up in the mental ward at St Mary's. The police put him on a 72 hour hold. Then Dean had his doctor hold him for fourteen days after he tried to commit suicide."

"We could lose a great musician, Gil. Nobody in town can play bass like Carl. He has so much talent!"

"Well, don't give up on him. He'll get good care there. Dean said he's already made some progress. Maybe they can help him turn things around."

They ordered the Fuji-Ya Special. It was a typical Japanese dinner with chopsticks. They were served green tea and then a bowl of rice, a bowl of miso soup, and then some pickled vegetables to nibble on while a Japanese chef prepared tempura--vegetables and shrimp-- dipped in a light batter and deep fried in sesame oil. It was all so light and crisp and such fun to eat. They were both blown away by tentsuyu dipping sauce. The kimono-clad waitress brought out the dishes, one after another, and arranged them with elegance. The shrimp was delicious and they were delighted by how the tempura deepened the flavor of the vegetables. They ate leisurely and reminisced about some of Dean and Carl's parties then moved on to Gil's adventures Up North. Sarah was fascinated by the Ojibwe sweat lodge. She felt sorry for old Harvey and his sorrow that lead to his demise. She didn't blame Gil. She was so happy about how the rural experience had brought out the best in Gil.

As happy as she was, the thought still crossed Sarah's mind that her jazz friend could go off the wagon at any time and turn into a slobbering drunk again. But she let it slide on by and into the void it appeared from. She was facing a well-dressed, healthy looking man. Instead of his old trademark faded jeans and worn shirts he wore a new pair of slacks, a new denim shirt and a bright tie. He was calm. He smiled a lot. He had a great haircut and was clean shaven. He wasn't at all like Mark Hamilton, the pretty boy preppy who'd been after her money. Gil never asked for anything from her and could be trusted.

After their meal, the waitress brought them each a fortune cookie. Sarah's read, "Love and romance will encourage commitment" and Gil's read, "A life-changing opportunity is coming to you."

Gil became quiet and somber. Sarah stared at him. "What's the matter, Gil? You look perplexed."

"I was just thinking about Boris. He's had another let down."

"What happened?"

"Well, you know Boris got ripped off last year by a cokehead musician that stole all the original music he was going to try to get recorded. He was looking for anything he could hock to get bread for his cocaine habit. He sold it to a recording studio in Chicago and the album was a hit!"

Gil took a break from feelings of anger rising from his core. "It got airplay in Chicago and New York. Anyway, Boris worked up new album material, including a beautiful ballad by Joe Citro, his trumpet man."

Gil looked sad. "He was all set with a deal to record it here with the Twin Tone Recording Studio, but it went bankrupt just before he could cut the record. The owner Herb Davis has it up for sale. It's a bad break not just for him but for all musicians because it's the only place here to record."

"What can Boris do now?"

"All he can do now is send out demo tapes, to Chicago recording studios, and take his chances for getting an audition. If he gets one the whole band has to travel there-- and that takes bread. Here in Minneapolis, Davis heard them play at a local club and offered to record them, with no audition at all."

"Why do you think the studio went bankrupt?"

"Herb didn't book enough commercial gigs to pay the bills, I guess. He liked recording artists, including jazz, but only pop music is selling and he didn't push that."

"Will the studio sell?"

"I don't know. I heard some big shot wants to buy it, he likes the location for a store or something."

"My God! Then there'd be no recording studio for the musicians around here at all!"

"That's the story."

"Well, I'll tell you what, it sounds like another job for Sarah, Jewish Wonder Woman! I'll buy it!"

"You would?"

"Why not? We probably could use a tax write off. We could record a lot of jazz here in the Twin Cities. I'll talk to my board of directors and our lawyers and buy it ASAP."

"Yeah! Sarah to the rescue! But hurry, Sarah, hurry, before someone else buys the place!"

31

STANLEY

Sarah had given Jim a thousand dollars to do a painting for her new apartment. She said she planned to order more work by him. With a steady client he could afford to rent a sleeping room above Gray's Drugstore in Dinky Town. He no longer had to sneak in and out of his art studio in the warehouse district where he wasn't supposed to be living. When he asked Sarah what subject she wanted for a painting she said, "Surprise me." He looked through sketches he'd made of the jazz musicians at Pan's Pipes and decided on a painting of Boris Simpson playing his sax in front of his band. Deeply pleased with the work, Sarah requested two abstracts and two jazz subjects, for her new recording studio, paying him three thousand up front.

On a visit to his studio, Sarah noticed Jim had Stan's junk art piece up on a wall. "How's Stan doing," she asked.

"Oh, he went back to New York City."

"New York City?"

"Yeah, that's where he's from. He started going to pieces when Cynthia dumped him."

"My teacher?"

"Yeah, the one he was having an affair with. She dumped him for her young handsome assistant and Stan flipped out. But it was more than that. He was combining heavy meds with liquor to keep himself going, but he flipped out. His parents convinced him he should return to New York. I got a postcard from him and he said that his folks set him up with a studio in one of their condos and put him on valium."

"What happened to all that artwork at his studio? Did he take it with him?"

"Nah, that's the most pathetic thing ever. It was all tossed in the dumpster behind his studio. He paid for two small paintings to be shipped ahead: the big paintings, his experimental work with fiberglass, and the junk art pieces--all trashed."

"Why didn't you take some of it, Jim?"

"I didn't realize he was going to leave so quickly. I was going to borrow a truck to get as much of his work as I could and store it for him. Next thing I knew he's gone, the place is empty, and there's a 'for rent' sign in the window. He could've been rich by now if he'd stayed here."

"What do you mean?"

"Last week an art dealer came over here to look at some paintings of mine to maybe buy. He saw that piece of Stan's junk art and went bananas! He raved about it. 'Did you do it, where did you get it, will you sell it?' He went on and on. I had to tell him there weren't any more, that the landlord tossed them into a dumpster when the artist left. The gallery offered me two grand for mine and I told him I'd never sell it."

Jim looked puzzled by the turn of events. "Then he doubled the offer, four grand and I still said no, it means more to me than cash. He said it was called 'junk art'. Hell, that's what we were calling it. Anyway, it's real hot, he says, it's 'in,' and fetching big prices and Stan developed it on his own, probably one of the first. He could've cashed in on it for a while. He could have started eating better, bought good whisky and grass, and found a new woman."

"That should never have happened to him like that, having to leave so quickly!"

"Don't I know it, but it did. The real tragedy is that the history of Stan's Minneapolis oeuvre was lost. It wasn't even documented in photos. All that work he did. It's gone, like it was never there. It's sad, man, and it really depresses me."

32

WOUNDED BY SONG

Earl Saunders lay dying in his bed. The 89-year-old jazz musician's heart was failing and he was too weak to reach the phone. He felt his life was slipping away and he knew medical intervention couldn't help him now.

His cat, Cassidy, knew Earl was dying and wouldn't leave his side. *The housekeeper's coming, She'll find us, me and my dear Cassidy, and she will take care of him. She also knows where to find the instructions I've left on what to do when I die. She'll also discover a generous payment for her last workday plus.*

Earl felt okay about dying in St. Paul because the Twin Cities had treated him well. There could never be, however—not in New York or Chicago or anywhere else on God's earth—a place as swingingly dynamic as was Kansas City, his birthplace in the 1930s, where he learned the art of swing and was grounded in blues. But the Twin Cities were mellow enough and musicians treated him with respect. Earl smiled knowing that he had robbed death of its *coup de grace*.

Death now was only an undramatic, informal end to a lifetime wounded by song. Each time he heard a beautiful melody for the first time, a song like "Stardust," or "Solitude," it wounded him deeply. Each encounter pierced him like a lethal arrow of ecstasy and left a stigmata in his heart which opened each time he heard that melody again. All his life he had rendered these songs as best he could. A few of his own songs had come to him as well, and one was coming on his deathbed when it was too late to try out on his sax. Perhaps it would carry him over to wherever God was taking him. He wanted to see his wife on the other side. He smiled thinking of Boris, the spunky kid who would now be THE HORN who would take over his throne. Just as his consciousness was slipping away, the housekeeper came into his bedroom, said a cheery hello and opened the shade of the window to the last light of day Earl would ever see in his present life. Still thinking of Boris, he said, "Well, I had a good run at it, now it's Junior's turn."

"Junior?" the housekeeper asked, but Earl never replied.

# # #

There was no funeral service for Earl. He didn't belong to a church, but Tommy set aside the next Sunday jam session at The Blue Note for a memorial tribute to Earl. In the meantime, Earl had made arrangements for his remains to be left at a St. Paul funeral home so people could come by there to pay their respects.

Dean and Carl, who had been very proud to be in Earl's band at The Blue Note and had maintained unheard of sobriety when they gigged with Earl, began to drink the moment they heard he died. They drank out of shock, they drank because they would no longer play side by side with genius, and they drank just because it had been a long time since they drank as much as they really wanted to.

They closed the bar at Road Buddy's when they learned of Earl's passing. Then went back to the crib and played blues records until they passed out. They woke up on the afternoon of the last day they could go to pay their respects.

Hungover, they set out to try and find the funeral home in St. Paul. Dean had some hair o' the dog, a couple of Millers and some shots of brandy, but Carl just smoked joints because for the first time in his life rum made him sick just looking at it.

It took two hours for the boys to locate the place. They had shared some joints on the way and went around St. Paul in circles, not a disgrace in itself, as even sober Minneapolis people often got lost venturing into St. Paul's irrational street layouts. They finally found the funeral home with just enough time to pay their respects. Dean told friends about the viewing the next day:

"There was nobody in there. It was too dark. We couldn't find the coffin. Carl was spooked. He got scared. 'WHERE'S THE BODY, DEAN?' he said real loud, 'WHERE'S THE BODY?' He looked like he wanted to bolt. Then he whispered to me, 'Let's get out of here!' and he dashed out the door. That's when we heard this creepy guy who just appeared from nowhere say, 'Hello, gentlemen, have you come to visit Mr. Saunders?'

'Yes, where is he?' I said. 'Carl was tugging at me to leave.'

'Why, he's right here, gentlemen. His ashes are in this urn. He was cremated, you know. Please excuse me, I have work to do.'

"I looked at Carl and we suppressed our laughter. Carl relaxed. We went up to this little urn that held all that was left of Earl and just stood there. I don't know what Carl was thinking, but I was thinking these are his ashes but Earl's gone somewhere; he moved on. Carl didn't say anything until we got outside and then he says, 'Ashes to ashes, dust to dust, Earl's gone, carry on we must.'

"And I said, 'Amen,' and we went home and started drinking again. Hell, I couldn't function for days after."

Sunday Dean and Carl were playing with Boris Simpson, who was the new leader of The Blue Note house band. Musicians came from all over to play in tribute to Earl. Boris kicked off with a soulful rendition of Charlie Parker's "Parker's Mood," which set the tone for the Kansas City style swing and blues that Earl especially loved.

33

MENTAL WARD AT ST. MARY'S

It was visitor's hours at St. Mary's Hospital and Gil signed in to visit Carl. They shook hands without a word. Carl's sullen expression belied his bright intelligence. Gil could sense the anger which was always a part of what kept Carl in motion. The big man would never be docile no matter what they gave him for meds.

"It's been a long time, bro. I've been up north drying out. Just needed to see you again, "said Gil.

"Look at me, man!" said Carl. "Do I look crazy?"

"No. you look like Carl to me."

"I asked the shrink if he was implying that I'm unhinged. He blabbered something in shrink talk, and I said, man, you must be around the bend yourself."

Carl pointed to patients around the room. "Look at these poor motherfuckers, man. They keep them so doped up they don't know where they are. They got me on more than I'm used to. They are pickling our brains! I'll end up a mush-head like a lot of these mothers. You got to help me, man. You got to try to talk to someone who can get me out of here. They had me in a strait-jacket for two days once. They can do shit like that."

When calmer, Carl asked about Dean and a few other musicians. Then the conversation seemed to have nowhere to go. Tears began forming in Carl's eyes and he suddenly grabbed Gil.

"Help me. Please!"

Two attendants came quickly and told Gil his visit was over. With the door locked solidly behind him, Gil turned and looked back through the thick glass. Carl was standing exactly as he had left him, his face tortured. Gil knew that look on Carl's face would haunt him forever. But who in the hell could he reach that would listen?

Gil left the mental ward completely depressed. He took off walking like he did the morning Tommy was killed at The Blue Note—only this time he was walking sober. He reached the Southside, his favorite neighborhood in Minneapolis. He thought he heard live music somewhere up ahead. As he got closer, he realized it was the blues, rough sounding, but strong. A black man opened a garage door and the music poured out. Gil recognized him. It was Sweet Charles and he played guitar.

"They workin' out in there," said Charles, "go in and grab yourself a beer."

"Thanks, man. But I'll just listen out here for awhile. What's this group called?"

"They be the 42nd Street Rhythm Kings. They jus' startin'."

After soaking up the blues that fit his sorrow for Carl, Gil cut through an alley. He saw a black woman tending her backyard garden. She was working compost into the soil and it struck him that the southside itself was a rich, deep compost of a neighborhood that jazz sprang from—rich, black soil with African roots, sweat, struggle, spirit: that all came out in the sound.

Late that night after returning to his crib, he found telephone message from Dean. 'A rich uncle of Carl's just come forth after a call from Boris and is sending money for Carl to be sent to Rochester for more help.'

Gil slept well that night… like he did when he was up north.

34

UNFINISHED BIZ

Boris was eager to get to that farm up north and woodshed, try out ideas for his new style and new voice. But he knew he had unfinished business with Sam Jackson, who'd stole his music, had it recorded in Chicago, and had steady checks coming in. He'd heard that Jackson had bought a new Corvette and had been free-spending, and ferrying around a bevy of funky women that he pimped. He continued to avoid Road Buddy's and places that Boris might appear.

But, Boris was patient. "I'll get him one of these days," he told Joe Citro. "He'll be getting careless from all that blow he's doing. I'll catch him as he goes down and pulverize his ass."

In his playing, Boris had gotten away from Coltrane's influence and that of Sonny Rollins. He was eager to get to that farm up north to woodshed and try out ideas for his new style, a new voice.

Boris needed to get away from everything for a while, away from the band, gigs, friends, Lucy, and just solo on his horn, reaching deep inside himself to get in touch with that wellspring of creativity, that source which fed his intuition.

He wanted to catch the last set of blues at a bar on Washington Avenue before leaving town. He was surprised to see Sam Jackson, with a floozy on each arm, come out the door and head for his Corvette parked in front. He ran up to Jackson waving his arms and yelling, "Step aside, girls!"

Sam's listless eyes turned crazed and he started running away. Overweight, short of breath, he didn't get far. Boris put his two fists together and slammed Sam on the back. He hit the sidewalk, skinning his face, his nose bleeding. "Please, man, have mercy," he pleaded while reaching for his pistol. Boris slammed a fist into Sam's mouth, grabbed the pistol and stuck it in his sports coat.

"Get up motherfucker!"

"Take it easy, man!"

Sam got up and started to run again. Boris chased him and slammed him down the same way, clubbing him on the neck this time and kicking him in the side after he hit the sidewalk. "I could kill you, you fucking snake, like you killed that drummer over north. I should take the keys to that Corvette you bought with my music, because it belongs to me. But I don't want it. I'm going to let you live and suffer like I did when you took my dream. It serves you right to suffer. Cocaine's gonna get you anyway. You ever get in my face again, motherfucker, I'll off you for sure." Boris began to walk away, then suddenly ran back and started kicking Sam repeatedly. "That's for Joe Citro, for his stereo that you ripped off."

35

BORIS WOODSHEDS

Boris arrived up north at Finn's farm after dark. Eric introduced his wife and kids, and then put Boris up in his studio. Boris went to sleep on the same cot Gil used while drying out from booze that previous winter. The next morning it was completely silent in the studio, which made Boris uncomfortable. He actually missed the cacophony that went on in the city day and night. He wanted to rush out the door with his sax and locate the field where Eric said he could play to nature, start his woodshedding immediately. But he relaxed when he saw Eric had the coffee all set up to brew. He knew he needed that before anything else.

When the coffee was ready, he poured a cup, opened the door, and stood there sipping. The unnerving silence of the studio was forgotten as he began listening to enchanting summer morning sounds, crickets and birds singing, the neighing of distant horses, a dog barking and crows in raspy primordial conversations. Here was a natural world where sounds rose and fell with beautiful, organic integrity and wholeness. He refilled his coffee cup, grabbed his sax, and walked out to the pasture gate letting him in, and latching the gate behind him.

Eric was at the corral feeding and watering his wife's horses. He cordially pointed out the path that would lead up to the best field for woodshedding. The walk was shaded by tall pines whose partially exposed smooth-worm roots crisscrossed the path. Boris was more excited on this walk than he had ever been on gigs with good musicians. He knew he was on a rendezvous with his inner self, a tryst with inspiration, something he had never done just for himself. Now he had a whole week of uninhibited blowing on a field.

Eric said the field was high up and secluded on all sides by woods. There would be no distractions or interruptions, no sleeping babies or old folks to disturb, no time limits, closing hours or critics—just himself to draw clear, clean ideas from.

The field opened out in front of him. It was vast, quiet and, best of all, there were no human beings anywhere in sight. Grasshoppers leaped to his side, dodging his footsteps. Birdsong broke out and now and a breeze lifted and stirred the leaves of trees around the field. Bees and dragonflies hummed along while the sun shown above, conducting the whole symphony of life with silent radiance.

Boris walked further into the field and stood for a while, looking about, taking it in. "Hallelujah," he said. "Hallelujah," then shouted, "HALLELUJAH!" Dropping to his knees, he opened his sax case; put the sax together, put the mouthpiece to his lips. First he honked and screeched, drunk-like with freedom, letting out wildness. Then he pretended he was John Coltrane doing a bar-walk which Lucy said humiliated Trane before he kicked horse, paying a lot of dues by taking a gig where he had to play raunchy R&B, strutting back and forth on top of the bar in front of drunks in a Philly dive. Then Boris aped Trane's breakthrough style and did some double-clutching, blowing those "sheets of sound" and the semi-garbled speaking in tongues of Trane trying to do the impossible, driven, and possessed. Then, shift in midflight to flow Bird-like through fabulous runs as fleecy and facile as Parker. He stopped a while to rest and then changed over to ballads, playing slowly, delicately lacing out filigrees of ideas which had been haunting him in fragments for years. He went on playing whatever came to mind, riding out associations. He tried to block out all logic for as long as he could because logic led to conventional modes of expression. For a while he played strange, all strange sounds in strange sequences, and he smiled at the thought of somebody requesting "play strange for me," instead of "Stardust." Strange was a kind of tool you could inject now and then to jar customers back into listening.

Melodies were coming, mellifluous, haunting, coming from memories of how the old horn men had rendered them, coming from how his mind had been playing with them since he had first heard them. Music began flowing through him in torrents, overwhelming him with joy and sorrow, his subconscious delivering seed ideas churned up from soul silt, ideas he could unravel and develop for years to come.

Later that day, Eric's children brought Boris up a bag lunch and a jar of lemonade made with honey and real lemons. He thanked them sincerely, realizing what an appetite he'd worked up. He tried to engage them in some conversation, but they said their dad had told them to leave Boris alone while he's up here; he needs to be able to soul search. But the boy turned and asked, "Boris, what does soul search mean?"

"Well, boy, that's a darn good question. I guess it means reaching way down inside yourself to try to find things that can help you live your life. Boris watched them as they left the field without any dallying, but he saw the boy duck behind a tree near the path down through the woods. He wanted to listen to his music.. Boris noticed how fascinated the kid was with his sax.

As he finished the delicious lunch and two brownies washed down with the homemade lemonade, Boris watched a red-tailed hawk circle above. It looked really fine up there drifting on the air currents. He decided to adopt it as a personal emblem to use back in the city as a reminder of the freedom of woodshedding.

During the retreat Boris realized how frantic his city life had become. He'd spent most of his life running around chasing time like it was running out. In his constant study of mathematics, he had encountered Einstein's theory that time was circular, that it really didn't exist. Back that up with the spiritual teaching that there is no death, that the soul is eternal. Yet, like most everyone else, he was still running about from gig to gig. *If the backdrop is really eternity why not try to act like it, believe you have enough time all the time.* This kind of mindset could take a lot of anxiety away. He decided to keep reminding himself whatever he was doing at any time was being done in eternity.

And the money thing? Best to stop chasing that, too. *Why do I play?* He then answered himself. *Because I love to play.*

When Sonny Rollins dropped out and went up in the Williams-burg Bridge to woodshed, was he thinking about bread? No. He was thinking about making his music pure. Up there the air was rare, the money all down below. He'd already been hailed as Bird and Trane's successor. He dropped out when he had it made to rededicate himself and search some more. Hell, they followed him with money after that.

The emphasis on the field workouts was spontaneous sound, uninhibited, naked like the cry that comes from a new born when it's slapped on its tiny ass to make it cry and clear its lungs. Bird said if you haven't lived life, it won't come out your horn. *Well, I been out here scuffling' since I ran away from home. When I play blues what's comin' out my horn is the time that the rats and roaches found my food stash when I was livin' in abandoned buildings. What's comin' out is the time a mugger put a switchblade on my Adam's apple, threatening to slit my throat if I didn't produce some bread which I didn't have, having spent my last dollar on beer, drinking all that day and half the night. It's the time a gang of white guys beat me bloody, leaving me passed out in a mudpile. It's about finding my Lucy in the hospital with a slashed arm. I play the loneliness that's embedded in our souls, loneliness that drenches the earth while each and every one of us carries the pain of separation. I walk the backstreets with the blues. In the meantime, people either respect you or they try to game you.*

What about fear? Fear is always down there too, in the subconscious in one form or another. He thought he'd gotten over the fear of whites, but leaving the city to go up north he ran smack into that fear stronger than ever. Knowing he was leaving the safety net of his own people and heading up to a domain of all white people, half of them probably redneck, fear was telling him he could go missing very easily. They could lynch him or kill him any number of ways and keep it quiet.

But once he met Eric Finn and his beautiful family, that fear subsided. He went to town with Eric once and the fear was right back again. Everyone stared at him. Boris knew damn well the little kids had never seen a black person before. But that fear gradually subsided, too. Most of the townsfolk actually tried to be friendly, or at least nice, in spite of their astonishment. All in all, a little fear is a good thing. It's that ancestral vigilance instinctively whispering that caution can save your life.

Hatred? Definitely in there with the fear as much as Boris would like to be rid of it. He still resented his militant father but had to thank him for dragging him around to all those different Air Force bases and their white schools. From that experience he got used to white ways and their dominant world. What he really hated was the system, how it kept blacks, and all minorities second class. It kept black music down while all the sentimental slop they put out made them millions. They covered up and ripped off original black music and took the money that that should go to the people who created it. They ran you out of downtown if you got strong in number, kept the liquor licenses for themselves and lord knows, someday a change would have to come.

On his last night at the farm, Boris fell asleep thinking how much he enjoyed being out on the land and about the ideas he was now holding for the band. *I'm coming back like a hermit from the desert, with my soul rejoicing.*

He woke up in late night and began wondering what it would be like to play in the field at night. He knew it would be his last chance to find out. He got up, grabbed his sax, and a flashlight, that turned out to be unnecessary. The land was flooded with moonlight and the field felt like a moonlit stage. During the day he'd spent a lot of time on the blues, but the night was calling for satin, for lavender, for dusting by The Muse. He started playing "Stardust" lovingly, giving himself over to the night. The lunar energy gave him an eerie facility. He wanted to express the softness of the moths that floated about the flashlight and drifted lyrically over the bosom of night. An owl sounded a HOOOO nearby and Boris took a pause in melody, and then sent a HOOOO back from his horn in reply.

Back in the city, Boris felt more self confident and motivated. He was happy to be back with Lucy again and resolved never to take her for granted.

Lucy was on a natural high of her own—she had been accepted to train and dance with a serious dance troupe that specialized in jazz dance.

36

THE FALLING DRIFTING LEAVES

It was early October and the leaves were beginning to drift down into the streets. Chuck and Jim were heading out to Ruth's house to pick up two of her paintings. Jim had invited her to show her work along with his at a Chicago gallery.

They found Ruth out on her lawn raking leaves. "Come on in," Ruth said, "I made coffee for us." She led them up the steps to the house. Jim, who by now was well aware of Ruth's wealth, had become accustomed to the expensive furnishings and the beautifully built old house; but Chuck was still amazed by the luxury of it. His immigrant parents struggled for years to afford a small house for a growing family.

"I picked out two paintings, Jim. I don't know if they're any good or not. Where are you taking them again?"

"To Hannigan's Gallery in Chicago, a place Gil told me about. The owner took two of my paintings and sold them right away. Good prices too. So I shipped him more. Now he wants to have a show for me there. He also told me if there was a painter I really liked to bring along a couple of their works, too. I chose you. He'll send you a consignment form to sign. He'll mail you a check when he sells the paintings along with info about the buyers."

Jim turned to Ruth to see how she felt about the deal. "If he really likes your work he'll ask you to send more and eventually have a show for you, too. He specializes in artists outside the Chicago area."

"Oh God, it sounds great! I'd better get busy."

"How's Rachel?"

"She's calmed down a lot. She's working on getting her GED. As you know, she was really shut down. I knew she was suicidal and it scared me to death. Again, I owe you a lot for getting me in touch with that detective friend of yours. He took Rachel and me to meet an ex-cop who runs a safe house for girls who want to get off the street. Rachel has gone and talked to those girls several times now about what happened to her, how she was almost killed before you and Chuck rescued her. She's got the will now to get back out there and do for herself again and to try to stay off drugs."

Ruth suddenly changed the subject. "I suppose you heard about my daughter Sarah and Gil?"

"Yeah, they're cooking up a scheme for Sarah to take over a recording studio," said Jim.

"Oh, that's all done. Sarah's lawyer managed to buy it for her before someone else did."

She turned to look at the two young men, her eyes sparkling. "What I'm talking about is that they're getting married!"

"What? Oh, my God!" Jim was speechless. "Ah, seems like it's a little soon?" he looked around the room in amazement. "Huh! I guess they both know what they want and… God bless 'em."

"When is the wedding?" asked Chuck, who was also very surprised by the news.

"They said soon, in Wirth Park, at some flower garden."

"You know Gil, is one of my best friends, but I didn't know he was serious about anyone," said Jim.

"Oh, Sarah was the one who proposed," smiled Ruth.

"Wow! No kidding? I always knew she was a take charge woman!" said Jim. "Well, I think it could work now that Gil is sober-- and stays that way."

"Yes, well, we all hope for that. I wanted a traditional Jewish wedding. But now that she's a Buddhist, she wanted one in the Zen way. So does Gil."

Ruth sat back down enjoying her time with these two good friends. "Do you know what Gil said when she proposed to him?"

"No. What?"

"I thought you'd never ask!"

Ruth turned serious as she continued. "I gave them this house as a wedding present. I told them they didn't need to keep it the way we did; but they gracefully turned it down--too many memories!"

Ruth had even more news as she concluded: "I'm considering moving to Phoenix, Arizona soon. Many of my friends from St. Louis Park live there now. Rachel loves the idea, too. It would be a new start for us. So we'll put the house up for sale in December."

Chuck and Jim finished their coffee, hugged Ruth, and headed for home.

# # #

Two weeks later, Gil and Sarah were married in the Eloise Butler Wildflower Garden and Bird Sanctuary in Wirth Park. A Buddhist priest from San Francisco, who was visiting Minneapolis, blessed them with chants and the ringing of the hand bell. While Gil and Sarah had obtained the marriage license, a justice of the peace handled the ceremony and later filed the marriage certificate. In a bow to tradition, Jim was Gil's best man and Mary stood up for Sarah. Boris Simpson and Joe Citro played "Oh Happy Day" on their instruments as the wedding party, that included Sarah's Uncle Saul, made their way down the hill in the warm afternoon sun amid the falling drifting leaves.

The wedding party ended up at Road Buddy's for a reception party and dancing to jazz.

-The End-

Thanks To:

Early readers Mike Bjerk, Ashley Charwood and Mary Lou M.

My sister Mary, Lonnie K. , my writer aunt Patricia K. and all my other friends and relatives who believed in me. To my writers group who kept me going.

To all the musicians who have given us joy, excitement and soul through the decades.

Father John Dolsini, Czech immigrant priest, who, when I was a boy, gave me a dictionary when he learned I wanted to become a writer.

My father who said, "WRITE THAT NOVEL!"

Special thanks to "Satchmo", Louis Armstrong, who changed my life when I first heard his records. And thanks to the living memory of the late great female jazz singer, Amy Winehouse.

And to all you readers who make a book come alive.

#